Florida's Ghostly Legends and Haunted Folklore

The Gulf Coast and Pensacola

Greg Jenkins

Pineapple Press, Inc.
Sarasota, Florida

green press
INITIATIVE

Pineapple Press is committed to preserving ancient forests and natural resources. We elected to print *Florida's Ghostly Legends And Haunted Folklore Vol. 3* on 50% post consumer recycled paper, processed chlorine free. As a result, for this printing, we have saved:

17 Trees (40' tall and 6-8" diameter)
7,088 Gallons of Wastewater
2,851 Kilowatt Hours of Electricity
781 Pounds of Solid Waste
1,535 Pounds of Greenhouse Gases

Pineapple Press made this paper choice because our printer, Thomson-Shore, Inc., is a member of Green Press Initiative, a nonprofit program dedicated to supporting authors, publishers, and suppliers in their efforts to reduce their use of fiber obtained from endangered forests.

For more information, visit www.greenpressinitiative.org

Inquiries should be addressed to:

Pineapple Press, Inc.
P.O. Box 3889
Sarasota, Florida 34230

www.pineapplepress.com

Library of Congress Cataloging-in-Publication Data

Jenkins, Greg, 1964–
    Florida's ghostly legends and haunted folklore / by Greg Jenkins.
        p. cm.
    Includes bibliographical references and index.
    ISBN 978-1-56164-399-8
        1. Ghosts—Florida. 2. Haunted places—Florida.   I. Title.
    BF1472.U6J47 2005
    133.1'09759—dc22 2004025871

First Edition
10 9 8 7 6 5 4 3 2 1

Design by Shé Heaton
Printed in the United States of America

Contents

Acknowledgments   vii

Preface   ix

Site Map   xv

Introduction *Florida's Unique Haunted Legends*   *xvi*

Pensacola: The Most Haunted City in Florida's Northwest *1*

1. The Pensacola Lighthouse   Pensacola .3
   Mysterious Blood Stains and a Foul-Mouthed Ghost

2. The Naval Air Station and Naval Hospital   Pensacola 12
   Eccentric Spirits and Ghostly Poker Games

3. Fort Pickens   Pensacola 22
   Empty Graves and Geronimo's Ghostly Presence

4. Pensacola Village   Pensacola 33
   Follow Pensacola Village's Haunted Trail

5. The Seville Quarter and Rosie O'Grady's   Pensacola Village 37
   Tales of the Bartender's Ghost and a Victorian Lady

6. T. T. Wentworth Jr. Florida State Museum   Pensacola Village 43
   Eerie Sighs and the Phantom Jumping Cat

7. The Dorr House   Pensacola Village 49
   The Translucent Lady

8. The Pensacola Little Theatre   Pensacola Village 56
   The Legend of Hosea Poole

9. The Lear-Rocheblave House   Pensacola Village 64
   Of Perfumed Ladies and Dancing Bones

10. Museums of Industry and Commerce   Pensacola Village 71
    Specters of Days Gone By

11. Old Christ Church   Pensacola Village 79
    Ghostly Monks in the Graveyard

Florida's Gulf Coast: Ghosts and Haunted Locations *87*

12. Island Hotel and Restaurant   Cedar Key 91
    13 Ghosts and More

13. The Royalty Theatre   Clearwater 103
    A Sea Captain, a Murdered Manager, and a Little Girl

14. Belleview Biltmore Resort and Spa   Clearwater 111
    Phone Calls from the Dead

15. Lover's Lane of Keene Road   Largo .121
    Still Late for the Prom

16. Haslam's Book Store   St. Petersburg 128
    Mr. Kerouac . . . is that you?

17. The Vinoy Hotel   St. Petersburg 137
    The Lady in White

18. St. Petersburg High School at Mirror Lake   St. Petersburg 145
    A Little School Spirit

19. Egmont Lighthouse   Egmont Key 155
    Beacon for the Dead

20. The Ritz-Carlton Hotel   Sarasota .166
    Loitering Phantoms of Ringling Towers

21. Ringling School of Art and Design   Sarasota 176
    Mary

22. Cracker Barrel Restaurant   Naples .185
    Nothing but Bad Memories

Afterthoughts   195
Appendix A: Tools of the Modern Ghost Hunter   200
Appendix B: Glossary   207
Appendix C: Ghost Research Organizations   217
Appendix D: Ghost Tours   222
Bibliography and Resources   228
Index   232

I dedicate this book to the memory of Mark Kuhlman, a good man who left us far too soon.

Acknowledgments

This book, *Florida's Ghostly Legends and Haunted Folklore, Volume 3,* is dedicated to all those who have the insight to look beyond the confines of conventional thought and media consistency. For exploring the evidence with an open mind and without undue judgment in order to find the truth, I wish to thank those personalities of the supernatural, the psychical researchers, and paranormal investigators that have afforded me the chance to explore beyond the regions of my own philosophies. Drs. Hans Holzer, Tony Cornell, Larry Montz, Loyd Auerbach, Barry Taft, Kerry Gaynor, William Roll, who first sparked my interest in the paranormal, and Dr. Andrew Nichols, Florida's own expert on the paranormal, who keeps my interest alive and strong today—I thank you all for the momentum you have offered me.

I also wish to thank Sheila Cavallo, a Florida-based psychic, for assisting me in my journey into the unknown in 2006. Thanks also to Ray Couch and Jack Roth, and the *Southern Ghosts Paranormal Research Team* for their insight and assistance in my investigations. WFLA AM 540, a great Florida radio station that kept me awake those late Saturday nights with ghostly tales and paranormal legends spun by Coast-to-Coast A.M. with Art Bell and George Noory— thanks for the inspiration that keeps me searching for those elusive ghosts everywhere.

I also wish to thank Kimberly Penkava, a good friend and fellow researcher, as well as the many paranormal and psychical research groups throughout the state that have assisted me with my explorations, and who carry on a passionate vigil toward the understanding and reasoning behind the many ghostly mysteries. Expressly, I wish to thank Betty Davis of Big Bend Ghost Trackers and the North Florida

Paranormal Research Group of Tallahassee, and Brandy Stark and the S.P.I.R.I.T.S. research team of St. Petersburg, another dedicated group, for their time and effort in exploring these otherwise extraordinary topics.

Finally, I thank Pineapple Press for having the vision to explore such topics as ghosts and the unknown, and to all those who have helped me make this book possible; the witnesses, the faithful, and those who keep Florida's unique, diverse oral traditions and enchanting folklore alive and well.

The purpose of this book is to continue the compendium on ghostly and haunted phenomena, as well as the many eerie locations found in the great state of Florida. It is also a registry of some of Florida's most strange and preternatural locations found in our cities, towns, national parks, cemeteries, and even in our own backyards. Some information, such as names and private addresses, is omitted for the sake of privacy.

During my investigations, which had taken me from one end of Florida to the other, visiting lonely cemeteries, old abandoned hospitals, and deserted communities, I had found myself in sheer awe of Florida's grand uniqueness. After interviewing hundreds of people over the last few years, I truly have been fortunate to learn even more of Florida's ghostly legends and haunted folklore—more than I could ever have hoped for.

Preface

Ghosts and haunted locations, life after death, and the shadows we sometimes see in the corners of our eyes were discussed at some length in my first two books, *Florida's Ghostly Legends and Haunted Folklore, Volumes One and Two.* Although one might think there could be no ghostly tales remaining in such a modern and sophisticated state like Florida, I offer yet a few more dark and rather creepy legends from the Sunshine State.

In volume one, I explored the darker aspects of Florida's haunted folklore in the southern and central regions of the state; though some of these tales inspire more dread than mere lore would, the reader went away with just a little more knowledge than before. Many of the stories I have researched have been passed down from generation to generation, where the legendary ghost in question is more a member of that family than something scary or evil. Still other spirits and ghostly entities appear to be the remnants of more brutal times in our history, acting as echoing reminders of the pain and torment they once suffered in life.

While writing volume one of *Florida's Ghostly Legends,* I had the opportunity to visit some of Florida's most exotic and beautiful locations. When exploring the sheer grandeur of the Biltmore Hotel in Coral Gables, I was amazed of the colorful history of this charming resort, as well as the turbulent past that for many of us time had forgotten. The exploits of the 1920s gangster "Fatty" Walsh and the Biltmore Hotel are legendary, and his spirit today is no less a notable figure than he once was, and is just as much the ladies' man today.

When my girlfriend and I dined at Caps Place Island Restaurant in Light House Point, we found more than simply a wonderful meal waiting for us. The distinct presence that so many feel there, as well as the scent of old cigar smoke whiffing through the air, certainly had us both looking over our shoulders, as if waiting for the spirit of old Theodore "Cap" Knight to walk out from the bushes. And, as I toured the Boca Raton Resort and Club only a few miles north, I couldn't help anticipating the jovial Addison Mizner strolling through the lush, ornate foyers of this gorgeous hotel, or his trusted servant Esmeralda tending to her host, leaving the scent of freshly cut roses wherever she went.

While investigating central Florida, including Tampa Bay, Orlando, and Cocoa Beach, I found myself in awe of the simplistic beauty Floridians are fortunate to enjoy year-round. But there is more than just beauty and a relaxing attitude to be found here. Central Florida's history will certainly speak for itself, and yet, there appears to remain an unseen reality to our state's history, which will sometimes show itself to the unsuspecting.

As I drove over the Sunshine Skyway Bridge on the west coast early one morning, I had hoped to see the hitchhiking ghost of a young girl who always searches for a ride to the other side. I gripped my steering wheel tightly as I remembered the horrible tragedy that took place there in 1980, and the many lives that were lost that early, foggy morning. When I walked through the huge marble mausoleum of the incredible yet eerie Myrtle Hill Cemetery near Ybor City, knowing that I was the only one there those late evenings, I did indeed hear the low whispers and out-of-place voices coming from the cold, dark recesses of this giant tomb—an experience that had me walking out of that frightening place in a hurry, with the hair on my neck standing on end.

As I explored the many haunted locations that south and central Florida offers, I knew I had to explore further. As I did so, I traveled up the state, surveying and collecting stories, in search of other time-honored urban legends and oral traditions that would otherwise remain hidden. In so doing, traveling to tiny hamlets like Micanopy, where you'll find the charming Herlong Mansion, and the mothering spirit of Inez Herlong-Miller, to the opulent Don CeSar Hotel, the crown jewel of Florida's romantic past, I surely knew I was fortunate to have encountered Florida at its best.

In volume two I investigated the northern regions of the state, as well as America's oldest city, St. Augustine. During my research into this region's haunted lore and spooky legends, I found a wellspring of never-before-heard stories. Legends like Dexter, the sad spirit who, though released from legal bondage for almost one hundred years now, repeats his nightly punishment of walking the cat walks and grounds of Henry Flagler's Old Jail in St. Augustine, and the mournful spirit of the Blue Lady who continues to make solemn rounds down the lonely corridors of Flagler College late at night.

As I explored a slew of haunted bed & breakfast inns and restaurants, all of which held one or more tormented ghosts of long ago, I found that the entire town seemed to have a spirited legend to it. As I continued my research in St. Augustine and other cities and towns in north Florida, I discovered the very creepy School #4 in Jacksonville, where tiny faces of long-dead children peer out from blackened, abandoned windows at weary late-night pedestrians and where strange moans and whimpers can sometimes be heard in the old deserted classrooms, for this was a school with a devilish reputation. As I traveled throughout the bustling city of Jacksonville, I found myself treated to many time-honored legends, like the eerie tale of the hanged women in the once-deserted Homestead Restaurant, or the sinister poltergeist who resides in the abandoned apartment #40 of the Carriage House Apartments, where all have sent chills down the spines of those who lived there.

Then there's the whaling spirit who paces the hallways of the old Blanche Hotel in Lake City, and the extremely haunted and dangerous Sunland Hospital in Tallahassee, where a plethora of strange events that echo a horrible and illicit past have alerted more than mere speculation for countless ghost hunters and paranormal investigators worldwide. Indeed, it seems the entire state of Florida is haunted, or as the old timers would say "hainted."

During my investigations, I had interviewed hundreds of people from all walks of life who have had personal experiences with the unknown. From homeowners and morticians to historians and policemen, and the enthusiastic ghost hunters, I have been afforded the chance to get the other side of these time-honored legends. Indisputably, I found myself being fueled by the intense aspects of history that Florida holds—both the good and the bad. As a result, I was able to find even more stories from the darker regions and creepy avenues of this great state.

After the successful review of my first two books on Florida's ghostly history, I was approached by many people who wanted to know more about the ghosts and spirits of the west coast and Panhandle of the state, saying that they had heard that there were many haunted locations in these areas, but so little had been written about them. I knew they were right, but in truth, if I were to report on every haunted legend and ghost story in the state of Florida alone, I would have to write a library on the subject. So I decided to do the next best thing—write another volume for the *Florida's Ghostly Legends and Haunted Folklore* saga. In this volume, I will take you even further into the Sunshine State's haunted realm, where what you read might just have you looking a bit closer at what was once taken for granted, and perhaps these stories will have you looking over your shoulder when that summer storm is raging outside, or when you're working late at night, alone in a quiet, deserted place. Maybe they will have you jump just a bit more when you hear an unexplainable thud in the darkened corner of your room—for who knows what's lurking there?

Though Florida offers many beautiful beaches and lakes, gorgeous hotels and landmarks, and of course many fabulous restaurants and cafés, there is nonetheless something else going on in the Sunshine State that is truly supernatural in nature. Though many of the things we see and speculate as the spirits of the dead may be nothing more than our imaginations—where perhaps these whispers and disembodied voices are in fact nothing more than the fear of the unknown, or an innate belief in the otherworldly—perhaps such things as ghosts do co-exist within our living reality. They may go unnoticed by some, yet by others they are seen, heard, and fully experienced. For some, ghosts are as real as you and I, able to inhabit our earthly realm as easily as we do, watching us, remembering, and wishing they too were alive.

Though there are many who will argue that ghosts are something actually explainable, something scientific, there are those who will choose to look beyond the fringes of rational thought and what we consider to be reality and simply believe. With that said, I invite you to once again prepare to go beyond Florida's bright, sunny days and step into the lesser-known, darker regions of our most haunted Florida.

Pensacola

1. The Pensacola Lighthouse
2. The Naval Air Station and Naval Hospital
3. Fort Pickens
4. Pensacola Village
5. The Seville Quarter and Rosie O'Grady's, Pensacola Village
6. T. T. Wentworth Jr. Florida State Museums, Pensacola Village
7. The Dorr Houses, Pensacola Village
8. The Pensacola Little Theatres, Pensacola Village
9. The Lear-Rocheblave Houses, Pensacola Village
10. Museums of Industry and Commerces, Pensacola Village
11. Old Christ Churchs, Pensacola Village

Florida's Gulf Coast

12. Island Hotel and Restaurant, Cedar Key
13. The Royalty Theatr, Clearwater
14. Belleview Biltmore Resort and Spa, Clearwater
15. Lover's Lane of Keene Road, Largo
16. Haslam's Bookstore, St. Petersburg
17. The Vinoy Hotel, St. Petersburg
18. St. Pete High School at Mirror Lake, St. Petersburg
19. Egmont Lighthouse, Egmont Key
20. The Ritz-Carlton Hotel, Sarasota
21. Ringling School of Art and Design, Sarasota
22. Cracker Barrel Restaurant, Naples

Site Map

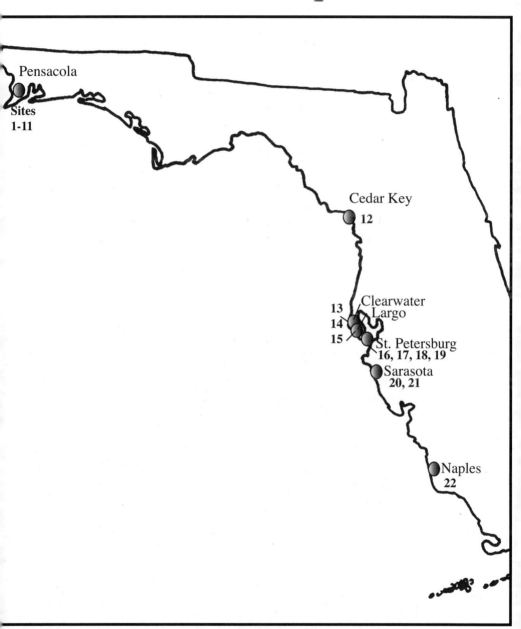

Pensacola

Sites
1-11

Cedar Key
12

Clearwater
Largo
13
14
15
St. Petersburg
16, 17, 18, 19
Sarasota
20, 21

Naples
22

Introduction

Florida's Unique Haunted Legends

"Traumatic events such as death release some sort of psychic energy that imprints itself on physical objects such as walls or furniture. . . . When people report seeing a ghost, they're seeing a replay of the imprint, like a natural hologram, rather than a disembodied conscience that's trying to interact. . . . It's as though places or objects are capable of retaining memories. . . . The brain acts as a type of VCR and plays back these types of events. . . ."
—*Dr. Andrew Nichols, Ph.D., Parapsychologist*
Associated Press, 2002

This quote from Dr. Andrew Nichols, parapsychologist, psychical researcher, educator, and chair of the department of psychology at City College in Gainesville, Florida, as well as author of *Ghost Detective: Adventures of a Parapsychologist* and president of the American Institute of Parapsychology, sums up a very rational and comprehensible view of that which we call a haunting. Dr. Nichols is not one to jump at every tale of the unknown, nor is he looking to confirm that every photograph of an orb or misty anomaly is proof of ghosts or life after death. No, he is a scientist first and foremost, so finding the facts is always job number one, meticulous research is second, and the use of precise scientific methodology third—uneducated speculation has no place in science, and equally, should have no place in serious paranormal research.

I had the pleasure of lecturing with Dr. Nichols last October, and am happy to consider him a colleague in the pursuit of truth within the realms of parapsychology and psychical research. Although his research is the direct pursuit of finding the facts of a spooky occurrence, the creaking doors and disembodied footsteps, it is my goal to dredge up the hidden history to the time-honored folktale and haunted legend. Though I have a firm belief in the reality of ghosts and spirits, mine is more the search for the story than that of the science of hauntings alone. I hunt out the creepy legend and the haunted folktale, digging as deep as I can go. In many cases, the haunted legend might just have an explainable answer, where our imaginations over many years had built up something much bigger than it should be. And sometimes, I find that one story that truly stands out and has little or no ties with a reliable explanation.

Though the endeavors of Dr. Nichols and myself seem vastly different, there is actually a close connection. Because the search for truth is our primary directive, and to hopefully demonstrate that the field of parapsychology and folklore are both respected and understandable professions, our agendas become clear. Indeed, the search for the haunted realm, whether it be in relating the ancient legends of spirits who haunt the living, or in proving that we are actually haunting ourselves, is the final question. To that end, it is my job to best relate the individual ghostly legend and the haunted tale, and then investigate as much as I and my colleagues can, and then offer the finished product to you, the reader. After all, in the end, you will be the judge—ghost or heated imagination?

As I began researching the concept of ghosts and haunted locations, all the while remaining grounded in the scientific endeavors of both psychical research and folkloric studies, I found myself indulging in the many individual ideals of what these vaporous entities are believed to be. Indeed, from the Swiss mountains to the jungles of Brazil, and from the fjords of Norway to the rich savannahs of Africa, and even the sunny beaches of Florida, people around the globe have believed in, seen, and felt the many separate guises of what we commonly refer to as a ghost or spirit apparent. Although no one truly knows for sure what these entities are, if they're just over-worked imaginations or the actual remains of a disembodied soul, many legends and folkloric tales have grown from such ideals nonetheless. And even though many rational, respectable and down-to-earth individuals have claimed to have encountered these strange wonders of our human existence, they remain in the thin ether of mythology.

Scholars and religious leaders believe that the human spirit may actually separate itself from the mortal coil and exist outside for a particular period of time. This time-span might last a few moments, or for many centuries, each having a purpose and time amongst the living. Though there appear to be many separate classifications of ghost, many parapsychologists refer to only a few traditional terms. The crisis apparition, for instance, is a spirit said to show itself to a family member as either a warning of danger to come or to give assurance that the apparition in question did indeed pass on. This type of spirit may be trying to tell the living that he or she is content with the afterlife and that the living should move on with their lives and not worry.

Other forms of spectral entities may seem to repeat themselves with a particular action. One example of this type of spirit would be the legend of a lady in white who is seen walking up the stairs of an old English castle every midnight when the moon is full. Though a little clichéd, this category of spirit is not necessarily an independently intelligent entity. In fact, most researchers believe that this form of spirit is nothing more than a recording. As with a video tape, CD, or DVD, the image or sound plays back when prompted by something—seen or unseen. Perhaps it's a particular time or place that activates this ghostly recording or perhaps it's a person that inspires this paranormal behavior; either way, this form of psychical incident has been reported since recorded time.

The poltergeist phenomena, though represented violently in most movies and books, are actually quite harmless. From the German root words *polter* meaning noisy and *geist* meaning spirit, the true representation of this phenomenon is more the prankster, or maker of bumps or knocking sounds than that of child-stealing, otherworldly monsters. This type of spirit might be responsible for atmospherically spooky phenomena such as phones constantly ringing when no one is calling, objects moving by themselves, or disembodied sounds, voices, and music. At its most active state, a poltergeist outbreak might intensify all the aforementioned attributes, yet might also end at a quicker rate. Regardless of the method of the poltergeist representation, it is usually a compelling aspect to psychical research and a definite source of intrigue for the folklorist.

Other varieties of ghost appear to have a definite intelligence, as if co-existing in our own particular reality and dimension and going about a particular task. Many scientists of the paranormal believe that such entities actually co-exist with us, but belong to a place beyond a thin veil between our physical reality and theirs. The classic haunting for instance, where cold spots of air can be felt, a creaking floor board in an empty house being heard, a door that slowly opens by itself, or perhaps the rancid odor of decaying flesh, may all constitute the possibility of what we call a haunting. Although these examples are of course stereotypical, as portrayed in the movies and novels, such things may be proof that a haunting is taking place.

Haunted locations can be a house, a hotel, an apartment building, or even a supermarket. Cemeteries and battlefields may have a preternatural residue, where vibrations of tragic events from the past may form "portals" for such ethereal entities like ghosts cross over into our realities. Many practitioners of the paranormal believe the whole world is in fact a haunted place, filled with a complex array of supernatural highways. Others simply do not believe, feeling that such events are nothing more than a settling house or wind blowing through an attic. Perhaps the reality of the ghost story is nothing more than a good legend that originated during a thunderstorm when the lights went out—the environment was just right for telling such a story, thus initiating a folktale that might last for centuries. Maybe that haunted legend is based on a factual event that once took place, but over years of storytelling, had developed into something a bit more than the original incident.

The paranormal investigator or parapsychologist may be a professor at a college or university, most likely trained in fields such as psychology, anthropology, folkloric studies, or physics. Such people study the possible causes and effects of alleged hauntings, or the presence of a ghost, and will use various scientific equipment and procedures to rule out the possibility of a more down-to-earth cause for the seemingly ghostly events. Although many ghostly occurrences, like a house shaking every day or night at a certain time, may in truth have logical explanations, such as a passing train in a nearby town, or even a subterranean river splashing against the earth basin below, not all eerie occurrences have such logical explanations.

Most of these highly trained people may truly want to detect the presence of said spirits and specters, yet reserve judgment until they have sufficient proof and scientific evidence for the existence of such entities. The ever-popular ghost hunter, who is becoming increasingly popular every day, is usually a lay person who may work an average day-to-day job and who has no formal training in the study of psychology or parapsychology. Notwithstanding, their devotion to this fascinating study into the unknown is as real and as determined as that of the scholarly professor or seasoned scientist. Indeed, these people may hold typical jobs by day, but when night falls, they take part in the rather spooky, nocturnal activity of hunting ghosts.

You might find these people creeping through an old abandoned building or graveyard equipped with digital cameras, video recorders, and a large array of pseudo-scientific gadgets in hopes of finding proof of life after death. This ghost hunter may have a ready supply of electromagnetic frequency analyzers, portable temperature gauges, hygrometers, infrared goggles, and a variety of other strange, science fiction–like devices, all available via the Internet. Without a doubt, the search for ghosts isn't just for the Hollywood ghost-buster anymore.

With that said; whether you are a scholar of paranormal and psychical research, an enthusiastic ghost hunter, or just someone who enjoys a good ghost story when the lights are low and the atmosphere is just right, prepare yourself for another selection of Florida's ghostly legends and haunted folklore that spans from the Panhandle down the beautiful west coast. Prepare for the unknown things that really do go bump in the night and remember that we are truly not alone.

Pensacola

Pensacola
The Most Haunted City in Florida's Northwest

Located northwest in the Panhandle of the state, resting serenely on the Gulf of Mexico, is beautiful Pensacola. With a rich history, this section of Florida has much to offer for visitors and natives alike. With the sun blazing down on the beaches and parks, and with many attractions and an active nightlife, it's no wonder why so many come here to play, explore, and just have fun.

Pensacola is also the home of the world-famous Blue Angels, which are based at the nearby US Naval Air Station. When visiting the naval base, you can view the decommissioned Blue Angel jets hanging in a diamond formation on display in the National Museum of Naval Aviation. When exploring the city and historic sights—such as Historic Pensacola Village, the Pensacola Historical Museum, Ft. Pickens, Ft. Barrancas, and of course the festive Seville Historic District—you'll glimpse Florida at its best. From historical forts that protected our shores during the Civil War to the modern bases that had trained sailors and pilots during every war and conflict since, it's simple to see Pensacola's importance to the United States and to Florida's unique history.

Pensacola and its surrounding area offers a wide variety of shops, bed and breakfast inns, restaurants, art galleries, and museums, as well as many recreational activities such as boating, diving, parasailing, tennis, deep-sea fishing, and golfing on world-class courses. In nearby Gulf Breeze the zoo, which has over six hundred exotic and native animals, and the botanical gardens, offer the peaceful, natural side of our great state. But don't be fooled by the beautiful scenery—there is a dark side lurking just beyond nightfall. Indeed, seekers of the unknown find a little something for them here, as well. Spirits and ghosts are certainly among the living here, as there are haunted houses, schools, and hotels, not to mention hospitals, plazas, and cemeteries.

Ghost hunters will not be disappointed here, as one only needs to look, listen, and prepare to explore with history in mind. As with anywhere reputed to be haunted, there seems to be a connection between hauntings and places of intense action, pain, and misery—and Pensacola certainly has such places. Hospitals and psychiatric centers are often rife with spirit activity long after the building itself has been closed or refitted for some other use. Schools and active locations such as malls and plazas are also reputed to echo the past, as are hotels, motels, bed and breakfast inns, and the common home and apartment complex. Pensacola has them all.

To kick off our ghost hunting investigations of Pensacola and the Gulf coast, I am beginning with the northwest section of the state and moving downward along the coast. Because Pensacola is a very large and lively place from a paranormal viewpoint, I will deliberate on its haunted locations accordingly. Furthermore, as there are most likely far too many locations to list, I am covering some of the most common localities in this region. As we move further down the coast, we will visit beautiful Sarasota, St. Petersburg, Clearwater, Naples, and other locations that are filled with haunted legend and ghostly folklore. Without question, you'll soon see just how spiritually active the state of Florida truly is. Therefore I invite you to, once again, prepare to go beyond Florida's bright, sunny days, and vacationing spots, to once more step into the lesser-known, darker areas of our most haunted Florida.

1

The Pensacola Lighthouse

"Mysterious Blood Stains and a Foul-Mouthed Ghost"

A Little History

Having been a true fan of all things nautical—coastal villages, tall ships and especially the majestic lighthouses across the coastlines of our great country—I felt that my first investigation into the ghostly lore of Florida's Panhandle and the west coast should begin with the Pensacola Lighthouse. This is a landmark with historical significance, along with a few spirits to boot. I found that this intriguing lighthouse offers the usual trappings, such as a stately home for the lightkeeper and his family, the cascading waves lapping the nearby shore, and the oaks and Australian pines swaying in the breeze. Indeed, the very image of the Pensacola Lighthouse is as picturesque as any antique postcard—but there appears to be so much more to this particular lighthouse.

When Pensacola, the state's second-oldest city, became a major seaport, there was a desperate need for a powerful lighthouse to guide the major shipping lanes. By 1824 Congress appropriated enough money for a modest beacon, to be called the Barrancas Lighthouse, which would hold a fourteen-inch parabolic reflector lens and be

3

fueled by a ten-whale-oil-lamp system. It was to be built on a raised section of land in order for the light to have the best effect visually. Unfortunately, this section of land and other similar spots nearby had been used as a cemetery, so the first order of business was to relocate the stone and wood markers to begin construction. As it was considered unnecessary to move the actual remains of those buried there, only a shovel of dirt to honor the soul beneath the marker was turned, and construction continued. The tower and a huge surrounding wall was finished in due time.

Regrettably, the lighthouse was simply inadequate for mariners of the day, and by December 1859 a new and more efficient lighthouse had been completed half a mile west of the original Barrancas Lighthouse. The new lighthouse was fitted with a state-of-the-art Fresnel lens, fashioned by the famous French crystal-cutter Henri LePaite. This new lens, which is mounted atop the 150-foot tower, stands 191 feet above sea level and emits eight intense beams of over 300,000 candlepower that can be seen more than twenty-five miles in all oceanward directions. During the Civil War, the expensive lens was secretly hidden in Montgomery, Alabama, so it would not be destroyed or stolen by Federal or Confederate troops. Thankfully, the valuable lens was returned safe and secure by 1869 and has continued to aid mariners ever since.

The first lightkeepers were a husband and wife team named Jeremiah and Michaela Ingraham. Jeremiah was officially appointed in1824 and served until he died in 1840. After his death, Michaela continued as the lightkeeper until she died in 1855. Although their time together was a notable passage in history, there have, nonetheless, been rumors about this duo. Indeed, reports of infidelity and murder have echoed from this historic landmark for many years. Were Jeremiah and Michaela the victims of foul play? History only knows. And apparently, history isn't saying much.

Over many years the ghostly legends would continue to grow out of proportion, than wane again to nothing, leaving any truth of the rumors to remain as much a ghost as the alleged spirits who are said to reside there. Indeed, legends came and went, just as the lightkeep- ers have done since the nineteenth century. The lighthouse would continue to guide ships in from hurricanes and foggy nights and watch over the people of Pensacola with little incident. Life was simple in old Florida, and that's the way folks liked it.

By 1938, electricity was finally installed and indoor plumbing replaced the outhouse and cistern wells, creating living conditions for twentieth-century comfort. Soon thereafter, the United States Coast Guard officially took command of all the lighthouses in the country, extinguishing the use of civilian employees for private service. To be a lighthouse keeper, one either enlisted in the Coast Guard or remained a civilian worker who was a pre-appointed employee of the U.S. government. This arrangement continued until the mid-1960s, when most lighthouses were automated, and many would become simple sub-stations for the Coast Guard. Thus would end the romantic era of lightkeepers along the nation's shores.

The lightkeeper's house, a two-story wood and brick home, is an elegant example of early Floridian architecture. This structure is complete with covered verandas and white picket fences, sporting high doorways, quaint windows, and cozy fireplaces. In its heyday, these verandas would have been laden with delightful flowerpots and wood rockers for that homey feeling. There would have been clothes hanging on lines, the lightkeeper's children playing in the massive yard, and an abundance of swaying trees as far as the eye could see. Today, however, there is a darker essence to the structure, and a rather sad and sullen feeling to the entire area. Though the lighthouse remains relatively the same in appearance and function, the original need of the structure and for a living keeper facilitating it has certainly changed.

Throughout the years there have been several lightkeepers who have overseen the safety of seafarers during both war and peace. And, though the lightkeeper's life and duties were for the most part typical, even to some extent boring, there have been a few notable points in Pensacola's history that should be discussed. Legends of sordid love affairs and ghastly murders, of unspeakable hardships and of heroic patriotism—this modest lighthouse has them all. More than just one ghost is reputed to stalk the grounds, hallways, and stairwells of this haunted lighthouse.

Ghostly Legends and Haunted Folklore

As the Civil War ended, life went on as normally as could be expected, minus a few earth-shaking events like the damaging lightning strikes of 1875 that burnt down most of the roof on the lightkeeper's home and the tornados that destroyed a good portion of the tower in 1877. Let's not forget the bizarre earthquakes that centered in Charleston, South Carolina, and rumbled on down to northern Florida in 1886. Of course, there were also two world wars and the Korean and Vietnam conflicts, but life went on as usual at the Panhandle lighthouse.

Over those many years, people have reported strange and downright paranormal occurrences here. From disembodied voices and echoing footsteps upon the 166 steps within the tower to cold breezes and icy grips from unseen hands, strange goings on in and around the old Pensacola lighthouse have always been detected by sensitive people.

This lighthouse, like so many other famous buildings and landmarks, carries an oral tradition of a famous event which makes it easy to realize how such legends can grow over the years, creating even more of a mystery. A case in point is the legendary murder and betrayal within the Pensacola lighthouse. Even though this horrific event allegedly took place more than 150 years ago, and even though there are no recorded documents of it, those who love a good mystery or ghost story will not question its authenticity.

As the story goes, the first lightkeepers, Jeremiah and Michaela Ingraham, appointed to run the lighthouse in the early nineteenth century, had faithfully served until Jeremiah died of either a heart attack or by a fatal fall in 1840. Another version is that the lightkeeper was repeatedly stabbed by either his wife or an unknown jealous lover. History tells us that Michaela continued as the lightkeeper until her death in 1855. If Jeremiah had been murdered, there was no recorded documentation to verify it. I had the opportunity to interview several people concerning this lighthouse, including Coast Guard personnel and local residents, and the facts of this crime remain vague from their point of view. What we do know about the fate of Mr. and Mrs. Ingraham is that they served honorably and with a clean record, with no legal arrest or intervention taking place. So who, then, is the spirit or spirits that haunt the lighthouse and surrounding compound? Though this remains the primary question, there are even more reasons for speculation.

The ghostly manifestations reported at the Pensacola lighthouse seem to point to a murder. In the main living area, near the fireplace, where the murder was said to have taken place, there is sometimes a dark red stain where the murder was said to have taken place. Some legends tell that on stormy nights, especially when there is an abundance of thunder and lightning, the stain appears and even gets moist. This type of haunting has a history, where many tell-tale signs linger on years after an event takes place. We will never know for sure if the appearance of this stain is evidence that a heinous crime took place.

If you visit the lighthouse and wander through the lightkeeper's home, you will see what appears to be bloodstains just to the left of the fireplace, and a few spots of long-dried blood, as if the victim wandered through the area before his death. Several local historians believe that there may have been a bed or even a group of beds in that area used as a makeshift hospital during the Civil War, which might support a more down-to-earth explanation for the stains. Even though the floor has been sanded and coated with a polyurethane layer, it still remains a mystery as to why a bloodstain would continue to appear after so many years.

Other ghostly phenomena are reported in and around the lighthouse and the adjacent home. On certain nights and during stormy weather, the sounds of echoing footsteps can sometimes be heard. It is said that when someone walks up the spiral steps within the lighthouse and sits in the middle section of the steps, that light footsteps and labored breathing can be heard even when the tower is empty. In addition, some witnesses have reported feeling cold blasts of wind rushing past them as they ascended the stairs, as if the foundation door had swung open during a November gale.

Recently, there was trouble with the light and the lens would not pivot properly, so a Coast Guard official was called to check out the problem and repair the light, if necessary. When he and his wife unlocked the main door of the lighthouse tower, both got the feeling that something was out of place and stood perfectly still to survey the situation. Within a moment they began to hear the low murmurings of a man swearing, as if annoyed. The cursing seemed to get louder and then stopped altogether. Though a little frightened, both the Coast Guard official and his wife entered to see who was in there, since all of the compound doors had been locked with heavy deadbolts. They searched the entire area and found no sign of an intruder or any evidence that someone had been there. Things were as they should be.

There were other, similar, incidents, witnessed by both Coast Guard personnel and locals. Strange laughter has occasionally been heard at the top of the tower and doors have been known to open and close by themselves. Door knobs slowly turned, but when investigated, no one was behind the door. There have been reports of icy hands gripping arms or hands when someone is climbing the stairwell, and on occasion there have been reports of faint images of a man with a beard wearing dark clothes, and a woman dressed in a heavy, dark green or gray dress seen walking around the compound; this was the style of clothing worn about a hundred years ago.

Although visual reports of the resident specters are rare, there has been evidence of "orb" activity in and around the lighthouse and surrounding areas. These small iridescent balls of light have been reported in clusters in the main living area and bedrooms of the lightkeeper's house. Such activity is believed to be evidence of spectral activity. Many ghost hunters, psychical researchers, and psychics have come here to investigate these occurrences over the years. Who haunts this lonely lighthouse is a good question, since people have lived and died here since its creation over 150 years ago, and having a lighthouse built on top of a forgotten cemetery is bound to make more than one restless spirit linger.

Afterthoughts

From almost the inception of lighthouses, guarding the shores and jetties of almost every port and waterway throughout the world, strange tales have followed them throughout history. Whether you believe the lighthouse beacon can attract spirits as a light to the Other Side or that they hold the ghosts of the past is entirely up to you. Personally, I do believe there is something going on at this lighthouse and inside the keeper's home. There is no recorded proof that a murder took place there, but after so many years with no record keeping, it is indeed possible to forget. When you visit this lovely, if a bit spooky, lighthouse, be sure to speak with the staff or with one of the Coast Guard liaisons, as they are sure to have a story to tell.

If you're lucky enough to be visiting on a particularly gloomy day, be sure to wait until everyone else has vacated the tower before climbing the stairs. Be sure to sit near the middle of the stairway and listen for the light, ever-so-faint echoes of feet walking on the stairs above you, and listen for the slight panting of breath. While in the lightkeeper's home, look for the bloodstain that is said to have been made from the violent wounds of the murdered lighthouse keeper of long ago. Who knows? Perhaps you too will have an unearthly experience to claim as your own.

Tours of the keeper's home are given from the first Sunday of May to the last Sunday in October, from 12 P.M. to 3 P.M. Be sure to check these times and schedules as they may change. For more information about the times and dates, call the Pensacola Coast Guard at 850-455-2354.

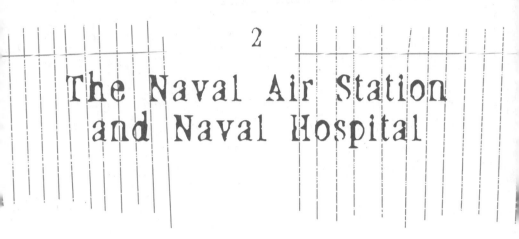

2

The Naval Air Station
and Naval Hospital

"Eccentric Spirits and Ghostly Poker Games"

A Little History

When visiting Pensacola, be sure to visit the Naval Air Station and the famous Whiting Air Field, located just northeast of Pensacola in the quaint city of Milton, in Santa Rosa County. The naval station, simply referred to as NAS, is one of the Navy's primary pilot-training and proving bases. The NAS also supports advanced training for the United States Coast Guard, Marine Corps, and Air Force, as well as a few allied nations.

Whiting Field is comprised of two separate airfields with one support base to oversee both. On any given day you might see a plethora of military aircraft soaring the skies of Pensacola and nearby towns. From T-34c Mentors to TH-57 Sea Rangers, including allied aircraft, visitors and natives alike will be treated to a unique display of aircraft in full regalia. However, it wasn't always like that. Florida's history is steeped in defined cultures dating as far back as the Spanish influence of the sixteenth century, when Don Tristan de Luna built his tiny colony where Fort Barrancas now rests. Until the purchase of Florida

Florida State Archives

from Spain in 1821, the banners of Spain, France, and England were flying over the port of Pensacola.

During World War I, Pensacola was still one of the few full-time air stations, with thirty-eight Naval Aviators, fewer than two hundred enlisted men trained in flying, and no more than fifty-five active, combat-ready planes. By 1918, after the Armistice Treaty was signed, the Pensacola air station increased its training and resources to a staggering 438 flight officers, 5,538 enlisted men, and more than 1,000 trained aviators. By the 1920s, there were combat aircraft, seaplanes, and dirigible balloons, as well as hangars and barracks lining the Corry Air Field for more than a mile up the beach. The Naval Air Station of Pensacola became known as the Annapolis of the Air.

When America was gearing up for World War II, NAS of Pensacola expanded once again by building better facilities, barracks, and air fields. By the late 1930s, several auxiliary bases were constructed to add to our air fleet. Saufley and Ellyson Airfields were commissioned for use. Three more auxiliary fields were added later: Barin, Bronson, and Whiting Fields, all named after early naval aviators. Once again, history was made with the help of Pensacola's brave fighting pilots and instructors.

By the Korean conflict, the major transition of technology had changed Pensacola from propeller-driven aircraft to jet-powered dynamos that would, in effect, change the course of the American military. By the 1970s, the NAS became the headquarters site for the Naval Air Basic Training Command. From that time to the present, the NAS of Pensacola developed into a base of high technology and advanced theory in air combat, housing the headquarters and staff of the Chief of Naval Education and Training; the Training Air Wing Six and its subordinate squadrons; the Naval Aviation Schools Command; the Aerospace Medical Research Laboratory and Operational Medicine Institute; the Naval Air Technical Training Center; a computer and telecommunications station; and the Blue Angels Squadron. It also houses the National Museum of Naval Aviation.

The Naval Hospital of Pensacola has been in continued operation for more than 175 years, practically since the birth of Florida as a state. It is one of the oldest and most respected navy medical facilities in the country. The hospital officially opened its doors in 1826, as a two-story rented home located just north of Fort Barrancas near the Bayou Grande. President John Quincy Adams assigned the first surgeon there, Dr. Isaac Hulse. For years, Dr. Hulse and his senior medical officer made sure the sick and wounded received the best care possible. Soon thereafter, the hospital would grow from that meager house on the bayou, to a fifteen-acre compound with more than twenty-five beds, a laboratory, and a surgical room. From there it expanded into the sprawling compound of buildings, as it stands today.

The present Naval Hospital of Pensacola has one of the Navy's few family practice residency-training programs, with an emphasis on comprehensive family care, including emergency, surgical, and obstetric care. This hospital serves active personnel, as well as veterans and their families, with in-patient and out-patient care. Along with this amazing aero-technology and medical care in sunny Pensacola, there also appears to be a hearty selection of ghosts, spirits, and paranormal incidents.

Ghostly Legends and Haunted Folklore

When we speak of ghosts and hauntings, we might ask ourselves what marks a place as haunted. Can a particular location embrace the exclusive spiritual essence of a person's soul? This question is difficult to answer, ghosts or hauntings cannot be truly defined. When we think of a place holding a memory, like that of a recording, the question is why? What causes a location to keep replaying a past incident in the first place? This is the question that applies itself directly to the Naval Air Station, the Naval Hospital, and surrounding buildings in the heart of Pensacola, Florida.

As I have toured this air base, its compound, and the adjacent lighthouse over many years, I was aware that the place was haunted. Sometimes you can be in a place and just know that there is something out of the ordinary about it. This could be in the way a building feels, or even catching a glimpse of something out of the corner of the eye. This can also occur while working alone in a location that emits a strange or unusual vibration or feeling, or is reputed to be haunted. This is the feeling I got while walking around the old naval base and surrounding complex, as I make a habit of researching a location as completely as I can before making any statements about a haunting. I simply report the findings—other people's experiences and my own. Indeed, Pensacola truly appears to be teeming with ghosts and haunted places. In any good haunted legend, there should be a playful ghost, a sullen spirit, and many odd occurrences to make your hair stand up, and the NAS has them all!

Likely to be the most popular specter on the premises of the naval base is that of Captain Guy Hall, an ace flyer and flight instructor with the United States Marine Corps, who met an untimely death while engaged in a training mission just after World War I. Captain Hall was an almost Hollywood-like example of what the marine corps pilots were to resemble, including a leather jacket, knee-high boots, and a rugged look that would have the enemy running in the other direction. When the Captain was off-duty or on furlough, he would enjoy a whisky or beer and an all-night poker game with friends and cohorts. Even though Captain Hall had died while trying to land his plane on Corry Field in 1926, he still enjoys his poker games, and no one is going to tell this marine to go home for the night!

Apparently, Building 16 is one of the many certified haunted locations throughout the naval base that has received more than its share of ghostly reputation. During the 1920s, the octagon-shaped building was used as the officers' quarters, which housed many pilots and servicemen. It stands to reason, then, that there might be various forms of haunted activity here. Base legend tells us that Captain Hall enjoyed playing poker so much that he still plays long after his death. The captain had the habit of dropping the poker chips on the table, making a loud crashing and snapping sound that could be heard throughout the barracks and officers' quarters. To this day, this sound can still be heard on certain nights, as a ghostly reminder of a good time long gone by.

Another interesting tale is the ghostly Commandant of Admiral's Row, a story of unfortunate circumstance and urban legend gone wrong. If you have the chance to drive up Admiral's Row on the base, after acquiring the proper permission, proceed up Johnson Street to Quarters-A. Here you will see a gorgeous home designed in the old Florida style with a touch of New England elegance—one that's said to be quite haunted. At one time, Commodore Melanchton B. Woolsey was the first commandant to reside in this stately residence during the nineteenth century. He was said to have been a stern leader, but also a little eccentric in his beliefs and mannerisms. Though he served without major incident and was well-liked by most of his subordinates and comrades, he was an individual who had to have things his way.

By the middle of the 1800s, a terrible outbreak of yellow fever was taking its toll on Florida and much of the South. Because of excessive rain along with the summer heat, the mosquito population was out of control. Current medical information was certain that mosquitoes were the culprits in carrying the dreaded disease, and the level of fear was high, especially for Commodore Woolsey. In fact, as naval legend tells it, Commodore Woolsey was so frightened of contracting the yellow fever that he gathered all of his important belongings and moved upstairs into the third-story cupola. There he received all his meals, having everything brought up to him in a wicker basket attached to a rope. The commodore took part in other protective rituals, such as lighting candles and drinking lots of spiced rum, which he believed would make an excellent tonic to ward off the yellow fever. He always had enough pipe tobacco for his pipe and took to wearing long-sleeved clothing even in the summer. By doing this, he fully believed he would be spared. He was wrong.

One day, when his orderly forgot to pack a fresh bottle of spiced rum in his daily basket, Commodore Woolsey immediately fell ill and died within a few days. Whether or not the good Commodore actually stayed alive by the regiment of spiced rum and tobacco is anyone's guess, but he is said to walk the cupola on many a late night, and sometimes his hand, arm, and part of his body can be seen as if descending the stairs. Others say he can be seen walking throughout the elegant home and even up and down the streets of this lovely section of the NAS.

Another spirit said to haunt this home is a lady in white, though she appears more translucent. This spirit remains a mystery. Some say that she was the wife of an important official on the base back during the First World War. Other suggest that she goes back further still to the Civil War, having been widowed and dying alone in the exact location where this elegant house now stands. Though no one is exactly certain who she was, what people do know is that she is seen walking throughout this home with a kind of glow, showing only the merest outline of an adult woman. Her identity will undoubtedly remain a mystery for the rest of eternity.

As we venture to the base hospital that has been in operation in one form or another since before the Civil War, it's not hard to imagine that such a location could be haunted by the spirits of those long deceased. If I were to list all the names of the people that died, and whose bodies were stored here, after disaster or war, the list would fill more than half of this book. Regardless, there is no doubt that there have been many strange events recorded here, such as lights that sometimes go on and off by themselves, or occasionally staff members will hear their names being called late at night. Shadowy faces have been seen through darkened windows, and it will sometimes get very cold in places where it should be warm. No one really questions these things, however; they simply ignore them and focus on their work. The exception is the night crew, the nurses, the orderlies, security guards, and the countless others who keep the operations going after the sun sets. These people are likely to be the first to observe the paranormal activities, and many there will tell you so.

In the interviews I conducted, I have been told that among the most startling events are the odd sounds that echo from the basement recesses, along with the clicks, snaps, and footsteps that can be heard on the stairwells. Of course, these sounds can all be attributed to logical, down-to-earth events rather than spooks and specters. Yet when the witnesses investigate these strange sounds, nothing can be found.

Other odd events include cold spots, and sometimes, a semi-warm breath may be felt on the necks of late-night nurses, female orderlies, lab techs, and others while they walk the floors at night. Apparently, whoever this spirit is, it still enjoys the run of the entire hospital, as almost every floor has some kind of haunted history attributed to it.

The old boiler room section, now used primarily as an engineering level, is thought to be one of the most haunted places in the hospital. Though this area is restricted to non-personnel, ask someone from the night shift, or if you are lucky enough to get permission to enter this area, walk down the stairs to where the pumps once stood. Wait there in the dark, and as legend has it, you will begin to hear voices echoing from that general area. On occasion, people have reported hearing the voice of someone asking questions, but never able to fully understand what is being said. The voice is reported as if someone talking from within a box. There is no record of whether this was the original location used for the storage of those who died after such disasters as the great yellow fever epidemic of the 1880s or during the unrecorded hurricanes and other disasters that had taken place over the many years, but many have suggested this possibility.

As this hospital and the entire naval base appears to be haunted by a cascade of spectral entities, it is plain to see that something uncanny is, indeed, taking place there. Are there ghosts roaming the halls and stairwells of the Pensacola Naval Hospital? Many believe so—even a few level-headed doctors and nurses. What's causing these ghostly manifestations and spooky outbreaks? Only the walls of this hospital, or perhaps its ancient foundation, know for sure. What is certain is that with the many pilots and military personnel and the medical staff and civilians who work both within and around the Naval Air Station and the Naval Hospital Pensacola, is that there is something going on there—something very strange and a little frightening.

Afterthoughts

Pensacola's history is filled with many horrific events which are equal to that of any other city in the United States. It has survived many hardships and tragedies, along with many hurricanes that blasted the shores, estuaries, and bayous, taking many lives in their wake, so it stands to reason that this city and the surrounding areas are teeming with spectral activity. Since this is Florida's second-oldest seaport and one of its oldest cities, there's bound to be psychic residue left in the recesses of the buildings and homes where so much activity took place.

Paranormal researchers, ghost hunters, and psychics visiting the Naval Air Station and the nearby hospital will find the entire experience a delight, as it is likely they will not leave empty-handed. Many researchers and ghost hunters have captured a plethora of photographic anomalies such as orbs and tornado-like spectral images known as vortexes. Some have captured what they believe to be the voices of the dead, through electronic voice phenomena (EVP) in the basement section of the hospital, as well as detecting other abnormalities while using gadgetry of various scientific significance, so a semblance of scientific proof has been attained.

When visiting the very active and festive city of Pensacola, be sure to enjoy the nightlife in nearby downtown and the historic Seville district. Enjoy the many antique shops and fine restaurants, visit the museums and have fun on the beaches, but don't forget to bring your camera. Since there are so many spirits reputedly haunting this area, don't be surprised if you bring someone or "something" home with you. Many believe this is one of the most haunted cities in the United States.

The Navel Air Station and Hospital is located at 450 Turner Street near downtown Pensacola. To get there; take I-110 to Exit 4 and then right on Fairfield Drive until you see signs for NAS Pensacola, which will take you to New Warrington Road. The hospital is approximately four miles from there. For further information or assistance, call the main information number at: 850-505-6601 or e-mail PAO@pcola.med.navy.mil or visit the Pensacola website at www.historicpensacola.org/visitorinformation.asp.

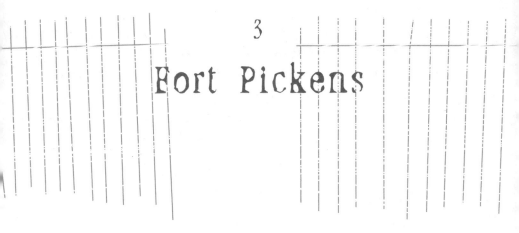

3

Fort Pickens

"Empty Graves and Geronimo's Ghostly Presence"

A Little History

On the westernmost shores of Santa Rosa Island, just seven miles from Pensacola Beach, lies one of Florida's most celebrated fortresses—Fort Pickens. Named after the Revolutionary War hero Andrew Pickens, this pentagonal garrison was built by indentured slaves, and completed in 1834 as a major military fortification to help defend Fort McRee, Fort Barrancas, and the Pensacola naval shipyard. Fort Pickens was originally designed by French military engineer Simon Bernard, who was hired by the United States as a consultant, and appointed in charge of engineers. Bernard began construction on the fort with new and improved concepts of design, radical to previous American fortresses. Although the fort's design was a rather new concept in relation to French-influenced fortifications and harbor defenses, Bernard made sure that Fort Pickens and the other forts were all calculated to work in concert when defending the harbor mouth and naval shipyard.

By the time the American Civil War had begun, Fort Pickens came to the forefront of all the fortresses due to its location in a

defendable position. Though the fort had been vacant since the Mexican-American War, and was somewhat rundown at the time, a Union officer named Lt. Adam J. Slemmer, stationed at Fort Barrancas and in charge of U.S. forces quickly determined that Fort Pickens was more impregnable than any of the other fortifications in the area, and made Fort Pickens the primary command outpost; it would remain under Union control throughout the Civil War.

Fort Pickens survived admirably throughout the war; surviving the brunt of Confederate attacks on many occasions without surrender, and never sustaining enough damage to necessitate its evacuation. After the war, the fort continued to act as the main defense against any possible attack that might arise, but it would need to advance greatly in combat technology to counter more modern enemies. By the late 1800s, there would be ten concrete-base gun batteries, including large cannons in the middle of the old fort designed for both sea and air attacks, which would supply ample firepower to keep an enemy navy or subversive army at bay. Instead of war, however, the once combat-worthy fortress would end up becoming somewhat of a famous military penitentiary, as it would incarcerate one of the most famous Native Americans in history—Geronimo, the notorious Apache Indian chief.

Though considered one of the most deadly and cunning Indians in American history, Geronimo and his warriors made a reputation for themselves as the murderous attackers of pioneer settlers and Mexican soldiers during the height of the Wild West era. Though his harsh reputation may have been more fanciful fiction than pure truth, he was one of last American Indians to formally surrender to the United States.

From 1885 to 1887, the legendary Apache chief was imprisoned at Fort Pickens, along with several of his warriors and their families. During Geronimo's stay here, he became somewhat of a local celebrity, and more of a folk hero than a dreaded enemy. Many of Pensacola's townsfolk came to see him and listen to his stories of adventure, as well as to learn of Indian customs. He would often sell the buttons from his wool coat to the locals as souvenirs, and sit for hours telling stories to women and children. Indeed, he became more a friend to the people of Pensacola than a caged military prisoner.

Geronimo was known to have had at least nine wives during his life, and was married to two women while he was held at Fort Pickens. And though incarcerated, he seemed to have made a somewhat regular life for himself, at least as much as possible in a prison. But, as his legend and presence had become so popular with the town's residents, Union officials decided to relocate the chief and his family to Fort Sill in Oklahoma, unbeknownst to the townsfolk. The famous chief and his family were moved out of Fort Pickens in the dead of night, so as not to excite the people, and Chief Geronimo would remain a prisoner of war the rest of his life, never to return to his homeland in the Mexican territories. He died on February 17, 1909, and was buried in Fort Sill's Apache cemetery. One of Geronimo's wives from Fort Pickens is buried in the Barrancas National Cemetery, now a part of the Pensacola Naval Air Station.

As time went on, and the legend of Chief Geronimo simply faded away, as did the need for coastal fortresses, an era of American history had ended. With the advent of modern warfare and weaponry, the old forts that once lined the United States became virtually obsolete by the end of World War II. The majority of these forts were abandoned and left to decay. Many of Pensacola's once-impressive forts were either destroyed or remained vacant and desolate until the U.S. National Park Service stepped in to save this portion of American history. They made extensive repairs to old Fort Pickens, and with great fanfare, it was reopened to the public in 1976.

Today, Fort Pickens remains a perfect example of the early nineteenth century military fortification. It was designed and built so well that it has hardly changed from when it was commissioned into service almost two hundred years ago. The fort, which is made of red brick of various shades, offers an antiquated look of great age to the modern visitor. Inside the fort, long subterranean tunnels leading from gun ports and around the bastion compound stretch like a great hand, as if reaching underground. These dark, damp, and rather cool tunnels are low and encrusted with a black slime over the moist sections of the stone and brick. And, though a bit creepy, these tunnels will offer visitors a look into the workings of a genuine Civil War fortress, as well as offering a look into the life of the soldiers who occupied it. The aged brick of the inner walls, which were once coated with plaster and paint, is now exposed in spots due to the pitting of time, giving the whole place the spooky look and feel of a dungeon. When visitors walk around the fort, and up the steep stairs, they will notice that there are great heaps of grass now growing on the rooftops of the covered tunnels, and the ancient cannons sit silent and still, forever welded in their final positions, as if dead to the world.

Although this once-active fortress appears somewhat desolate and disregarded by the rest of the populace, there have been many reports over the years that strange things and paranormal events have taken place here in the dead of night; such things have had some visitors, and even a few park rangers, looking over their shoulders to the sounds of disembodied footsteps, and long, echoing gasps from the dark corners of the silent tunnels. Some believe that the restless spirit of Chief Geronimo walks these forsaken halls and tunnels of the prison he once called home—others believe there's more than one ghost inhabiting Fort Pickens.

Ghostly Legends and Haunted Folklore

Since at least the early 1970s people have experienced strange events in and around the fort throughout the day and night. For many of those who had paranormal experiences, the primary report was having the feeling that someone or something was watching them from the darkened corners of the tunnels and around the entire bastion. However, from time to time, some have heard disembodied footsteps and the sounds of moaning or gasping all around the fort's perimeter. Indeed, sometimes, when park rangers lead lantern-lit tours of the fort, or organize nature walks through the surrounding area, they and select patrons may comment on these strange sounds. And, though these people will continue their tour, occasionally looking over their shoulders in the process, almost all have said they had the eerie feeling that something was watching them the whole time.

Physical evidence, such as photographs of orbs and vortex phenomena, which are tornado-like, smoky anomalies, have turned up on visitors' film after professional developing. It's also common for electrically operated equipment, like digital cameras and video recorders, to be drained of power. And on occasion, fully charged, unused batteries have been found to be entirely drained, especially when inside the fort's tunnels. Strange buzzing sounds have been detected on videos when played back, and sometimes shadowy images will turn up on the video film, or the film will turn out completely black. The audio will sometimes function improperly as well, capturing what some believe to be voices of the dead through a phenomenon known as EVP (Electronic Voice Phenomena). Either way, there seems to be some kind of electromagnetic disturbance taking place around Fort Pickens that has yet to be explained.

Other oddities that have been reported within the fort's compound have ranged from muffled voices to an occasional scream, as if from a soldier giving a command. In addition to this, witnesses have claimed to have seen the silhouettes of men walking on the tunnel rooftops or on the beach area around the fort when the moon is out of sight. Sounds of people working, complete with the echo of grunts and the resonance of shovels digging their way through some unseen plot of earth, have been detected by some visitors and late-night workers. And, if that isn't enough, odd lights—as if from a campfire—have been seen by the occasional park ranger from within the tunnel areas. When investigated, the strange light dims and extinguishes all together before the hapless park ranger can find the source. Though a mystery to some, a few feel this may be the spirit of Chief Geronimo reliving his old habits; as records show, Geronimo and his warriors would often make small campfires along the southern walls where he once lived, and though much of the original section is gone today, several psychical researchers consider the great Indian chief's noncorporeal presence a distinct possibility.

Another possible theory, one which appears logical for many local paranormal investigators, is that the misplaced grave markers, which sit just outside the fort, are the causes of the ghostly antics. Apparently, this small, rectangular, fenced cemetery near the front section of the fort holds the original gravestones for a plantation family who are actually buried under one of Sherman Airfield's runway strips across the bay in what was once Fort Barrancas. As the bodies remained unmarked in their resting place, with only the stones moved, some believe that the spirits of this family are not amused by this dishonor, regardless of the military's need of their land for an airfield. Although there are few records to support the facts about these plantation owners, local legend tells us that it was a large family who lived near Fort Barrancas since at least the early 1800s. So the possibility exists that the restless spirits of this long-dead family may be responsible for the paranormal activity recorded here. Perhaps the stones themselves are holding energies that are somehow causing these eerie events, or perhaps there's some other preternatural explanation that has yet to be discovered.

Another section of Fort Pickens that seems to carry some ghostly activity is the park rangers' offices, which were once used as the fort's summer homes. These individual offices, which lie just around the main compound, can feel very isolated and creepy after dark. If an investigator gets the chance to walk around this area, she or he will notice a distinct aura of loneliness here, as if the entire place is cut off from the world. When a park ranger stays late, it would not be too surprising if he had a spooky experience himself, as many before him have had. Without a doubt, there have been several official and unofficial reports that something weird goes on at Fort Pickens after dark, and though most of these reports may be considered unsubstantiated, at least one park ranger did admit that he would not work in the office alone because of the unusual and unsettling events he had experienced, even though this park ranger claims not to believe in ghosts.

Who or what haunts this ancient fortress is still very much a mystery. Even though many paranormal investigators conclude the events recorded here must be that of the famed Indian chief Geronimo, others feel the emanations, though possibly due in part to Geronimo's presence, might be due to the many slaves who served as manual labor building the fort, and who lived and died here in the early nineteenth century, as well as the plantation family that now rests under a once-busy airfield. These attributes, along with the possibility of the aforementioned empty gravesites, as well as many unmarked graves near the fort and all around Santa Rosa Island, may all constitute the haunting experiences. Perhaps there is much more to Fort Pickens than we actually know, as history certainly has a knack of concealing the facts. One thing is for sure—something truly weird is going on in old Fort Pickens.

Afterthoughts

When visiting Fort Pickens, remember that the brick and mortar construction may hold within it the very sounds of history itself. These bricks may in fact hold within them the psychic impressions that are responsible for the ghostly activity; the entire fort itself may indeed be a haunted realm that simply relays its historical information over and over again like a great recording device that renders the ghostly occurrences a matter of scientific fact instead of supernatural entity. Perhaps this is true, or perhaps the residue of a once-living person, which some might refer to as a ghost, is indeed a very common thing: that our whole world is a haunted place. Whatever the case, old Fort Pickens, which has seen many harsh and violent times, appears to have more than just history attached to it. As the Civil War conflict was certainly the worst on American soil, such begrudged feelings may linger on long after the bodies have decayed, and the possibility of a restless spirit or two may indeed inhabit this dark and somewhat foreboding place.

Whether or not Chief Geronimo haunts the silent corridors and tunnels of this fort is truly anyone's guess. Perhaps the ghost is more memory than entity, as some researchers have speculated. But one thing is for sure—more than a few self-proclaimed psychics have declared that they have seen and felt the aged chief walking around the southernmost sections of the old fort, where he was said to live while incarcerated here. Other psychics are certain that these agitated emanations are those of angry slaves who tilled the earth and built the fortress here, that their souls are restless and spiteful. Still others seem to believe that the entire island is itself a haunted place, where spirits of the dead come and go as freely as you and I to our everyday places. What of the empty graves? Do the spirits of the old, long-forgotten plantation still search for their proper gravestones? Some believe they continue to haunt the place that refuses to surrender the stone markers that bear their names—stones that hold the proof that they were indeed once here too.

When planning a getaway to Fort Pickens, be sure to bring plenty of water and maybe a snack. Bring sunblock and bug spray too, as the summer months can bring in plenty of mosquitoes along with the abundant sunshine. If you wish, you can make a weekend of it, as the park offers a campground and a fishing pier for nature lovers. As night falls, you can take a hike around the island and fort for a uniquely Floridian experience. Hurricane Ivan battered Fort Pickens and the Gulf Islands National Seashore in 2004, causing extensive flooding and destroying several buildings. Fort Pickens and a good portion of the Santa Rosa Island has been closed to vehicular traffic. So be prepared to walk a little if the roads are still under repair.

When exploring the fort and surrounding summer houses, you may wish to bring a camera, a tape recorder, and a video recorder as you walk through the spooky tunnels and dark corridors. When it's quiet, turn your tape recorder on and ask questions of the spirits that reside there. When taking photographs or filming, don't be surprised if the batteries run down quickly, even if they're brand new—spirits are believed to love energy and will consider your battery-operated devices a light snack.

Remember the many lives lost there, and the misplaced gravestones that honor no one beneath them. Try to recall the intense and rather spectacular history of Florida's past, as, for sure, the many ghosts who are said to walk this old fort remember quite well. If you hear footsteps behind you while walking through those dark tunnels, don't be alarmed, it may only be Chief Geronimo telling stories of adventure to unseen patrons of Pensacola's past. If, however, you hear the disquieting grumblings and moans of the misplaced plantation family looking for their gravestones, politely apologize and perhaps leave a flower or two on those empty graves out of respect. If all that doesn't quiet the restless dead, then hasten your steps out of old Fort Pickens as fast as you can.

The Fort Pickens main gate is located about a quarter of a mile east of the entrance gate to Fort Pickens on State Route 399 in Pensacola. For more information about Fort Pickens, Santa Rosa Island, and Gulf Islands National Seashore, as well as camping sites, hotels, and park services, contact the Fort Pickens Visitor Center at 850-934-2635 or 850-932-2257. The center is open daily from 9:30 A.M. to 5:00 P.M., and offers informational pamphlets on the local nature and fishing, as well as maps, park information, and books about Pensacola's rich history. There is a free daily guided tour of Fort Pickens at 2:00 P.M. that lasts about forty-five minutes.

The Fort Pickens Fishing Pier and Campground is located about *seven miles from Pensacola Beach on the western end of Santa Rosa Island. The campground features paved parking areas, picnic tables, and grills, as well as water and electric hook-ups. A spot can be rented for $20 per night. For further information, directions, and reservations, call the National Park Reservation System at 800-365-2267, 850-934-2623, or 850-934-2600, or you may visit the main website at www.nps.gov/guis/planyourvisit/fort-pickens.htm.*

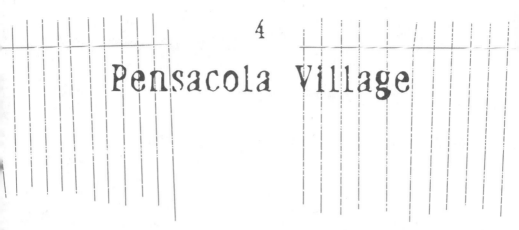

4

Pensacola Village

"Follow Pensacola Village's Haunted Trail..."

A Little History

Downtown Pensacola is without a doubt one of the liveliest places in the northwest section of Florida, not only due to its vast military presence and vacation crowds, but also because of its active nightlife and festivities. There is something for everyone in sunny Pensacola and the surrounding towns and villages.

Pensacola is also known as the City of Five Flags and Florida's First Place City, as well as the Cradle of Naval Aviation. It is believed by many to be older than St. Augustine, the Spanish settlement on Florida's northeast coast. Although there is some debate surrounding the dates of an official or organized colonization, many historians and archaeologists believe that there was a European settlement here many years before Pedro Menéndez de Avíles organized the first Spanish colonies in St. Augustine in 1565, and even before Ponce de León sailed the shores of St. Augustine in 1513. According to many archaeologists and historians this area of Florida has far more history and legend attached to it than was previously believed.

Kevin M. McCarthy

Julee Cottage in Pensacola Village.

Pensacola and its surrounding townships contain naval military museums and the historic Seville district and provide great scuba diving opportunities. But it also has an antiquated side, where old Florida homes and living history exhibits line the streets, highlighting its beauty and historical significance.

The Historic Pensacola Village proves a wonderful showcase for late nineteenth-century architecture, its indoor and outdoor museums, and the many gorgeous homes, such as the Dorr House, the Lavalle Home, and Julee Cottage. The village also includes educational centers like the Museums of Industry and Commerce and the T. T. Wentworth Jr. Florida State Museum, where you'll have the opportunity to see Florida's history of technology and commerce in action.

Just behind the museums you'll find the colonial archaeological trail. Here, you will find actual remains of a late eighteenth-century British fort, along with costumed actors to demonstrate authentic machinery and farming techniques used during this period; you'll also see millinery textile and cooking customs that professionally re-create lifestyles of colonial-era Florida. This is a great place to learn and teach, as schools across the state and country have done for years, but there's still so much more to this often neglected part of Florida.

Be sure to visit the Quayside Gallery, one of the largest art-cooperative galleries and educational centers in the United States, and the Pensacola Museum of Art, located inside the old city jail. Visit the Pensacola Cultural Center, home of the Pensacola Little Theatre, and the beautiful Bayfront historic districts—here, you will find the ever-active Rosie O' Grady's, where you can sample their famous "Flaming Hurricane" cocktail, or head on over to Lili Marlene's World War I Aviators Pub, a long-time favorite gathering place with Pensacola residents. There's also Apple Annie's, famous for its frozen daiquiris, and The Palace Oyster Bar for that down-home feeling, great seafood, and assorted beers. Shanahan's, probably one of the best seafood restaurants in all of Florida, is also located there.

When visiting this section of Florida and its surrounding towns, remember the history that occurred here for more than five centuries. Try to recall all the battles that had occurred during those turbulent years. Remember also the active history that took place in this quaint village with its antiquated homes. Some places still hold the images and vibrations of so long ago, which seem to repeat themselves over and over again in cyclic fashion.

Follow Pensacola Village's haunted trail and see for yourself if there's something lurking behind you or hiding in the darkened areas of this quaint setting. Prepare to venture these semi-ancient buildings in search of unseen entities that are said to walk in the wee hours, repeating their final moments on earth. Hunt the otherwise elusive specters that have been quietly making history since before European explorers walked these beaches. But don't be surprised at what haunted evidence you find here in sunny Pensacola, as there is a very rich history here, and one that apparently has more ghostly activity than previously known by ghost hunters and folklorists like myself.

We shall begin with some of the main haunted attractions within the village and Seville Quarter. I'll start with the primary sights listed, and from there you may conduct your own research. Indeed, you might be surprised just how much ghostly legend exists here, and just how many such tales the locals know and will be happy to share with you.

The Pensacola Village is open Monday through Saturday 10:00 a.m. to 4:00 p.m. Tickets for individual tours may be purchased at the Tivoli High House Gift Shop, located at 205 E. Zaragoza Street in downtown Pensacola. Adult tickets are $6.00, tickets for children (ages 4–16) are $2.50, and discount tickets for senior citizens (65 and older), active military personnel, and AAA members are $5.00. Guided tours of the French-Creole Lavalle House, the 1871 Dorr House, the 1832 Old Christ Church, the 1890 Lear-Rocheblave House, and the Barkley House are offered daily at 11:00 a.m., 1:00 p.m., and 2:30 p.m. For more information call 850-595-5993 or 850-595-5985.

To get to the Pensacola Village, take I-10 to Exit 12, I-110 South. Exit I-110 at 1C (Garden Street). Go left at the first light onto Tarragona Street and follow Tarragona Street to Church Street to the parking lot on the right.

5

The Seville Quarter and Rosie O'Grady's

Pensacola Village

"Tales of the Bartender's Ghost and a Victorian Lady"

As you begin your ghostly journey into the darker regions of Pensacola, it might be wise to begin in the historic downtown Seville Quarter, located on Government Street. One of my favorite eateries there is Rosie O'Grady's Bar & Grill, where the good food and spirits are always welcome after a long day of sightseeing and ghost hunting. This particular restaurant appears to have a ghostly employee on its staff—a ghost by the name of Wesley.

When I interviewed a waitress about Wesley, she only had general information for me. He was once a faithful customer who enjoyed the restaurant's fine dining and festive nature, and had a great knowledge of mixed drinks from all over the world. He enjoyed this restaurant so much he later became a bartender here. The waitress informed me that he worked the afternoon and happy-hour shifts, sometimes until the bar and restaurant closed. This she knew through word-of-mouth, since she was a new employee, and hadn't had any paranormal experiences. There were others, however, who had.

Ghostly Legends and Haunted Folklore

As I was staying in the Pensacola area for a few days, I knew I had to

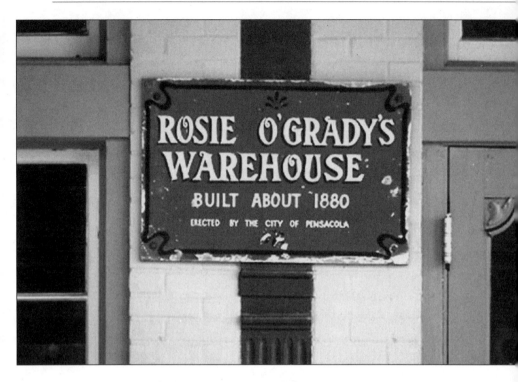

get more details on this story, as the legend of Wesley seemed to have various angles to it. Apparently, there was, indeed, a man named Wesley who lived in town, and who was a long-time patron of the Seville Quarter, specifically Rose O'Grady's. He did work there between 1991 and 1993, and many claim to have known him personally. The problem with this legend is that the specifics are difficult to pin down, as no one knows exactly when he worked there, or for how long, the exact circumstances of his death, or even what he looked like. Although it would seem that this would create more disbelief about a ghost or haunting, many people still believe in this elusive specter.

After speaking with several waitresses and waiters and a few bartenders about the haunted legend, I was able to conclude that Wesley worked at the restaurant in the early 1990s; was a man in his late thirties or early forties; was tall; had short, receding dark hair; and, after a few years working both at Rosie O'Grady's and throughout the Seville Quarter district, died as the result of a heart attack. There were many variations as to where he died, some being that he died on the front stoop of the restaurant, within the restaurant itself, or while at home. In fact, most believe that he died as he was cooling off in a walk-in beer cooler behind Rosie O'Grady's one early afternoon. The description of his spirit differs from person to person, as some remembered him as a tall, dark man, while others remember him as shorter and having light hair. Either way, his spirit has a definite appearance all its own.

Of the reports of Wesley's ghost—if, indeed, it is the former employee—is that he's more of a smokelike entity that lurks around the corners of the restaurant and throughout the Seville Quarter late at night. This spirit is said to have a human form, sometimes almost solid with augmented facial features, such as heavy eyebrows and dark eye sockets, and sometimes a simple human outline that hides when spotted. Others report only the feeling of being watched after hours, when the manager and staff are preparing to lock up. Sometimes a restaurant staff member or patron will spot Wesley walking around the bar or near the bathrooms. Indeed, people have also witnessed this loyal worker throughout the entire Seville Quarter compound walking under the New Orleans–like building awnings and porches with his head lowered. On some occasions, this spirit appears to be mischievous. His presence is felt in the downstairs men's bathroom, turning the water and the hand dryers on and off while people are using them. Indeed, this spirit does seem to be more prankster than spook.

There is yet another spirit said to haunt the upstairs area, the business offices, the historic districts, the Seville Quarter, and along nearby Romano Street. This feminine spirit is said to be the ghost of Sarah Wharton, the daughter of a well-to-do Pensacola businessman, and a hapless victim of a pirate raid during the early nineteenth century. It was while Sarah and her father were taking an evening stroll down Romano Street that the vicious attack took place. Pirates landed nearby and murdered several people immediately, but when one of the scoundrels saw the beautiful Sarah, he ran quickly to take her as his prize. This pirate killed Mr. Wharton with one shot from his black powder pistol, and then snatched up the hysterical woman in his arms, and began to run back to the docks where a longboat was moored. Sarah, however, in a fit of rage, began fighting the thug by biting, scratching and hitting as hard as she could. In the process, Sarah gouged out one of the pirate's eyes with her diamond ring, forcing him to drop her. In his anger, the pirate drew his cutlass and lopped off her head with one blow, her lifeless body falling limp in the city street. Since that time many people, both locals and visitors alike, have reported seeing the vision of a Victorian-era lady silently gliding down Romano and other local streets. Some believe that Sarah enjoys the silent Seville Quarter long after the party crowd goes home.

Some have reported seeing a woman dressed in old-fashioned clothing silently walking past office doors, or hearing knocking sounds coming from empty rooms and closet spaces. On occasion, this spirit plays with the office copy machine, turning the device on and off and making copies of absolutely nothing; the paper exiting the machine will be pure white, or black and hazy, as if someone lifted the cover while the machine was printing. Whether this is simply a late night worker's imagination has rarely been questioned, since far too many people, including workers, local patrons and visitors, all know of the enchanted Seville Quarter and its playful ghosts.

Afterthoughts

When visiting the festive Seville Quarter, prepare to make a day and night of it. There's always something to do here. As you walk these wonderful streets, remember those who made their living here over the years, and the many who lost their lives in the process. Don't forget the bartender and his somewhat spooky yet playful legend, and the unfortunate lady who met her end at the hands of a murdering pirate. There seems to be a ghost around every corner.

From a ghost hunter's point of view, the spirit of Wesley may very well be a repeating phantasm, where it is more or less a psychical playback of the once day-by-day lifestyle of a person. The fact that there is interaction in the downstairs restroom implies this spirit is somewhat intelligent and aware of its actions and the reaction of the witnesses. Because playing with the living in a lighthearted manner would take a form of consciousness, Wesley might appear as something more than a mere recording of past actions. Then again, there may be more than one spirit residing within the Seville Quarter property.

Sarah Wharton may be the emanation of Pensacola's earlier residents who had died in the area. Perhaps the nicely paved roads and brick lanes of this village are in fact covering some obscure graveyard of yesteryear? We may never know for sure. What we do know is that there is something going on here that simply cannot be overlooked. When conducting your search into the preternatural world of Pensacola's downtown village, feel free to ask the locals and those operating the stores, restaurants, and bars their opinions on the paranormal. You just might be surprised at how open they are about their ghosts.

If conducting a ghost hunt here, be sure to follow any rules given, and be sure to ask the local shop owners and venders for information as they are sure to have many stories. Or, take the guided "The Haunted Ghost Tour" offered by the Pensacola Historical Society. Tours normally operate for two weekends in late October, usually starting around 6:30 P.M. on midnight on Fridays. To learn about dates, times, and locations of tours and story times, call or visit the Pensacola Historical Museum.

The Seville Quarter is located at 130 East Government Street in downtown Pensacola. For information on shops and restaurant hours you may call 850-434-6211 or e-mail info@rosies.com for general inquires or visit the Pensacola website at www.historicpensacola.org/visitorinformation.asp.

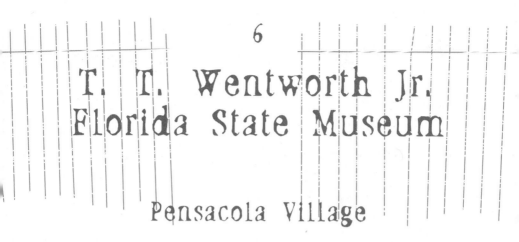

6

T. T. Wentworth Jr. Florida State Museum

Pensacola Village

"Eerie Sighs and the Phantom Jumping Cat"

A Little History

The T. T. Wentworth Jr. Florida State Museum, located in the Ferdinand VII Plaza on Jefferson Street, is part of the Historic Pensacola Village Museum complex. The building itself resembles the famous Alamo mission in San Antonio, Texas, but with a unique Floridian charm. This structure was originally built in 1907 as Pensacola's City Hall, but it has had many other uses over the years. With its symmetrical design, graced with wide overhanging eaves, an arched entry porch, and a second-story arcade, topped with a red tile roof, this building offers a turn-of-the-century flair reminiscent of old Florida. Indeed, the entire museum is a storehouse of fascinating historic artifacts ranging from practically every aspect of west Florida's history, to that of the truly strange.

The museum's first two floors hold both permanent and traveling exhibits showcasing Florida's unique past. Here you will find everything from strange metal devices that look suspiciously like tools of torture, Civil War paraphernalia, swords and ammunition, cattle droving equipment, and various weird artifacts—including a mum-

mified cat! On the third floor, there's a hands-on exhibit for children called "The Discovery Gallery," complete with fun artifacts to touch and examine, as well as many other learning devices to keep kids interested and occupied.

Though this museum is relatively small compared to bigger city museums, it captures the very essence of early twentieth-century architecture and the post-Renaissance influence which Florida once boasted. It is important to remember the simplistic and humble beginnings of those early days, which by today's standards would be far too rustic to endure. Regardless of the past, however, the T. T. Wentworth Museum will prove both educational and entertaining for every member of the family, including those interested in the paranormal. This museum harbors a little strangeness that cannot be ignored, especially by those working in the building after hours. It is during this time that unexplained things occur.

Ghostly Legends and Haunted Folklore

During my initial research into the unknown many years ago, I became aware of several strange aspects of paranormal research—both from a psychical and philosophical point of view. According to many scholars and researchers, objects may very well act as repositories of ghostly vibrations. As many museums are noted for having some artifacts with questionable backgrounds, such as swords, daggers, and guns, it stands to reason that such objects and tools of death and destruction may hold within them residue from a past horrific event. As many of these items were used to kill people, some of these relics may have absorbed the carnage and violent vibrations created by their users, making them a vehicle for a haunting.

Throughout history there have been legends of haunted objects and cursed antiques. Many people have claimed that a family heirloom, such as an old mantel clock or pocket watch, for instance, is haunted by its former owner. The Hope Diamond, for example, is believed to kill whoever owns it, as is the Woman of Lemb statue. The artifacts found in King Tut's tomb are believed to have killed those who removed them from the crypt. Indeed, if such a thing is possible and nonliving objects can be haunted or cursed, then we might consider the contents within the T. T. Wentworth Museum to be possible examples of this phenomenon.

This hypothesis may shed some light on the ghostly goings-on in this museum, as there are several artifacts that bear close investigation. Most notable is the mummified cat which sits as though content but ready to pounce. Many have claimed the feeling of something rubbing up against their legs, with a wispy feel to it, followed by a slight draft of air. Anyone who has owned a cat is sure to know this particular feeling, as cats have the uncanny habit of sneaking and jumping out of nowhere, at any given moment. Apparently, one cat continues to act like its old self regardless of its current condition.

On many occasions, museum workers have reported seeing small objects simply fall over on tables, including artifacts under glass display cases. Sometimes, these small knick-knacks will gently fall over in a row, as if something was leaving a trail of disarray after it walked by—just as a cat would do. If you're lucky, you might catch a glimpse of a small tan-colored critter walking around through the corner of your eye, or see the faint shadow of a small animal under a display area or table creeping out of view. To date, no one has identified the phantom creature, which remains a curiosity at the museum. Apparently it's not the only thing roaming around this interesting locality.

Other ghostly events to take place inside the T. T. Wentworth Museum are the inexplicable voices that are heard throughout the complex on all of the floors. These voices are just outside of range, meaning that you can almost hear what is being said, except that the words are muffled, as one employee told me, "as if someone were speaking from under a pillow." According to several staff members, strange voices and the sound of footsteps echoing from the hallways and display rooms began during the late 1980s, when major reconstruction work was taking place inside and around the museum. A few days after a major overhaul had begun inside the old museum, workers began hearing voices of an old man, who sounded perturbed and upset about something. This was not so much a fit of rage, but the kind of grumbling one might hear from a cantankerous old man who was simply fed up with something and was being vocal about it. This voice and a few others can be heard in the early morning and late evening in the museum.

Among the odd sounds and voices heard here, there is also the distinct sound of someone sighing as if terribly bored. These sounds have been heard throughout the day and evening hours, as if coming from behind the listener. You might hear such sounds from around a corner as you're studying a display case or in the restrooms. Several people have claimed that they had heard someone sighing several times while they were using the facilities, only to vanish when the witness would immerge from the stall. Whether or not this is indeed a ghost remains to be seen, as the disembodied sighs are only occasionally heard.

Some have suggested that this spirit is the remains of an alleged murder that had taken place on the grounds almost one hundred years ago. There was a rumor that a murder took place in one of the many offices that once existed within the Wentworth building during the 1900s or early 1920s; I have been unable to locate any hard evidence to support such an event. Regardless of the facts, however, there have been several presences detected within the structure over the years. In fact, several local and visiting psychics have reported feeling at least three entities residing in the T. T. Wentworth Museum, and according to one psychic, there is also the playful spirit of a cat roaming the hallways too.

Afterthoughts

Who and what haunts the corridors and display rooms of the T. T. Wentworth Museum is a good question because no one is quite certain as to who these spirits might have been in life, or if they wandered in from another location in Pensacola village. Some believe that these restless ghosts were here long before the building was constructed in 1907. Some claim that there was a small cemetery on this location dating from colonial times, but no one is absolutely certain. Still others have suggested that there was once a small wooden home on the property that burned down during the 1860s or 1870s. Again, no one is sure of this.

When you walk throughout the museum during the morning hour, right as it opens at 10:00 A.M., you might hear the low voices from another era, muffled and subdued. You may also see something small creeping on the floor out of the corner of your eye, but don't be surprised if it disappears if you try to look for it. There's something going on inside this well-maintained museum, even if the facts are unclear. One thing is for sure, you will have the opportunity to hear about some of Pensacola's ghostly history right here, so don't be shy in asking—Pensacola's residents are proud of their ghosts.

Visiting hours to the museum are Monday through Saturday, from 10:00 A.M. to 4:00 P.M. For more information or directions, you may contact the Tivoli High House Store at 850-595-5993, the T. T. Wentworth Jr. Museum at 850-595-5990, or the administrative office at 850-595-5985 or visit the Pensacola website at: www.historicpensacola.org/visitorinformation.asp.

7

The Dorr House

Pensacola Village

"The Translucent Lady"

A Little History

The Clara Dorr House—located on 311 South Adams Street, resting serenely across form the Old Christ Church—is one of the most often visited historic homes in Pensacola. This beautiful home was built for, and primarily by, Clara Barkley Dorr in 1871, the widow of lumber tycoon Ebenezer Walker Dorr. The two-story Dorr Home was designed in the Greek-Classic Revival style, popular with many Southern homes of the day. It is painted in charming saffron yellow with white trim and sports an elegant balcony on the upper floor. The entire home is furnished with gorgeous antiques, including mirrors, paintings, and period wood-burning stoves ranging from the 1850s to the 1890s, giving it the perfect feel of authenticity. The grounds are tailored with shrubbery and gardens, complete with seasonal flowers to enhance its charm.

The Dorr home and the historic district of Pensacola have an illustrious past that could highlight any television miniseries. Ebenezer Dorr, father of Ebenezer Walker Dorr, was Escambia County's first sheriff when Florida officially became a state in 1821, and it is

believed that one of his grandfathers rode alongside Paul Revere during the Revolutionary War. Later, poet John Greenleaf would write *The Branded Hand,* a series of controversial antislavery poems, which directly honored the Dorr family and their homestead.

Over the many years, the home has been used for city- and county-wide functions such as benefits and charity get-togethers. It has served as a foundational backdrop for local politicians and as an icon for Pensacola's banners and travel brochures. Undeniably, the Dorr House is one of Pensacola's most prized artifacts of architecture and family lore.

Today visitors enjoy walking through this lovely landmark knowing that not only has so much history taken place here, but that a little part of that history continues today, since there appears to be a ghost haunting the home and surrounding property. Though the exact personality of this spirit is uncertain, many of Pensacola's residents believe it's none other than Clara Barkley Dorr, the home's original matriarch.

Ghostly Legends and Haunted Folklore

Although there seems to be a cast of ghostly residents lurking around the avenues and corners of Pensacola Village and throughout Florida's sunny northwest, and having investigated more legends than I can count, I can honestly say that I rank this classic ghost tale among the best. Clara Barkley Dorr lived during the height of the nineteenth century, having survived the carnage of the Civil War with considerable ease. Indeed, having been left almost $52,000 from her late husband's lumber company, and having the home free and clear from debtors and land offices, she and her five children were left relatively well-off. Mrs. Dorr lived in this house until 1896 and loved every corporeal moment of it, so it is quite understandable why she would choose to remain in her lovely home. Outside of a few guided tours a day, and a scant few city functions, Clara Dorr still has her home to herself and evidently, she doesn't want to leave.

My interviews with residents and Pensacola Village staff have revealed quite a bit of evidence regarding the Dorr House hauntings. It seems that over the years there have been many people who have reported various odd occurrences, as well as capturing strange visual oddities on both video and photograph. Some have taken photos of those ever popular "orbs," and "vortexes," those strange, tornado-like anomalies that sometimes appear in haunted locations. On video some have caught faint images of human forms darting around corners or behind furniture. Local ghost hunting groups have reported the same evidence, as well as capturing strange voices on audio tape. These strange muffled voices, captured through Electronic Voice Phenomena, have been recorded on both floors of the house, as well as throughout the gardens. Though there is no positive proof from a scientific point of view regarding EVP or photographic evidence, many amateur ghost hunters and paranormal researchers believe such to be inescapable proof of consciousness after death.

Many of the assigned tour guides have reported that various items, such as antiques and small artifacts, move seemingly by themselves. On occasion, these items may disappear altogether without a trace, only to reappear long after the staff and personnel gave the item up as being stolen or lost. Many researchers, as well as some of the staff members, believe this is done by one of the Dorr children who died here at a very young age. Others believe the mischief is conducted by the curious ghost of Clara Dorr herself, who had an active interest in knick-knacks and similar oddities.

The Dorr House, as with most homes of that period, has a formal sitting room designed for the ladies of the day. In this room a lady would have the opportunity to tie, tuck in, or fix anything out of place, and basically prepare to meet her family and guests in order to appear proper and ladylike. This sitting room has a floor-to-ceiling mirror for those touch-ups, as well as several high-back chairs known as "fainting chairs," which were actually used to catch a poor corset-clad woman about to faint after wearing her corset over a long period of time. Because these chairs were used to offer women a chance to rest and regain their composure, they were very popular. This room was also used as a place where ladies could relax for a few moments before meeting their guests, so one can imagine the importance of such a room.

Over the years there have been many reports of people seeing a faint image of a woman dressed in nineteenth-century garb sitting in one of the fainting chairs. Most feel this is Clara Dorr, who is said to have sat there on many occasion while the children were falling asleep or while resting between household chores. Moreover, legend tells us that when a female visitor stands in front of the mirror, she will feel a tugging on her clothing, especially if she's wearing a short mini-skirt or shorts that ride up too high. As wearing such a garment would have been blasphemy in Clara Dorr's day, some feel the tugging is a kind gesture asking the lady to show some modesty and cover up.

Other oddities such as smelling freshly cut roses throughout the house are also quite common, as is feeling cold spots where there should be no drastic change in temperature. These and other paranormal events reported within the Dorr House seem to point to the classic form of haunting. As roses are believed to have been Clara Dorr's favorite flower, and cold spots are almost universally believed to indicate the presence of a spirit, most psychical researchers conclude that there is irrefutable evidence of a haunting. In addition, some people have reported hearing soft crying coming from the sewing room, a room once used as the family sick room. Who this spirit was in life is uncertain, though local legend points to a child who may have died during the yellow fever outbreak during the 1880s, an epidemic that claimed hundreds of lives. Though history seems to be uncertain, historians tell us that at least one child died in the house during the epidemic.

Although these ghostly tales are certainly interesting, the most intriguing aspect to the Dorr House legend is that of the translucent lady. Though there have been many tales of misty or almost invisible ghosts to haunt a location, the Dorr House's translucent lady seems to have all the features of a nineteenth century woman, holding all the creases and pleats in her gown, as well as her bodily features. Her image is almost like an unfinished draft of a person, not wholly present, but much like that of an actual person.

The translucent lady is said to appear as a younger woman around the age of thirty to thirty-five who is almost always seen dancing in one of the upper rooms of the house. This happy spirit is said to leap and jump from one side of the room to the next, then effortlessly glide about the room. In almost every report, this spirit is said to dance in this manner and then fade to nothingness. On several occasions, the translucent lady has been spotted on the balcony, staring silently at the churchyard across the street or upon the quiet streets of the village late at night. This more pensive vision of the spirit is said to appear when she is unhappy with something, such as a favorite piece of furniture being moved or the way the gardening was done. These things seem to bother her and she sulks when such simple things, such as respecting the arrangement of her home, are ignored.

It's hard to say just when is the best time to see the translucent lady of the Dorr House. Some say she is seen mostly during the summer months, when the humidity is raging and the mid-day storms are brewing. Others say she can only be seen at night, long after the tourists and the party crowd have gone home, and the night is silent and dark. No one knows for certain. The ghost of Clara Barkley Dorr—the translucent lady—may surprise you when you visit; she has been known to do that from time to time.

Afterthoughts

When visiting the Dorr House, remember that this was the owner's pride and joy, specifically designed and overseen by the lady of the house. Clara Dorr was a strong-willed and determined woman of substance, and one who always demanded her way—nicely and elegantly, of course. Though this particular ghost story is far less dramatic than a Hollywood film, it feaetures the noblest form of spirit—the mothering spirit.

Whether this is Clara Dorr reliving her younger years before her husband's death is anyone's guess, though many feel that Clara Dorr haunts the building because she loved and cherished her home. Indeed, Clara Dorr was a fine example of aristocratic stateliness of old Florida culture, at a time when honor and class meant everything.

A few psychical researchers have classified the paranormal events at the Dorr House as that of a poltergeist, largely because of items being moved around or taken, and then being returned to their original locations at a later date. However, as these events have taken place over a course of many years, far longer than that of typical poltergeist occurrences. Other noted paranormal investigators almost always argue that these events resemble a classic haunting, even when various forms of psychokinesis are evident.

The dancing spirit and her pensive stare off the balcony do indeed appear to be that of a classic haunting, which many believe to continue to this day. When visiting the Dorr House, be conscious of the little details such as the fainting chair room, the sick room, and the balconies, for these locations appear to be the primary sites of paranormal activity. Likewise, if you notice a vague or wispy image out of the corner of your eye, or perhaps the feeling that you're being watched, just know that you may indeed be under supernatural observation.

The Dorr House is on the tour listing for Pensacola's Historic Village, and is on the National Register of Historic Places. It is located in the Seville Square Historic District, on the north end by Government Street. To get there, travel on Government St. to Taragona St., then left on Zaragoza Street. The Dorr House is open Monday through Saturday 10:00 A.M. to 4:00 P.M. and closed on major holidays. For more information call 850-595-5985.

8

The Pensacola Little Theatre

Pensacola Village

"The Legend of Hosea Poole"

A Little History

The Pensacola Cultural Center, located on 400 South Jefferson Street, is today's home to Pensacola's more refined side of living, having served Pensacola's citizens with culture and class for many years. Although this is the location of fabulous operatic performances and top-notch concerts, it did not begin this way. During the Great Depression, money issues made it almost impossible for the average person to afford this type of culture. Toward the end of the Depression, an organization called the Works Progress Administration began creating numerous theater companies throughout the country in order to ease the many unfortunate realities of the day. Pensacola's local civic drama troupe recognized this rare opportunity, which would offer work for actors and artists, and quickly organized their group to benefit their township. In less than a year, the Pensacola Little Theatre opened its doors to the public.

The Pensacola Little Theatre opened with their first performance in the old Chamber of Commerce auditorium before relocating to the nearby Pensacola High School. Their first production was a one-act

Florida State Archives

show entitled *On the Park Bench,* a romantic comedy of the day. Things at the theater were fine until the late 1940s, when a portion of the building collapsed after a heavy storm, crushing most of the rehearsal area and storage rooms. Since this put a heavy damper on their future plans, they devised a plan to raise money to find lodging elsewhere. The board of directors initiated a fund drive, and success-fully earned enough money to get started. The theatre also received a $20,000 matching loan from the Federal Government, which expe-dited their plans, and secured a successful era of shows and concerts for Pensacola audiences. By 1952, a new auditorium named the Quonset was constructed and they were back in business.

This wonderful new structure was complete with dressing rooms, a large rehearsal hall, and an extra-large stage, costume- and prop-stor-age rooms, including equipment and storage shops. Indeed, the Quonset playhouse was perfect for their needs, and they went on to produce many shows, offering Pensacola's citizens the wonderful craft of song and dance for many years. Sadly, by the 1970s the Quonset auditorium began to deteriorate to the point of being hazardous. When the Fire Commission demanded the installation of new and expensive equipment, along with other major improvements, the need for up-to-date lodging was once again a necessity. By 1977, the beloved Quonset was sold, and the Pensacola Little Theatre packed up and moved to the recently renovated Florida Movie House, located at 186 North Palafox Street. But they still needed a permanent home to call their own.

As the Pensacola Little Theatre was seeking assistance once again, they found that there were many other nonprofit arts organizations with similar needs, so all of the organizations met with the Escambia County Office of Commissioners to make plans to correct the problem. The small group of artists and entertainers was deeded the old Escambia County Court of Records Building, as well as the old jail house, for a combined juncture of arts and entertainment. And so, this rather spooky, abandoned, early-1900s landmark was to become the Pensacola Cultural Center, home to the Pensacola Little Theatre. Here, after extensive renovations, Pensacola's new cultural center seems to have it all, even though it took many years to get to where it is today.

At present, the Pensacola Cultural Center and the Pensacola Little Theatre is also home to the Pensacola Opera House, the Kaleidoscope Ballet Company, the West Florida Literary Federation, the African American Heritage Society, and the Pensacola Children's Chorus. This cultural center complex has a beautifully designed rehearsal hall, a state-of-the-art theater with 474 seats on three separate levels, and a children's theater called the Tree-House Theatre, to introduce Pensacola's young to the arts. Indeed, the Pensacola Cultural Center is one of the oldest continually producing community theatres in the southeastern United States, and shall, no doubt, remain so for the next hundred years.

The one aspect of the newly renovated County Court of Records Building and adjacent jail house that the new tenants did not understand was this location's history. This antiquated complex had seen much over many years of active use; it held a place in the legal arena, which involved everything from probate litigations to death sentences. Apparently, after many years of such use, and then sitting in abandonment for many more years, it stands to reason that the arrival of new tenants, along with the stirring of old dust and even older memories, had somehow awakened something from its dark past—and his name was Hosea Poole.

Ghostly Legends and Haunted Folklore

Many people consider the legend of Hosea Poole to be based more in myth than in fact; this is inconsequential, as the paranormal activity that has been reported within the Pensacola Cultural Center and the Little Theatre over the years is proof enough for many witnesses. According to local history and documentation, a man named Hosea Poole was the last man hanged inside the confines of the old jail. His crimes reportedly range from murder and embezzling town funds to conspiracy and treason. Whatever the crime actually was, this man was sentenced to the fullest extent of the law—death by hanging!

The paranormal activity experienced within the cultural center varies from electrical problems—where the lights will turn on and off without human intervention and elevator doors open by themselves—to props and personal items mysteriously moving or disappearing, only to be found in another location at a later time. Although the majority of these events take place where the old county jail was located, these strange occurrences also take place throughout the entire complex and theatre.

On one frightening occasion, while a staff member was in her office attending to her clerical duties after hours, she heard the distinct sound of the elevator approaching her floor. Because she had left her office door open, and because the elevators were close to her office, the dinging sound of the elevator doors opening was recognizable. The office worker thought this was a little strange, but told herself that it might simply be another late worker, or perhaps a security guard making his rounds. She dismissed her concerns and retuned to her work so she could get home before it was too late. While she was reading over her papers she saw a dark figure of a man walk quickly past her open door. When she lifted her head to see who it was, the man disappeared out of sight. When she called out to inquire who was there, she did not get a response. She got up to peek out the door, but the hallway was empty and silent.

On another occasion an operations manager and a maintenance engineer were working late in the main auditorium laying new carpet in the orchestra pit; both claim to have seen a man sitting in one of the audience chairs. As they looked at each other, and than back toward the chairs, they noticed that the man had moved to another chair across many rows to the opposite side of the complex. He was reported to be dressed in a dreary-looking suit and had a withered, gaunt face. His eyes were dark and set back in almost hollow sockets. As they continued to stare at the man, he simply faded away.

Though those who have witnessed this somewhat depressed-looking apparition say he certainly startled them, they all agreed they were not really frightened of him. They seemed to accept this vision as the ill-fated Hosea Poole. Though many late-night workers have attributed such ghostly goings-on to the former prisoner, some claim to have seen and felt other lively spirits throughout the cultural center. Apparently, there may be a ghostly spirit of a little girl roaming the grounds, but who she was in life is a mystery.

During an interview with one of the theatre workers, I was informed that this youthful specter was that of a girl around the age of ten or eleven. She is said to wear either a blue or green summertime dress similar to those popular in the 1920s and 1930s. Though there have been several variations of this little spirit's wardrobe, her physical appearance has been reported as whimsical and nonthreatening. She is said to be neither sad nor angry, just a curious child. Indeed, many have reported the feeling of being watched, but in a playful manner, as with a child playing hide-and-seek. For those who have actually seen this spirit, most say they have seen a little girl running or skipping out of sight, whether behind a book shelf or beyond the wall in a corridor. Often giggling can be heard ever so lightly, and her presence is always playful and never scary or unpleasant.

As with any location that's ripe with history and legend, we can expect to find at least a few ghosts, and the Pensacola Cultural Center boasts a few more than those mentioned above. Evidently, a few of the early actors and entertainers have chosen to remain—or in this case, transplant themselves—with the modern troupe, for all time. There have been a few reports over the years of shadowy people on the stage, as if rehearsing for a big show that will never be seen. Some of these specters are said to have been dressed in dramatic clothing, sometimes looking extremely antiquated, sometimes comical, but always with a flair that would otherwise be out of the ordinary. As these early actors and entertainers had fought hard to establish their craft when money was tight, and secure for themselves a place in Pensacola history with great vigor, it makes sense that, with their vehement tenacity, their spirits would remain here. Something that practically every employee at the cultural center believes in is the existence of the sometimes spooky and mischievous specters, along with the sometimes playful and childlike spirits that freely roam the stage and confines of this wonderful establishment.

Afterthoughts

Although the existence of Hosea Poole and his spooky exploits remain a topic of controversy for some, others, have no doubt that the condemned man's spirit is present. Even if his continued earthly existence is often in question, other local luminaries and Pensacola townsfolk swear to both his once-physical presence and his spiritual one. Whether or not this man really died in the jail's confines is irrelevant for the workers here, as they will graciously relate the tale should you ask one of them. The ghost of the little girl is the real mystery. While some believe she was the child of an original actor with the troupe, others contend that she wandered in from another location in the area. Indeed, one employee stated that she might have been a victim of a house fire that happened during the early 1900s in the village, and that when the original house was destroyed, her spirit wandered into the County Court of Records Building and has been there ever since.

Though these paranormal events are indeed reminiscent of a haunting, due largely to the interaction of these specters, it is also plausible that these events are psychical emanations or replays of actual events in history. The little girl was certainly at an age full of playful glee and happiness. If she did die in a fire long ago, as some researchers believe, then she simply continued on with what she knew, not truly understanding or believing she had died. Many psychics also claim that many spirits are unaware of their passing and simply continue to exist, thinking that nothing has changed. Having no concept of the passage of time, this little girl is simply playing hide-and-seek forever.

The good-natured actors on the Pensacola Little Theatre's stage may represent the literal recording of once-live events, perhaps being drawn there or "activated" by the vigor and excitement of present-day actors and entertainers. Like many reports of such events, the ghost in question responds in the same fashion over and over again, unaware of the presence of others. Unlike the spirit of Hosea Poole, who has been reported operating machinery and everyday appliances or staring at the living, and then disappearing altogether, this would appear to be more sentient in nature. Though these classifications are vastly different from each other, this science is certainly understandable, albeit a little frightening.

The Pensacola Cultural Center and the Little Theatre, their staff and patrons are proud of the ghosts who roam here. In fact, they have dedicated a portion of their autumn events to the unknown with a series of spooky shows. Stage Fright Productions presents such shows as *Trilogy of Terror* and *Jailhouse Shock: Hosea's Revenge,* just a few of the playful interactive shows and events to take place during the Halloween season. You'll be able to hear some of the best stories any time when you visit; be sure to keep an eye out for the creepy cast of characters appearing there.

The Pensacola Cultural Center is located on 400 South Jefferson Street in the downtown district. Box office hours are Monday through Friday, 10 A.M. to 5:30 P.M. For more information on upcoming events and show times call 850-432-2042.

9

The Lear-Rocheblave House

Pensacola Village

"Of Perfumed Ladies and Dancing Bones"

A Little History

The Lear-Rocheblave House is yet another beautiful showcase home in the Historic Pensacola Village, located on 214 East Zaragoza Street. It was built by John and Kate Lear in 1890, but was later purchased by Benito Rocheblave and his family, giving it the hyphenated name we know it by today. This two-story beige home with white trim, surrounded by a stately white picket fence and a yard lined with live oaks and other native trees, is a fine example of early nineteenth century style construction. With several spacious rooms situated on multi-tiered asymmetrical floors, a quaint living room and sitting room, along with basinlike windows that offer a light and airy feeling, it's easy to see why this was a home designed for a large family when America knew a simpler, more tranquil lifestyle.

Although both the Lear and the Rocheblave families lived in this beautiful home for many years, much of the home's exact history remains in question today. The local historians agree that the original lady of the house was of old northern stock and was content with homemaking and fond of dancing, as many women were during that

time. Many also know that the later owner, Benito Rocheblave, was a rough tugboat captain who ran guns and ammunition to Cuba during the Spanish-American War. Most believe he was a cruel and angry man in life, with a reputation of being quite jealous. And though oral tradition may falter with the exact details of what actually took place here so many years ago, some feel that Benito's mischievous spirit lurks here, as well as a cheerful one, who enjoys the reminiscence of the dance, when the graceful gliding of the waltz was ever so popular.

If such events are not enough for the modern ghost hunter, there is also the historical account of a university archaeology project that stored human remains in the house while excavations were taking place at the nearby Christ Church. It was during this brief period that legends began to circulate about the ill-resting bones that lay in rotting wooden coffins—legends that these bones moved, shook, and even danced throughout the old Lear-Rocheblave House in the dead of night.

Ghostly Legends and Haunted Folklore

Though many old homes and buildings may take on spooky reputations regardless of whether a true haunting or paranormal event actually took place, a building's location or appearance can certainly stir one's imagination. Though this may be true with many homes, the Lear-Rocheblave House appears to be the exception—at least for a few witnesses.

Most of the ghostly occurrences took place around the time when an archaeological dig was being conducted in the late 1980s by students from the University of West Florida. The dig was taking place in the nearby Old Christ Church Cemetery and adjacent grounds. Apparently, while the dig was underway, the students unearthed three decomposing coffins of the church's early rectors. The students agreed to send the fragile bones and the contents to Florida State University the following week in order to have X-rays taken, as well as have a thorough medical examination performed on each of the remains. This was for the purpose of determining the living habits of these men and their exact causes of death, and then to report the findings in scholarly journals and lecture halls everywhere. It was necessary to store the expensive equipment, as well as the coffins and their remains, in a well-secured place during the evenings so the research could continue without delay during the day. The best place seemed to be the Lear-Rocheblave House since it has an excellent electronic alarm system. So, the students and university staff, after securing permission to use the premises, began storing their tools, cameras, and the various artifacts in one of the large downstairs rooms. The museum staff locked the doors securely and activated the alarms. They went home thinking all would be safe and secure for the night. But they were wrong.

When the museum staff met the students and their professor in the morning, they disarmed the security system, opened the door, and let everyone in. When they began to collect the equipment, they walked over to check on the artifacts. To their surprise, they found that the human remains, the bones that were once almost perfectly placed in their coffins, had been scattered around within each individual coffin, as if each had been lifted up and shaken violently. Some of the skulls were found near the feet, some of the arms were found where the legs should have been, and legs where arms should be. All was out of order, as if an earthquake had taken place in the night.

Naturally, this event had everyone concerned. There was no evidence that anyone had been in the building after it had been locked—if anyone had entered, a recorded message would have been found on the alarm system control box. As the students investigated further, they also noticed that small fragments from the long-dried bones were found in various locations outside of the coffins, meaning that whoever was meddling with the skeletal remains must have been hitting them on the floors, as if they were using them as drumsticks. That would have been the only way for these dustlike fragments to have gotten all over the wood floors. Either that, or as one student said, "maybe the bones got out of the coffins by themselves and started dancing." From that point on, strange incidents began taking place throughout the Lear-Rocheblave House.

While the bones were being returned to their final resting places during a simple ceremony for the three rectors, one of the students from the university's archaeological dig team noticed a strange and wonderful thing. He noticed three men dressed in dark robes walking past those attending the funeral, as lively as any living people. Two of these monklike figures were gleeful, with a bounce in their step, while the other seemed more pensive and carried a large book under his arm. The university student just watched as the three figures continued to walk right through the wall of the old church, disappearing from sight. When the student asked if anyone else had seen the vision, he found he was the only one. From that day on, the scent of roses can be detected in and around the old churchyard, as well as within the Lear-Rocheblave House, where no rose bushes exist.

The legend of the dancing bones is certainly an interesting story to tell when the lights go out during a Floridian summer storm. Indeed, this tale remains a favorite with Pensacola citizens, but there are still other weird incidents which took place within the Lear-Rocheblave House. Incidents such as books, paintings, and other objects moving around the home in an erratic manner, as if a small child had been playing with them during the night. Lights are some-times seen turning on and off by themselves during the night. There also seems to be a feminine spirit here too—a lady who enjoys the gentle fragrance of an antiquated perfume.

As legend tells us, a female spirit is said to sashay through the home long after hours, sometimes leaving the light scent of a lady's perfume behind. This ghostly woman has also been seen from time to time, and is said to be dressed in a light purple or lavender gown from the nineteenth century. She has been observed dancing happy and carefree inside this home through its darkened windows late at night. Though no one is quite certain who she was in life, most suspect that she is Ms. Lear herself, the original lady of the house, who is simply enjoying the quiet confines of her beloved home.

As for old Benito Rocheblave, there have been a few rumors of his presence, as well. Several of the town's youth have reported seeing the dreary sea captain over the years. They claimed that a strange-looking man with a thick dark beard is seen staring out of a top-floor window with his arms crossed. He just stares down at the street, as if he is unhappy or in deep contemplation. And though this specter is hardly ever seen, he does get the blame from time to time for some of the more mischievous events that occur in this lovely home, specifically when things go missing and reappear a week or two later. Who knows, perhaps there's a variety of spirits roaming this quaint little home of so long ago? Perhaps you, too, will spot the sea captain staring down at you some late evening, or perhaps you will smell the faint scent of a lady's perfume while you walk across the floor where the old bones once danced.

Afterthoughts

With so many old homes listed in the Pensacola Village tour, all with a long line of history attached to them, it shouldn't be too difficult to suppose that there could be spirits of former owners roaming about. Perhaps, as many psychical researchers and paranormal investigators believe, there may remain a sentient or recorded "essence" of a human soul that continues to remain in or near a particular location. Perhaps the lady of the house so enjoyed her evening waltzes with the man she had loved in life that she continues to do so today. Perhaps her gentleman always commented favorably on her delightful perfume, and that's why she continues to wear it decades after she departed this world. Maybe the sea captain continues to this day to contemplate his actions during that long-ago battle.

What about the dancing bones of the three rectors? Did these long-dead pious men dance around their coffins in delight at being freed from their tombs or in anger at being disturbed? We may never know for sure. What we do know is that ever since the students unearthed those bones, strange and even uncanny events have been reported within the lovely Lear-Rocheblave House. Coincidence?

The only way you can be sure of whether this location is truly haunted is to investigate for yourself. Walk around this beautiful home and see if you can spot the eerie and somewhat sinister-looking face of one of the owners, and try to catch the sweet perfumed scent of the dancing lady spirit who swirls and glides through the old home late at night. You might just get lucky.

The Lear-Rocheblave House is on the tour listing for Pensacola's Historic Village and is on the National Register of Historic Places. Tickets can be purchased at the T. T. Wentworth Museum for a small fee, and for the cost of the ticket, you can also visit several other haunted locations, such as the Dorr House and the Museums of Industry and Commerce. The Lear-Rocheblave House is open Monday through Saturday 10:00 A.M. to 4:00 P.M. and is closed on major holidays. For more information call 850-595-5985.

10
Museums of Industry and Commerce

Pensacola Village

"Specters of Days Gone By"

A Little History

The Museums of Industry and Commerce—located at 200 and 201 East Zaragoza Street, toward the end of the Pensacola Village—are original structures built during the late 1800s for various purposes, ranging from lumber storage to office space. Today both structures offer an intelligent look at Pensacola's nineteenth-century industrial age, and its city- and state-wide practice of economic commerce. The museum itself is constructed of two warehouselike buildings, which are united by iron ties, wood, and mortar. Each complex stores various exhibits of machinery and similar artifacts from west Florida's industrial periods. Because Pensacola was high in many natural resources, such as rich woodlands and estuaries that offered plenty of lumber for loggers and marine life for fisherman, several high-profit jobs such as brick making, lumber cutting, and railroad construction, as well as the fishing and icehouse businesses, were born and prospered during those early years. By the 1920s, Pensacola's industrial boom had secured a place in the American economy and, in the process, paved the way for future development and commerce for its citizens.

The Museum of Industry exhibits the original Pensacola Lumber Train, The Piney Woods Sawmill, and The McKenzie-Oerting Ship's Chandlery, along with other aspects of original businesses which literally made Pensacola what it is today.

There are excellent examples of Pensacola's historic presence by way of the many antique photographs of the workforce in action throughout the entire complex, as well as there being a plethora of written documentation for the curious to see just how much effort went into Florida's early business customs.

As you continue through the Museum of Commerce, you'll find a reconstructed streetscape from the mid to late 1800s, complete with a detailed pharmacy, a hardware store, a print shop, and a toy store, all eloquently stocked with genuine artifacts from the nineteenth century. Each store and shop contains various tools, books, musical instruments and records, photographs, and toys from this era, all donated by a variety of companies and personal collectors from throughout Florida's west coast. The print shop, for instance, has one of the best collections of antique presses and typesetting equipment in the entire Southeast. In the pharmacy there are original flasks, beakers, and pill bottles from the nineteenth century adorning the walls, display cases, and countertops of this authentic-looking establishment. In the main section you will find educational displays and even a bona fide collection of horse-drawn carriages to show the visitors the rich and diverse history of Pensacola's fair trade and commerce.

Though there is much to learn from these two museums, from Florida's business practices to the methods of commerce used over a century ago, you will find all you need to know here. And along with the historical artifacts and the educational lessons, there also appears to be something a bit out of the ordinary.

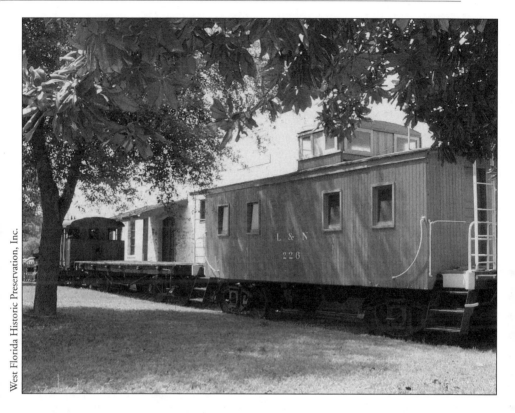

West Florida Historic Preservation, Inc.

Ghostly Legends and Haunted Folklore

Of the many local legends of ghosts and haunted locations through-out Pensacola, only a few have truly given me the creeps. If a location is dark and gloomy, or if terrible things took place there years earlier, or it has a haunted history, I may have a few personal reservations on such things, and let it go at that. Other places however, may have a lit-tle something more to offer in the area of strangeness that will have me looking over my shoulder while walking out of such a darkened place of ill repute.

Having worked in very spooky places, from the medical examin-er's office, to psychiatric hospitals with high-level security, I have had my share of creepy and downright frightening experiences. And, even if there is a logical explanation and commonplace reasoning behind a spooky legend, we may, nonetheless, have adverse feelings. In my first book, I included the story of Myrtle Hill Cemetery and its large mausoleum. I related to the reader just how disturbing this place is, and how it had affected my fellow investigators. Although we all knew this location was indeed a creepy place, with all the trappings of a haunted location, we also knew that many of our feelings were explainable and quite logical in every respect. Regardless, we were still excited— though some of us were downright terrified.

My experience with both the Museums of Industry and Commerce echoed my earlier experiences at Myrtle Hill Cemetery, which had me looking just a little deeper and listening just a little harder as I investigated the grounds. It was while visiting Pensacola last year that I got a personal experience with the unknown. While taking the tour of homes in the village I decided to talk with some of the people running the museums and inquire if I could interview the staff about their ghosts, and maybe take some photos after closing hours in order to get some clear inside shots. I was granted the interview and told I could come back just after 4:00 P.M.; they would give me some information about their ghostly happenings and allow me to take a few photos. I knew I was in for a treat.

As it was getting late, and the clouds were getting dark, I knew I had to hurry over to the museums before the afternoon storms hit. I arrived just in time as the rain began to fall hard, and the lightning flashed as thunder sounded loudly around me. Luckily, a staff member saw me at the door and let me in before I got drenched. As I entered a now deserted museum, the first thing I noticed was just how dark and cool it was inside. Though our summer storms can cool down a hot building rather quickly, it seemed a bit too cool here. As my guide walked around with me to explain some of the exhibits, she explained that many of the antiques, tools, and other paraphernalia were authentic pieces from many collections across the state. I was informed that many of the items came from deserted or run-down buildings around Pensacola, and were salvaged for the museum. Some of these pieces came from personal collections that were part of original businesses in town.

As we walked further, I asked her about the haunted legends regarding the two museums, and if she thought they were haunted. She said that there are a few ghostly stories involving the antiques, as some people think they're cursed. As we continued to walk around the displays, she told me about voices and laughter and of strange knocking sounds being heard all through the night, especially during the off season. She also explained that some of the staff had seen the shadows of people walking around corners when they were sure the building was empty and locked. Others have complained of hearing the distinct sound of footsteps echoing all throughout the complex and getting the feeling that they're being watched when they knew they were completely alone.

Toward the end of my interview, I prepared for my photo shoot. I had a new Minolta 35-millimeter camera with all the accessories, so I was prepared for anything. I took photos of the various tools and machinery in the main display areas, as well as the other artifacts throughout the museum. As I did so, I continued to listen to the stories and the ghostly legends of Pensacola and the museums which I explored. When I arrived in front of the "streetscape" section, which held the turn of the century facades and storefronts, I began photographing the glass beakers, pill bottles, and other paraphernalia in the pharmacy, as well as the creepy toys and dolls in the makeshift toy store. I just knew they would make great photos of my Pensacola journey—or so I thought.

Just as I was finishing up, a loud crash of thunder sounded and shook the building; enough to make the lights flicker twice and then go out altogether. It remained dark for a few moments until the lights came back on, only to cast an eerie glow throughout the entire complex. It seemed colder inside too, and as began to comment on the temperature, both my guide and I heard an odd sound coming from the toy store display. As we looked at each other, we both started toward the noise. As we approached, we both witnessed a small toy, which resembled a train or motorized cart lying on its side, with its small wheels moving by themselves. Coincidence or not, both she and I were a little unnerved.

Although this may have happened as a result of the shaking building during that thunderstorm which knocked over the little toy, thus prompting it to move as a result, one can only imagine the strange feeling we got, nevertheless. The coldness could have been attributed to an efficient air conditioner or to the humid air, which was cooling rapidly. Although these are the first questions to ask in such a location, and certainly when experiencing such strange events, it's easy to see why so many people over the years might believe these museums are haunted.

If such spooky events are not enough for the intrepid ghost hunter today, then let me just say this: When I returned home, and turned in the full roll of film to a reputable developer, the photos taken within the Museums of Industry and Commerce were the only ones which did not turn out. Each photo, though clear and bright around the edges, was blackened in the middle sections, as if someone's fingers were in front of the camera's lens. And, though I do not claim to be best photographer around, I certainly know to keep my fingers away from the lens when shooting. It seems that for whatever reason, someone or something did not want me taking photos inside the museum that day—perhaps the spirits there are a little camera-shy.

Afterthoughts

My investigation of the Museums of Industry and Commerce, though free of a screeching wraith, did appear to have some strangeness to it. The thunderstorm may have created the perfect atmosphere for anyone in search of ghosts. This much is understandable. The only thing that may stand out as a paranormal event might be the overturned toy with the moving wheels. The skeptic might simply think the event was cause and effect, whereby the thunderstorm caused enough vibration to dislodge the toy, turn it on its side, and cause its wheels to move. Although this is a logical hypothesis, we have to ask ourselves, why would this toy after almost one hundred years start working on that particular day?

What about the haunted toys and antiques? History has given us many examples of such things in legends and folklore. We can see similar traits in the antiques and artifacts found in the T. T. Wentworth Jr. Museum. The mummified cat, for instance, which sits in eternal slumber, may still have a little life to it, if we are to believe that an artifact can indeed be haunted. Perhaps the little toy of so long ago has, as some psychical researchers might suggest, an ethereal attachment to it. It may be that the child who loved that little toy had permeated it with his or her own psychic residue, in effect, haunting it for years to come.

When visiting these museums, enjoy the rich history that is found here. As you walk around the displays, remember the hard-working people and the personal livelihoods that made Pensacola, and all of Florida for that matter, what we see today. When you look at all the interesting artifacts, the items of everyday life during the nineteenth century, and especially the eerie little toys that line the artificial storefronts, remember that living children once enjoyed them—children that are long dead.

The Museums of Industry and Commerce are on the tour listing for Pensacola's Historic Village. Tickets can be purchased at the T. T. Wentworth Museum for a small fee, and for the cost of the ticket, you can also visit several other haunted locations, such as the Dorr House and the Lear-Rocheblave House. The museums are open Monday through Saturday 10:00 A.M. to 4:00 P.M. and are closed on major holidays. For more information call 850-595-5985.

11

Old Christ Church

Pensacola Village

"Ghostly Monks in the Graveyard"

A Little History

This wonderful example of Pensacola's religious freedom is located at 405 South Adams Street, across from the Clara Dorr House. This lovely church was constructed in the early 1830s and was commissioned in 1832. The Old Christ Protestant Church is one of the oldest surviving church structures in Florida; it remained in its original condition until the Civil War, when the majority of the church's congregation fled to Alabama. It was during this time that Union soldiers seized the church and the adjacent homestead for use as a hospital and officers' barracks for their troops. It remained this way for almost five years.

After the war, Union troops throughout Florida returned to their northern homes and returned the confiscated church, and other indentured properties, to the congregation. Unfortunately, the church and surrounding property was left in an appalling state. In the end, it would take Pensacola's citizens until 1879 to finish the much-needed repairs, which cost close to $5000.

Throughout this landmark's long and illustrious history, it has

Florida State Archives

served as a church, a hospital, and a library. It was abandoned for many years and then restored and used as a church again. Most recently the complete restoration of the Old Christ Church has been funded by the City of Pensacola and the state of Florida and the church has been rededicated as a functioning place of worship. It remains a beacon of pride for the faithful and a jewel of history for Pensacola Village's residents and visitors.

Inside this lovely church you will find the typical trappings, albeit the finest furnishings one might ever see. The floors are original, made of polished pecan tree wood, and the pews are made from sycamore trees. The ceiling is curved to resemble the hull of a ship and the windows are modest, yet pristine in fashion and design, much as the pulpit and adjoining lectern is unpretentious, but exquisite. All in all, the old Christ Church will find favor with both the novice antiquarian and the seasoned aficionado of classic Floridian architecture. If a vivid and illustrious history isn't enough for the average sightseer, then there's a little something extra here, especially for the paranormal investigator and the novice ghost hunter. They may be interested to know that a merry band of spirited monks are said to inhabit this antiquated church and grounds. And a few have experienced a most gothic scene here in sunny Pensacola!

Ghostly Legends and Haunted Folklore

When I first read about this particular legend, I couldn't help remembering those old Hammer Film Productions from the 1950s and 1960s. These horrific events would almost always take place in an old graveyard, with an even older church or rectory in the background. There might be horse-drawn carriages racing through the darkened moors, and perhaps the appearance of a priest or monk to help the protagonist in his noble efforts. I never expected, however, to find such a gothic anecdote in my own state of Florida.

As I began my ghostly research into the realms of Pensacola folklore, I was told time and time again to research the Old Christ Church and its three roaming phantoms. I took the advice and began my quest. Evidently there were three rectors of the old church who were buried in the now nonexistent churchyard. These church rectors were each buried over the course of time during the mid 1800s. They remained there undisturbed for many years until renovations took place in the early part of the twentieth century. The three bodies were exhumed and hastily reburied just beyond the churchyard in three unmarked graves, and remained so for an unprecedented length of time. Over the years there were more changes made to the face of the church, including a new section of floor placed over the three old graves, which were eventually forgotten.

The three rectors, who meant so much to the people of nine-teenth-century Pensacola, were now virtually gone from memory. Many years later, people became interested in the history of the church, when the University of West Florida got involved with an archaeological project headed by Dr. Judith Bense of the university's Archaeological Institute. Indeed, they would unearth more than just mere artifacts—they would unearth the bones of the three rectors, and, in the process, unearth their festive spirits as well.

On a warm summer day the university students unearthed these bones that strange things began to happen. Because the original town records identified Rev. Frederick F. Peake and Rev. David D. Flower as two of the original rectors, the students knew at least two sets of the remains must belong to them. Figuring out who the third set belonged to would prove to be the biggest problem. As they carefully removed the decaying coffins, they gently set them aside until they could find a suitable location to store them while the dig continued. The archae-ological team was granted permission to set the bones, along with their equipment, inside the Lear-Rocheblave House up the street. Because it has an excellent alarm system and security patrol outside, this was deemed the best place. And, as you know if you read "The Lear-Rocheblave House" (see page 64), the paranormal events that took place there were quite incredible. But that's another story. What happened one steamy day at the Old Christ Church is downright astonishing.

It was after the students had completed their analysis and returned to the church to rebury the remains of the rectors that one individual had a very strange experience. Just after the three bodies were reburied beneath the church floor in an elaborate ceremony, a University of West Florida student named Gary Powell saw a ghostly ensemble—though apparently he was the only one who could see it. As the story goes, while the ceremony was taking place Mr. Powell saw what he claimed were three men dressed in robes like those a monk would wear, complete with dark robes and stoles around their necks, walking past the crowd of people gathered to witness the reburial. He claimed that two of the men seemed happy, as they carried on in laughter and glee, and another, more robust, man walked behind the two monks. In his arms he carried a large black book embossed with a gold leaf cross. Unlike the first two men, this one was sadder, more solemn in nature. Mr. Powell continued to gaze at the odd, out-of-place figures until he looked down at the three new coffins that now held the earthly remains of the past rectors. As he looked up to watch the ghosts, they walked right through the church wall and completely vanished from sight.

The young student was now beginning to see things in a different light. When he asked others attending the ceremony about the ghostly procession, he found that no one else saw anything out of the ordinary. Mr. Powell was so moved by this experience that he went on to head the first section of a documented research paper for the university, which also included his paranormal experience. Though many psychical researchers believe this event to be a psychic recording of past events, including the emotions of each rector, some feel there is something more going on here.

The earlier events at the Lear-Rocheblave House, where the bones were stored overnight, and later found in a shambles around the house, as if the bones were dancing around after dark, is certainly something to be looked into more closely. The events experienced by Gary Powell appear to be a finishing touch to the whole story, as if the monks were letting one living person know that they were set free from their earthly bonds.

Perhaps the later event was to thank the students and Pensacola citizens for remembering them by way of a fitting and respectful burial. Later on, Mr. Powell told his story to other students and friends attending the ceremony, and asked if anyone else saw the ghostly trio, or if anyone had a paranormal experience. Though most denied any such experience, he did find that the carpenter who made the new coffins for the three rectors saw what he believed to be their three spirits staring at him and smiling as he worked in his garage a few nights before the ceremony. Although the coffin maker shook his head a few times in disbelief, finally walking out to see the robed figures engaging in conversation and, to his surprise and amazement, he witnessed the three mysterious men fade away into the darkened night.

Whether or not the Old Christ Church is still haunted by these three ghostly rectors is unclear. For two lucky individuals, however, the question of whether ghosts really do exist has been answered. Perhaps these three spirits have gone on to a better place, having shown up one last time to say goodbye. It could be that their images may be seen from time to time as a spectral recording playing over and over again, only to be spied by a lucky few. Maybe you, too, will catch a glimpse of the three rectors of Old Christ Church inspecting the place they once called home.

Afterthoughts

The Old Christ Church is a must-see exhibit for anyone interested in early American architecture and history, as well as for those interested in the paranormal. This structure is truly a beautiful example of Florida's religious heritage that is steeped in the saga of our state's illustrious past. Be it war or famine, financial upheavals or natural disaster, the Old Christ Church survived it all through thick and thin. So when visiting this wonderful landmark, bear in mind the incredible history of this church throughout time, and the effect it has had on so many lives ever since. Remember the souls who made it what it is, and who still linger on today.

Although I haven't had an experience of the paranormal type while visiting the Old Christ Church, I still quite enjoyed visiting. I found the church and the surrounding area to be very peaceful, and on one occasion, I sensed the rich, sweet scent of roses all around me, almost as if I were standing in a rose garden. In the Christian context, this historically means a preternatural type of blessing on a location. I took this as a good omen and consider this church a true holy place.

When visiting the Old Christ Church, feel free to inspect the lovely furnishings and décor. Sit upon the beautiful pews when the church is still and silent, and see if you can smell the light fragrance of sweet roses as you imagine the three rectors giving sermons to parishioners of long ago. Who knows, maybe you will hear the faint laughter of the jovial spirits of Old Christ Church.

The Old Christ Curch is on the tour listing for Pensacola's Historic Village. Tickets can be purchased at the T. T. Wentworth Museum for a small fee, and for the cost of the ticket, you can also visit several other haunted locations, such as the Dorr House and the Lear-Rocheblave House. The museums are open Monday through Saturday 10:00 A.M. to 4:00 P.M. and are closed on major holidays. For more information call 850-595-5985.

Florida's Gulf Coast

Florida's Gulf Coast
Ghosts and
Haunted Locations

Traveling downward from the northwestern Panhandle of the state, we enter the grand region of Florida's west coast, a truly tropical paradise. From the quaint fishing village of Cedar Key to the lively city of St. Petersburg, ghost hunters and other visitors will find everything from antiquated architecture to the fully progressive amenities of a big city. The growing cities of Sarasota and Clearwater share these attributes and a particular charm that only Florida's west coast can offer.

During my life here in central Florida, I have been fortunate to have experienced the delights of Florida's west coast and all it has to offer, from the action-packed football games of the Tampa Bay Buccaneers, to a refined show at a theater, I have had the opportunity to experience the beauty that many simply take for granted. I have also been privy to several other aspects of Florida's west coast that may fall under the category of the paranormal or preternatural. In my excursions throughout this region, I have investigated many of the creepy avenues and reputedly haunted locations that would have some entertained and others thoroughly terrified.

Whether treading through darkened cemeteries and mausoleums, or through the stately hotels and bed & breakfast inns that exist in abundance here, there seems to be something else co-existing with the living—something downright uncanny.

In my first book, *Florida's Ghostly Legends and Haunted Folklore, Volume One,* I related my experiences inside the haunted mausoleum of Tampa's Myrtle Hill Cemetery, and of catching the sweet but out-of-place scent of a ghost's cologne within the magnificent Tampa Theatre. I wrote about the sad phantom hitchhiking girl who sometimes terrifies drivers crossing the Sunshine Skyway Bridge, and of the dapper spirit who walks the halls of the delightful Don CeSar Hotel in St. Petersburg. I thought that my paranormal investigations were virtually exhausted, until I started looking more closely into the deep and intriguing folklore of Florida's west coast.

Over the past few years, I have had the chance to further my research into the realms of the unknown, effectively uncovering even more stories of ghostly visitations and haunted locations throughout this region. In fact, because there are so many stories and legends, I am only able cover a fraction of them. For this reason, we shall investigate a few of the most tantalizing legends from St. Petersburg and Clearwater to Sarasota and Naples and a few places in between.

On this journey we will explore the beautiful Ritz-Carlton Hotel in Sarasota, where there's far more than a simple elegance waiting for you. Then we will travel to the Belleview Biltmore Hotel in Clearwater, where the guests might get a phone call from the beyond in the dead of night. Later we'll go to a lost little road in Largo, where the overly concerned spirit of an ill-fated prom queen tries to educate the young about drinking and driving.

We will continue our investigation into a haunted bookstore in downtown St. Petersburg, where you might find something lurking among all of the books and magazines. Then we head on out to Egmont Key, where the spirits of the dead from across the ocean are said to meet at the lonely lighthouse that beckons the departed to enter the island's ethereal sanctuary. Finally, we will enter a haunted restaurant in Naples, where the tormented apparitions of its murdered staff are believed to tamper with equipment, and re-live their sad, painful last moments of life in both a frightening and playful manner.

Throughout our paranormal journey in and around the Gulf coast region of Florida you can experience the strange and mysterious. Hopefully, after doing your own investigations, you will be able to validate these sometimes festive, sometimes frightening legends as true. So, when visiting the region of Florida, be sure to enjoy the many sights and events, and relish the beauty this area has to offer. Whether you're enjoying the splendor of the nature parks, walking on the beautiful white sand beaches, or even shopping and sightseeing, be sure to remember the fascinating history linked to Florida's Gulf coast.

While staying in one of the magnificent hotels or bed & breakfast inns, try to keep an eye out for a ghost or two, as you might be surprised at just how many spirits may be spending their vacation with you. When enjoying one of the many fine restaurants or bistros here, ask your server if there are any haunted legends about that location, or tales of the supernatural—what she or he tells you may just have you looking over your shoulder. While taking in a show or play at one of the many theaters or playhouses, keep in mind that many of the denizens of the spirit world might enjoy a night out too, and that the empty seat next to you might actually be occupied by an unseen patron. Anything is possible in the world of the paranormal, and Florida's Gulf coast has more than its fair share of weird happenings and downright spooky occurrences.

Perhaps the things you will experience while on your journey will be nothing more than a common occurrence—something with a rational explanation, such as the low rumbling of a distant storm or a tree brushing up against your window in the dead of night. Perhaps the shadowy forms you'll see out of the corners of your eyes are nothing more than the phantoms of a heated imagination. Perhaps the whispers and disembodied voices are in fact nothing more than a passing wind. Or perhaps the odd feelings and events you are witnessing are actually something quite strange in origin, something from beyond our understanding, such as the spirited residue of the dead—

the ghosts of the once-living trying to say hello from beyond the grave.

Now, I invite you to prepare for this final journey into Florida's haunted realm, and into the Gulf coast's lesser known, darker regions where ghosts and spirits abound. You might be surprised at what you find!

12
Island Hotel and Restaurant

Cedar Key

"13 Ghosts and More"

"Cedar Key might well be called the last outpost of the Florida Keys, inasmuch as it is the only remaining group of islands which has not been touched by the lush-plush of the resort hotels. . . . There are no nightclubs and where the hustle-bustle honk and screech of traffic is unknown . . . it's like going into Never-Never Land."
—Ron MacIntyre, *Cedar Key: A Way of Life*

A Little History

The Island Hotel and Restaurant, a truly beautiful bed & breakfast inn located on the shores of the quaint fishing village of Cedar Key, Florida, has entertained vacationing fishermen and sportsmen, the rich and famous, along with starry-eyed newlyweds for over 150 years. This truly delightful hotel, which continues on to this day, possesses a singular charm that can only be found in the old Florida style.

The inn was constructed in 1859 by two inspiring businessmen: Major John Parsons, a direct descendent of John Adams, and his partner, Francis E. Hale. The two entrepreneurs had envisioned Cedar

Florida State Archives

Key to be the crown jewel of all the islands in Florida, and a great location of opportunity. They anticipated scores of people and their money being ushered in by the Florida Railroad, and the economic opportunity that would generate from their enterprise. They opened the township's first general store and post office in what is now a part of the hotel. Parsons and Hale continued to build on the site, using a time-honored Floridian method of mixing shells with ground limestone and sand to make up a tough seashell concoction for the foundation and wall structure. This strong mixture, called "tabby," along with huge oak beams as support, not only created an antiquated and rustic appearance, but made it possible to withstand some of Florida's worst storms and hurricanes.

Sadly, the outbreak of the Civil War forced the future of Cedar Key and other developments to come to a halt, as Union troops used the tiny island as a strategic port, later invading and burning down almost every building there, except the Parsons and Hale General Store. After the war, the island and the hotel prospered until a massive hurricane came barreling through the islands and the west coast in 1896; almost everything was destroyed, including a good portion of the hotel. The hurricane wiped out the island's cedar industry and, consequently, wiped out the small community as well. It was the beginning of harsh times for the community and many packed up and left for brighter opportunities. Sadly, the hotel would remain a listless and decaying hulk.

In 1914, Langdon Parsons, son of Major John Parsons, sold the building to a man named Simon Feinberg, who then changed the inn's name to The Bay Hotel. The Bay Hotel was managed by an unscrupulous man named Marcus Markham, who is believed to have been involved in the illegal liquor trade. As local legend relates, it was during the 1920s that Simon Feinberg found case loads of illegal liquor, along with grain alcohol, still being stored in the hotel's attic. At the same time a mystery befell the hotel and Cedar Key's history. Apparently, while Feinberg and the hotel's manager were having a dinner meeting concerning this illegal venture, Feinberg became mysteriously ill and died the next morning of what was later thought to have been food poisoning. Whether coincidence or murder, no one is quite sure, but while remodeling was taking place in the late 1990s, the remains of copper piping, metal canisters, and glass jugs, all commonly used to condense liquor in stills, were discovered in the dusty recesses of the hotel's attic.

Over the years there have been many owners running this old hotel, all with new and different names to make it their own. Names like The Cedar Key Hotel and Fowler's Wood would grace a newly renovated hotel marquee, until yet another would-be proprietor would take the reins. During the Great Depression, the hotel operated as a speakeasy until it almost burned to the ground, and finally closed due to a lack of business. For more than twenty years the once-ornate hotel and adjoining annex would sit in an almost dead state, literally rotting to the ground until fortune intervened.

By the mid 1940s, two new owners named Loyal "Gibby" and Bessie Gibbs took control of the dead and decaying hotel and fixed it up to its former glory—no easy task. A fresh coat of paint was applied, new furniture and mattresses were purchased, and a bar and restaurant were newly designed. The new owners were then just about ready to put the once-noble hotel back into the limelight. Gibby took the job as bartender, where he was a natural, and Bessie took control of the dining room and balanced out the hotel's finances after hours. It wasn't long before the hotel and bar would once again become a popular gathering place for locals and visitors, and gleaned a nice reputation in the process.

During the years that Bessie and Gibby ran the hotel, many famous and influential people enjoyed this wonderful landmark's offerings. Indeed, Florida's Governor Claude Kirk would often make weekend trips to the hotel to enjoy the fresh seafood and strong drinks in the Neptune Bar. Other famous people, such as Tennessee Ernie Ford, Vaughan Monroe, Frances Langford, Myrna Loy, Richard Boone, and even Jimmy Buffet, also took advantage of the gentle and refined atmosphere of the beautiful Island Hotel.

Without a doubt, Bessie and Gibby not only made a name for themselves, but they also served their tiny island community with all the love and pride they could possibly muster. By the 1970s Gibby had passed away and Bessie was suffering from advanced arthritis and spinal degeneration, which confined her to a wheelchair. When her health did not improve, she sold the Island Hotel and Restaurant to Charles and Shirley English, thus ending a famous era in Cedar Key's history. Bessie would continue to live in her beloved island home until

1975, when sadly she lost her life in a house fire. Both Gibby's and Bessie's ashes were scattered in the Gulf of Mexico overlooked by their beloved hotel.

The Island Hotel and Restaurant has seen many more owners since the 1940s. Today the establishment is cared for by Andy and Stanley Bair, who continue to make this wonderful location the perfect place for anyone wanting to get away from it all and just relax. This splendid hotel and restaurant has since been listed on the National Register of Historic Places, and there is little doubt as to why it is one of Florida's most famous and beloved bed & breakfast inns. As there are so few permanent residents on the island—most of them retirees, artists and skilled craftsmen—it's easy to see why many view Cedar Key as a true-to-life link to Florida's past, and a utopian community as well.

With the colorful art festivals in the springtime that exhibit the talent of local artists, where paintings, sculptures, wood carvings, and various crafts abound, the spirit of this delightful community will prove favorable for the art critic and novice alike. The seafood festivals which are held every fall are always a joy, as they not only celebrate Cedar Key's fishing heritage and active industry, but will surely satisfy the most hearty seafood aficionado every time.

I have been fortunate enough to have experienced these festive events that Cedar Key hosts, and, of course the simple splendors that are always offered by the Island Hotel and Restaurant. Although my vacations there have always been filled with fun and entertainment, whether scuba diving in the nearby Gulf, or just enjoying a lazy evening sitting on the hotel's balcony watching the sun go down, I have always felt that I was not quite alone there. No matter how serene my room felt, or how quaint and charming my dining experience was, there was always the feeling that someone was watching close by.

Even though my opinions might seem biased, I would be surprised if anyone staying in the Island Hotel and Restaurant didn't feel the same way, for there's something else here besides the guests—something spooky.

Ghostly Legends and Haunted Folklore

It shouldn't be too much of a surprise to learn that such a charming inn as the Island Hotel and Restaurant is haunted. As it has seen Florida grow from its beginning as a state, it's not hard to imagine the events this location has seen. Having survived the perils and tribulations of the Civil War, two world wars, and the Great Depression, all of which taxed our great nation to its limits, the Island Hotel and Restaurant survived, even if it was a little rough around the edges. Indeed, much like the state of Florida itself, this hotel has endured killer hurricanes, terrible tropical storms, and tornados. It has survived disease, corruption, and financial hardship. Through it all, this lovely inn has always continued proudly on its way.

As I investigated this charming hotel, and the quaint island it rests on, I found myself truly falling in love with its simplicity and natural wonder. When I asked about the ghosts that might inhabit the hotel and grounds, I was assured that it was, indeed, haunted. I sat down with a few locals and staff and began recording some of the ghostly legends. The hotel staff insisted that there are at least thirteen authentic spirits occupying the hotel, as related by many psychics who have stayed here over the years. And though they are not all classified and accounted for, they are worth mentioning.

The first and possibly most historically important specter is that of a little African slave boy around the age of nine or ten, who died here during the Civil War. As legend tells it, this young boy worked for one of the original managers in the Parsons and Hale General Store and Post Office, where he would sweep and generally help out around the store. One day, while this boy was working in the store, he decided to steal some candy off the shelves, which the manager witnessed. He chased the boy out of the store with threats of a beating. The boy, scared for his life, ran as fast as he could and was never heard or seen from again. Life went on and the mystery of the missing slave boy subsided, and eventually was forgotten. Nevertheless, strange things were beginning to happen around the general store and grounds.

Curious events started to happen such as objects and goods in the store would often turn up missing, or were later found in odd places, and peculiar noises were sometimes heard in and around the store after hours. Soon the locals began to think the general store was just plain spooked, or as they would say in those days, "hainted." The basement of this area and the annex, which is now under the main hotel, was said to have a little ghost living there, who enjoyed jumping out of dark corners or grabbing the pants legs of a bystander, sending that person running out of there post-haste.

These events would continue for about a year or so, until the cause of that haunting was finally identified, at least for the manager and the locals. It was while the staff was cleaning out the basement's cistern-well that they discovered the skeletal remains of a young boy found at the bottom, covered with silt and slime. Evidently the boy may have climbed into the cistern to hide from the pursuing manager and gotten trapped, or perhaps fell in a top well and drowned. Even though history is unclear as to whether the boy ever received a proper burial, one thing is for sure—the basement is still reputed to be active with a playful little ghost who still tugs on the clothes of the living. The ghost often will be seen hiding behind boxes and furniture, or will sometimes be heard fumbling with the cistern's trap door toward the back of the hotel's basement. Either way, this little spirit can even cause a grown man to race out of that cellar while looking over his shoulder.

Another popular ghost spotted in the hotel is that of Simon Feinberg, the ill-fated hotel manager from the early 1920s. This hapless spirit is said to walk around the hotel from the evening into the wee morning hours, where he might check up on the guests or inspect the hotel, making sure all is well and clean. Because he was such a staunch businessman in life, having owned property all over Florida, it stands to reason that he would continue to do so in death. The staff feels that Feinberg's spirit is more a wandering spirit, and one who is mostly harmless. Although he met an untimely end from an unscrupulous cad, his upright and cultured mannerisms appear to remain steadfast in the afterlife. The best times to observe him will only be possible if you are staying the night at the hotel—usually on the second floor. One staff member told me that you may catch the faint odor of cologne just before he makes an appearance. If you sit still in one of the inside chairs, you might see him slowly walking across the floor with his hands behind his back, carefully observing the premises, just as any good manager might do today.

Another ghostly legend revolves around rooms 27 and 28, where the spirit of a murdered prostitute is said to occasionally make visits to the guests. Apparently, when prohibition was the law of the land, the hotel wanted to help those in need of a good stiff drink, so they opened a well-stocked speakeasy and brothel for some of Florida's less law-abiding citizens. This makeshift bar and brothel was said to have had a good selection of ladies to help entertain and sell drinks to thirsty customers, which seemed to be a good idea at the time. Unfortunately, some of these customers were anything but gentlemen, and a few of them were downright deadly. Though there is little actual documentation to support these events, many of the island's luminaries and historians believe them to be true, nonetheless. As the story goes, there was a kind and caring lady who worked in the brothel. She got involved with a rather rough thug who didn't take no for an answer. Although no one is quite sure where this poor lady of the night was buried, or what caused her demise, her spirit is said to linger in the hotel on moonlit nights, appearing to guests occupying those two rooms, which at one time may have been one large suite.

The spirit of this unlucky lady has been reported to be wearing a flapper-style dress with fringes or tassels on the ends. Some have reported the dress to be a light yellow or pale in color, and her hair is dark and short, with a face that is a soft white with full, dark red lips. When a lucky guest gets a visit, she will gently sit on the side of the bed and lean over to kiss him on the cheek. Then the apparition sits back up with a loving smile and simply fades away—truly an invigorating surprise for any male guest to get in the middle of the night.

Another spirit which is observed quite often is that of a Confederate soldier, said to stand guard on the second-floor balcony. Though the identity of the spirit and reason for his visit is unclear, many think he was a soldier assigned to protect someone of importance, such as a Confederate general, when the hotel grounds were secured by Southern troops just before the Union troops arrived to take command of the island. He is most often seen early in the morning just as the sun begins to come up. He stands at what is known as a "loose attention" where the guard is certainly alert, but somewhat relaxed, as if this is his one and only duty. Because this is quite common for low-ranking soldiers, it's a good bet this was the ghost's primary function in life. Everything else about this particular spirit is a complete mystery. Regardless of his anonymity, many of the hotel's guests have seen this vigilant spirit over the years.

Now that we know a few of the Island Hotel's time-honored spirits, it's time to remember the most popular, and seemingly the most dominant, spirit of all—Bessie Gibbs. Since 1946, when Bessie and her husband, Loyal, bought and renovated the old Island Hotel, until the day she died, every ounce of love and patience went into the investment they both called home. Bessie spent almost three decades in the hotel, where she was as full of character and life as imaginable, so it's not hard to believe that her lively spirit remains in what was most likely her favorite place in the world, and where she had some of the best times of her life.

Bessie's ghost has been witnessed in one form or another within the old hotel since at least the late 1970s. Many people, both staff and visitor alike, have reported strange incidents occurring in room 29, where Bessie lived for many years. Lights flicker on and off, icy cold drafts will be felt even in the summer months, and some will actually see an apparition resembling Bessie walk right through their room in the dead of night. As if that's not enough, she is believed to move furniture around and even play tricks on some of the guests. Some of her recorded mischievous actions include locking a guest out of his room and lightly placing a cold hand around a guest's neck as he or she passes her room.

A few years ago the hotel allowed a séance to take place in order to spiritually resurrect Bessie Gibbs, and to find out about the many ghosts suspected to live there. The results were very interesting as those conducting the séance knew very little of the hotel's ghostly lore. When their findings matched the experiences of the hotel's many guests, everyone realized it was Bessie.

Over the years, many psychics have come to the hotel to experience the spirits for themselves. Although most left with more than enough information about the jovial Bessie Gibbs from the other side, some were thoroughly convinced that there are several other entities coexisting in this charming hotel. Among the spectral guests, there are at least two Native Americans, a tall dark man dressed in antiquated clothes, and a fisherman complete with slickers and fishing gear, as well as several others that have yet to be identified or channeled by psychic mediums. The one thing that all of the visiting psychics and paranormal researchers agree with is that there are at least thirteen spirits in the Island Hotel and Restaurant, and possibly more, making this one of the most haunted spots in our journey.

So if you're looking for cold spots, unexplained breezes, and strange drafts from nowhere, the Island Hotel is a good place to start. If you don't mind sharing a room with one of its original occupants from one hundred or so years ago and if you don't mind a feeling of being watched or followed, then this is the place for you—the Island Hotel and Restaurant, one of Florida's most haunted places.

Afterthoughts

The active medley of spirits believed to exist in this hotel is certainly notable. Many paranormal investigators, psychical researchers and psychic mediums have made pilgrimages here in search of the preternatural, and very few have gone away empty-handed. In fact, almost everyone I interviewed believes without a doubt that the Island Hotel is haunted. If you wish to discuss the subject of ghosts and hauntings, you'll find a very receptive staff here. Not only will they openly admit to their haunted workplace, but they will actually sit down and talk to you about their experiences, which is a very happy occasion for the serious collector of paranormal legends and ghostly folklore.

If you are looking for a hotel that is truly a timepiece to the past, and a bit off the beaten trail, then the Island Hotel and Restaurant will be the perfect place for you. If you're seeking a truly spectral hotspot that will be sure to enlighten your senses, then this is the place. Our busy lifestyles might question a hotel that doesn't have television sets in the rooms or loud nightclubs nearby, but you will realize rather quickly just how enjoyable and relaxing the simpler way of life can be. While sitting in the rocking chairs that line the balcony, you can watch the sun go down on the Gulf. You can then adjourn to the beautiful King Neptune lounge and bar for a lazy nightcap to end a wonderful day on the enchanted Cedar Key. If you're an angler, then you won't have to travel far to get the best catch on the west coast, because the whole island is just perfect for a day of fishing and swimming, or for just getting back to nature.

The Island Hotel is as romantic and as filled with ambiance as can be imagined. Just as an old Florida hotel should be, there are no televisions or telephones in the rooms of the main hotel, and some of the rooms even have old-fashioned claw-foot tubs. Each room has its original hand-cut wood walls and floors, and are centrally air conditioned and heated. Cedar Key is about fifty-eight miles southwest of Gainesville, at the very end of State Road 24. The hotel is located at 373 2nd Street, in Cedar Key, Florida. For information, directions, wedding occasions or reservations, call 352-543-5111 or 800-432-4640; fax 352-543-6949.

13

The Royalty Theatre

Clearwater

"A Sea Captain, a Murdered Manager, and a Little Girl"

A Little History

Located at 405 Cleveland Street, in the older section of downtown Clearwater, there exists one of my favorite haunts when visiting the west coast—the beautiful and stately Royalty Theatre. The elegant design of this theater echoes a more refined era of Florida's past, when style and manner reigned supreme. It has seen a time when gentleman wore top hats and ladies carried parasols, as well as the age of fast cars and even faster people and lifestyles. Yet, through it all, the Royalty Theatre has retained its noble stature and placement in Florida's distinctive history.

Constructed and established in 1896 as the Capital Theatre, this classic structure, complete with a large balcony mezzanine and offering 533 seats with all the furnishings of a classic Hollywood theater, is one of the oldest and most stylish landmarks on Florida's west coast. Though this theater has seen many incarnations since its inception, the theater's original beauty remains steadfast nonetheless. Beginning as a vaudeville theater and movie house, it was once the home of

famous headliners and starlets of the day who displayed their legendary talents, and made history in the process. From Fred Astaire and
Ginger Rogers dancing up a storm on the polished wood plank stage,
to Bob Hope keeping the audience in stitches, the old theater was
responsible for prime entertainment and culture for the city of
Clearwater for decades. Frank Sinatra, Sammy Davis Jr., Liza Minnelli
and Elvis Presley were among a few of the famous personalities who
made the Royalty Theatre a legend.

From 1914 to the 1940s, the theater patriotically offered its services to house military troops during World War I and World War II.
In the 1950s, the theater was used primarily for weekend stage events
and double-feature matinees, which continued into the early 1960s,
when a topical storm from the Gulf of Mexico virtually destroyed the
main structure and flooded the orchestra pit and lower seating area. It
even tore down the hand-carved façade at the front of the building.
After a short hiatus for repairs, the theater reopened to the public and

continued to function as a well-loved theater.

By 1983 however, the Royalty Theatre suffered harsh competition from the Ruth Eckerd Hall Opera House and Theatre, a new theater house for the performing arts in nearby Tampa. Complete with up-to-date amenities and with more parking spaces for the west coast's growing population, this newer complex for the arts would spell certain doom for the elegant Royalty Theatre. By 1995, the theater's executives decided to close its doors for public performances and leased it out to the Calvary Baptist Church. It was used as a church and a theater for various religious events and performances. Fortunately, with the aid of a local Greek artist and philanthropist named Socrates Charos, his wife Dru, and the Clearwater Historical Society, repairs and much needed refurbishing of the theater began. By 2000 the Royalty Theatre had a grand reopening to the public.

Today, although still recognized as the Royalty Theatre, it's known primarily for the Museum & Performing Arts Academy, where a dance studio aids in instructing countless youngsters in dancing and the performance arts. Indeed, the handsome Royalty Theatre, which has provided an elegant place for world-class entertainment for more than one hundred years, is responsible for honoring the arts and patrons of the arts in all its guises with a class that very few establishments can match. And, though the Royalty Theatre shall always rank as one of Florida's most prized historical landmarks and contributors to the education of the arts, it also appears to be the home to more than just the eager patrons of the arts, opera critics, and movie-goers—this theater also appears to be the home to an odd variety of flamboyant phantoms.

Ghostly Legends and Haunted Folklore

This wonderful theater has been reputedly haunted by at least three spirits since the 1960s, where each ghost is quite distinctive. It was to my benefit that the proprietor and various local ghost hunting organizations were more than happy to share their knowledge of the three ghosts with me. Evidently, a local St. Petersburg ghost hunting group known as S.P.I.R.I.T.S. (Servicing Paranormal Investigators Reporting Information through Study), overseen by professor Brandy Stark, has been conducting research into the Royalty Theatre's alleged entities and has been able to collect a good amount of history and urban legend regarding them. To date, the primary spirits seen, heard, or otherwise witnessed are a sea captain, a one-time manager of the theater, and a lurking little girl. The exact identification of two of these spirits is a mystery. The other spirit, as well as the most often seen is known as Bill, who is believed to have been that of a long-dead manager whose ghost remains in the place he once called "home away from home."

Although it is often difficult to get the exact information of a crime or murder from the police or other law enforcement agencies, sometimes you can get lucky getting information from the staff or other workers from the location of the crime scene. Apparently, there was a man named Bill who had managed the theatre in the 1980s. He was tall and carefree in nature, and was said to have some effeminate mannerisms. He was known to be a good man who loved both his work and the theater, to the point that he considered his job more a labor of love than a job. He even thought of his workplace as a second home.

As the story goes, while working one afternoon in the mid 1980s, Bill was accosted by two or more drunken patrons. Apparently they had noticed his effeminate mannerisms and started calling him names; what started out as simple harassment ended in physical attack, which resulted in Bill's death. Though the particulars were hard to find, we know that he was murdered in the balcony area. The fate of Bill's murderers is unknown, but Bill's untimely passing was certainly a shock to everyone, especially to the theater's staff and patrons.

The first sign of a ghostly presence appeared soon after Bill's death, about the time a series of renovations were taking place in the theater. While a worker was repairing some electrical components on the balcony, he tripped over some wires and a toolbox. Just as he was just about to fall over the balcony the worker felt a cool grip around his shoulders, and he was gently pulled to safety. When the thankful worker regained his footing and turned around to thank whoever it was who had saved him, he found the balcony was completely vacant. He had been saved by a ghost! Since then, patrons, students at the dance academy, and visitors have felt the presence of the kindly manager, gently coexisting with them. Though an exact identification is difficult to ascertain, most people simply believe the spirit of Bill has chosen to remain in this lovely theater as a guardian who assists the patrons from potentially deadly mishaps and provides an enjoyable occasion for all who love the arts as much as he did in life. Indeed, it is a wonderful legacy.

Another spirit said to inhabit the theatre is known as "The Sea Captain." This somewhat out-of-place specter has been witnessed by the proprietor himself, Socrates Charos. According to Mr. Charos, when he first took command of the Royalty Theatre he was "formally" introduced to one of its ghosts. As he walked through the main door one morning, he was approached by a man of average height who wore a dark blue jacketlike coat from another era. He had a goatee and piercing blue eyes, and he wore a large hat like that of a fisherman. At first the new owner thought he was an actor, as this strange apparition offered his hand in good faith. After shaking hands with Mr. Charos, the fisherman proceeded to walk right through the unsuspecting owner. As the spirit went on his way, Mr. Charos noticed that the apparition had no legs, just the ends of the long dark blue coat.

As time went on, other strange things began taking place, such as out-of-place noises and banging sounds, as well as ungentlemanly behavior. Evidently, this scallywag of a ghost was known to be very rude to the ladies; it was not uncommon for a female patron to feel the icy disembodied hands of the captain running up her legs, or worse, having her derrière pinched or slapped. If this wasn't enough, the nasty sea captain began pitching a fit on the main stage, where he would scream and yell in the night, and make all sorts of unnerving noises such as banging pots and pans together and stomping up and down on the stage. He became quite a nuisance.

As this ghost's bad behavior continued, Mr. Charos felt he had had enough and called in a priest, who performed an exorcism on the stage and throughout the theatre grounds. This seemed to have worked, as the ill-behaved sea captain has apparently moved on to the Other Side or perhaps back out to sea. Though various religious ceremonies are usually enough to dispel an unruly spirit, they will sometimes come back. So don't be surprised if you hear that this interesting, if a bit salty, spirit returns to the Royalty Theatre.

The last spirit known to inhabit the stately theater is that of a little girl. And though her identity is a complete mystery, most simply refer to her as Angelica or Angelina. Her first recorded appearance was in the 1960s, shortly after the storm that caused a lot of damage to the theater, during the first renovations. She is described as a young girl around the age of ten, dressed in early American style clothing, somewhere before the turn of the century. It is widely believed that she died during that era. The little spirit is said to be friendly and enjoys music, song, and dance, which makes some paranormal researchers believe she was the child of an early actor or actress who may have died during the yellow fever or influenza outbreaks of the 1900s.

This little spirit is mostly benign in her actions and is only seen from time to time. When people do witness her childlike form, it's when she's dancing and frolicking about. If you're lucky, you might spot this youthful specter on the balcony, on the stage, or behind the curtains. She is most often described as wearing a fluffy yellow dress but she sometimes wears blue or green. She wears a bow in her hair, and is almost always seen with a smile on her face. She's just a happy little spirit who makes the Royalty Theatre home, and she's not afraid to let you know it.

Over the last few years, several ghost-hunting groups and serious paranormal investigators have researched the theater and its active spirits. Over the course of time, many have witnessed several odd things; they have also collected photographs of the ever-popular orbs and other strange misty images that cannot be explained. Furthermore, the enigma of Electronic Voice Phenomena (EVP) has also yielded evidence of something residing in the theater, where out-of-place sounds and voices have been recorded. Several people, both believers and nonbelievers, have experienced weird events such as lights turning on and off by themselves and chandeliers swaying back and forth without any apparent reason. It's safe to say, something para-normal is going on in the stately Royalty Theatre

Afterthoughts

When visiting the lovely city of Clearwater, be sure to drop by the magnificent Royalty Theatre and the Museum & Performing Arts Academy. If you can, try to see a show here, as every performance is an event not to be missed. Be sure to ask the proprietor Socrates Charos and his lovely wife Dru about the fascinating ghosts that exist there, as they are both very open about their experiences.

When walking around this beautiful theater, enjoy the timeless architecture and the golden furniture and façades. Stay after the show when the rest of the guests are ushered out and sit in one of the now-vacant seats. Sit still for a few moments and simply listen. You might be surprised at what you hear; maybe, just maybe, you'll catch a glimpse of a little girl who died a century ago. Perhaps you will feel a cold hand on your shoulder as to help you safely out of the theatre, free from accident or harm. If so, be sure to thank Bill, the theater's former manager. If, however, you spot the sea captain, that nasty rogue of long ago, be sure to tell the staff immediately, so a priest can send him back where he belongs—to the open seas!

Without a doubt, if you're looking for a strange group of ghosts, the Royalty Theatre is certainly a good place to start. Indeed, though many paranormal investigators and ghost hunters have little doubt that this location is haunted, most are uncertain as to the reasoning of their presence being there. Though the entity known as the sea captain seems mismatched for a theatre, some speculate that he may have died at sea and wandered into the theater after he died. Since the ocean is very close to the Royalty Theatre, this is one popular opinion. Another idea is that this is the spirit of an actor who was very much in love with one of his theatrical roles. Either way, this is one spirit who needs to work on his manners.

The Royalty Theatre is located at 405 Cleveland Street in beautiful downtown Clearwater. For information on show times and events, for dance class times and dates, or to schedule a party call 727-441-8868; fax: 727-447-2277. E-mail: Socrates@RoyaltyTheatre.org.

14

Belleview Biltmore Resort and Spa

Clearwater

"Phone Calls from the Dead"

A Little History

The Belleview Biltmore Resort and Spa, a masterpiece of the early nineteenth century, is located on a thirty-foot bluff and nestled on the western Intracoastal Waterway in the beautiful township of Belleair, just west of Clearwater, Florida. This marvelous hotel is probably one of the best loved landmarks, and best kept secrets on the Gulf coast. The Belleview Biltmore is considered by many historians to be of great significance, as it is one of the last remaining grand hotels from this period in all of Florida. The Biltmore Hotel was built in 1897 by railroad tycoon Henry B. Plant as an ending destination for his southbound railroad lines, to offer a convenient way to deliver his guests to the hotel and the lovely township. As this would also increase the number of tourists vacationing in his hotel, and in nearby Tampa and St. Petersburg, Henry Plant's vision proved both wise and profitable.

Upon arrival, guests would be welcomed by swaying tropical palm trees and huge live oaks draped with Spanish moss. They would experience the exuberance and elegance of the Victorian ideal toward social rapport and class, where every niche and block would be perfect in

every detail. As there were several early-nineteenth-century homes built around the hotel grounds to serve Mr. Plant's family and friends, as well as visiting dignitaries, the Biltmore became a township in and of itself, complete with a general store, stables, and various shops to handle all of the guests' needs. From laundering to shoe shining, the visitor here was completely pampered in every way. The beauty of the Biltmore is undeniable, as its dark-green sloped roof and white wood-sided exteriors eloquently demonstrate the class and love of this generation—especially in its extensive hand-crafted woodwork through-out the interior of the hotel. With its collection of antiques and semi-modern amenities, there's little doubt why this elegant resort hotel is so beloved. Sadly, the Biltmore is one of few standing hotels con-structed by Henry Plant still in use as an active resort, so keeping the Belleview Biltmore alive and well is of paramount concern for the managers and staff here, as well as to the guests and residents of the beautiful town of Belleair.

Once inside this glorious resort, you will find 244 beautiful guestrooms, each uniquely designed to inspire and gratify the guest in every way. While some rooms have ornately sculpted fourteen-foot ceilings, with period mahogany furnishings and luxury linens, others may have personal refrigerators and decorative fireplaces with views of Clearwater Bay and the Gulf of Mexico. Either way, anyone staying here will find this resort among the best in the world. In addition to the services provided by the resort, such as the Beach Club, that can handle any party, business meeting, convention, or wedding, your every need will be met with professionalism and courtesy.

Be sure to visit the hotel's historic museum, compete with artifacts and photos from over one hundred years of Biltmore history. There's also a complimentary ninety-minute walking tour that explains the hotel's unique and interesting history, presenting some of the two miles of hallways and underground passages throughout the hotel. Without a doubt, this is one of the most elegant hotels in all of Florida. Indeed, when a guest of the Biltmore Hotel Resort and Spa, you'll certainly be in good company. The Biltmore has hosted many famous people and dignitaries over the years, including Presidents George Bush Sr., Jimmy Carter, and Gerald Ford, along with Joe DiMaggio, Babe Ruth, Thomas Edison, Henry Ford, and even the Duke of Windsor and former British Prime Minister Margaret Thatcher.

It may also interest the guest to know that since the hotel's grand opening, a few of the hotel's lesser-known guests have apparently chosen to stay at this remarkable resort where they had vacationed so long ago. Evidently, the Belleview Biltmore Resort and Spa is just too delightful to leave—even for the afterlife.

Ghostly Legends and Haunted Folklore

The Belleview Biltmore Resort and Spa is indisputably one of my favorite places to visit and stay. There is an old-world charm to the place that enlightens me every time I visit. Though there seems to be a darker side to this lovely hotel resort, I can't help recalling Stanley Kubrick's 1980 film *The Shining* every time I visit, primarily because so many ghosts are said to walk the halls and hidden passageways here. And though there have been no reports of evil spirits roaming the grounds here, there seems to be a plethora of ethereal entities coexisting in this lovely hotel nonetheless.

Rumors of ghosts lurking within this grand hotel probably date as far back as the 1900s, when guests began complaining of hearing strange noises in the upper floors late at night. Of course, the fact that the hotel is one of the largest wood-frame buildings in the United States might suggest that such noises are nothing more than the creaky wood settling. Perhaps this is a logical and down-to-earth explanation; nevertheless, this does not explain the many strange occurrences reported by both guests and staff members over the years.

Of the most noted paranormal occurrences to have been reported are the incorporeal phone calls said to come from a closed-off room in an unused section of the fifth floor. If that's not strange enough, these phone calls are said to come from an old rotary phone which has no cord connected to it. And because such older phones have the cord permanently attached to them, it's safe to assume it had been cut or torn off, which should make it impossible to receive or transmit any calls whatsoever. This being the case, that phone should never work again, let alone begin ringing. When I interviewed a few staff members about the mysterious phone and its ghostly ringing, all were willing and even proud to tell me stories of their haunted workplace. Most told me that that phone is no longer in that shuttered room, and has actually been gone for several years. Others have informed me that the phone was actually much older and had been in that room since at least the late 1930s. Some say they believe that the phone is still there, and that it continues to ring on various late nights, sometimes waking guests on that floor, as well as frightening the maids and staff working in that area. The ringing ceases, however, when security or maintenance goes up to investigate.

Although there may be more to this story, almost everyone knows about the eerie phone and its late-night ringing. Several people over the years have divulged to me that a few of the hotel's staff members had actually found the phone and picked up the receiver to inquire who was calling, only to be greeted with light breathing sounds—and nothing else. On at least three separate occasions a startled employee answered the phone and heard a faint, echoing voice on the other end simply saying "hello . . . hello?" Moreover, this voice was reported as sounding like a woman who was calling from an outside location with a lot of wind or rain blowing, making her words almost impossible to understand. On another occasion, many muffled voices, as if coming from a distant conference room, were heard, which had that particular employee racing away when he noticed that that phone wasn't even connected to an outlet. Were these phone calls from the dead? Many believe them so.

If you are lucky, you might get permission to see this creepy, sealed-off and unused section of the fifth floor, which resembles an unfinished construction site from the turn of the century. Ragged discarded lumber sits in piles, along with old rugs, boxes, and various artifacts from the hotel's past. You'll smell the heavy scent of pine from the unfinished timbers and see a foggy haze that seems to permeate everything there. Most feel that they are being watched, as if many eyes are constantly upon them, or as if something unearthly waits, ready to lunge from behind a rafter or beam. In some sections it is so dark that it is almost unbelievable. Indeed, the feeling here is one of dread and apprehension.

The other oddities that occur within this elegant monument to the past include disembodied voices being heard throughout the empty hallways and from within the huge candlelit ballroom. Here, low muffled voices are sometimes heard and the chandeliers are occasionally seen rocking back and forth by themselves. There are also reports of faces being seen from outside the hotel late at night. On occasion, when a security guard is making his rounds or a late-night worker is closing up and leaving for home, he or she will notice a face staring at them from one of the many small windows on the fifth floor. Sometimes there will be a cascade of faces staring down on an unnerved witness—faces that appear to be foggy. When someone investigates, there will be no sign of anyone on the other side of those windows, nor any trace that anyone was ever there.

In addition to these creepy happenings, there are other spirits said to lurk the dark avenues of this charming hotel resort. Among them, there appears to be a myriad of ghostly children who are sometimes heard running down the hallways of the upper floors, especially the fourth and fifth floors, in the wee hours of the morning. Their tiny faces; some smiling and some grimacing, are occasionally seen peering out of the darkened windows in the dead of night. On occasion, a few of these youthful specters have startled more than one late-night employee by shaking the leaves on potted palm trees or knocking something over. These pranks are accompanied by eerie giggles. Still others have reported actually seeing two or more children running out of view on these upper floors, only to disappear when pursued.

If you're staying a weekend at the Belleview Biltmore, you might hear the story of "Maisie," the spirit of the grief-stricken lady who constantly searches for her lost pearls. Hers is a story of love and possession. Indeed, history tells us that when Morton Plant, the son of railroad tycoon Henry B. Plant, met this charming woman named Mae "Maisie" Cadwell Manwaring, he fell head-over-heels in love with her. Since the beautiful Maisie was a married woman, he had to make another move in order to have her. What did he do? He paid Maisie's current husband $8 million to walk away from his marriage. Apparently the money sounded good, because Morton and Maisie were soon married, and thus the legend began.

Soon thereafter, Morton bought his not-so-blushing bride a set of pearls from Pierre Cartier with a net worth of $1.2 million. She so loved those pearls that they were around her neck almost all the time, especially when there was a fancy function or stately banquet going on. Indeed, it must have been quite a commotion when she lost them. Though no one is quite sure how this happened, the loss of her pearl necklace was enough to drive her to a deep depression that lasted the rest of her life—and into the afterlife. Over the years, the ghost of Maisie has been seen wandering the halls looking for her pearls. A ghostly apparition would be seen bending over and looking in small, out-of-the-way places and under tables as if searching for something lost. Her spirit has been witnessed by many employees and guests alike, resulting in a time-honored legend that has lasted through the ages.

There is speculation, however, that this spirit is not the ghost of Maisie, but that of a woman who jumped to her death in the 1930s. This woman, named Anne, is said to have been a new bride honeymooning with her husband at the hotel when she took her life. Hotel records tell us that her husband was killed in a car crash while the two newlyweds were staying in the hotel; it was this tragedy that prompted her to leap from the fourth floor balcony of the Presidential Suite to her death. To date, a spirit of a woman dressed in white has been seen since at least the 1950s. Exactly who she was in life may be a mystery, but she has become a part of this grand hotel resort's history, with much love and admiration, as well as becoming the subject of many hotel ghost hunts.

There are a few more ghosts believed to haunt the hallways, rooms, and closed-off areas of this charming hotel. Stories of a tall dark man riding the elevators have been reported here; apparently he enjoys spooking not only the guests, but a few staff members as well. In addition to this, there is an unseen spirit who enjoys spooking the kitchen staff by placing a heavy hand on the shoulder of an employee, only to quickly disappear as soon as the startled employee turns around to see who it is. Sometimes this pesky spirit makes its presence known by rattling the pots and pans from a darkened corner of the kitchen. This almost always happens when there is a lone female worker in the room. Needless to say, there is little doubt by staff and long-time guests visiting the Biltmore that there are a few amusing spirits here.

A few years ago the Biltmore was featured in a segment of the *Weird Travels* television series, a popular program hosted by the Travel Channel. Not only did the producers and staff make with a great show, they also came out with a few personal experiences they could not explain. Indeed, more than one crew member told of having a weird experience or seeing something they could not explain. Almost the entire crew witnessed the lights flickering on and off on the upper floors, as well as hearing faint voices echo from various places.

When all is said and done, the Belleview Biltmore Resort & Spa does appear to have something going on. Maybe it's not one of the most haunted locations on the west coast; but it is certainly a location worth investigating. Even if you're a staunch skeptic, you may find yourself walking away feeling a little different about ghosts and haunt-

ings, as so many others have over the years. And even if you don't
believe, you will have one of the most relaxing visits imaginable; you'll
want to come back again and again.

Afterthoughts

When investigating this wonderful hotel resort, try to remember the
lives that passed through these stately halls, and those who stayed in
these luxurious suites, as well as those who played here and died here.
Try to remember that in every splinter of wood and grain of stone, a
memory is stored like a great recording device. Whether it's Maisie
pacing the halls in search of her lost pearls or the tall dark man who is
assisting those riding his elevator, remember that these actions were so
strong in their lives, that each vibration and recording had survived
through the ages, even beyond death.

The Belleview Biltmore is proud of its ghosts, so much so that it
hosts a few ghost hunting excursions that will take you deep within
the hotel's rich history and educate you in the popular methods used
by modern paranormal investigators. Led by a team of paranormal
investigators from Orlando Ghost Tours Inc., two individual tours are
offered to the public every Saturday night, taking guests through the
stately ballrooms, hallways, lounges, and even the closed-off areas of
the hotel, which are said to be haunted. During the course of the tour,
you will receive a working education in parapsychology and the investigation of paranormal phenomena. The trained staff walks guests
through the grounds, explaining the hotel's many amazing stories at
the same time. On the tour the guest will have the opportunity to uti-
lize actual equipment in order to get an up-close and personal idea of
parapsychology in progress. This is a fun and educational tour
designed for both young and old alike.

In addition to the ghost tours, there are other spooky events taking place around Halloween, where the friendly Belleview "ghosts"

host a weekend of fun and festivities for everyone. From haunted houses and mystery dinners to historical tours and a masquerade ball, the guest staying the weekend will have more to do than imagined. The hotel also offers a safe place for the kids to enjoy Halloween by having a costume and pizza party, with pumpkin painting and light spooky movies held in the ballroom and the hotel's amphitheater. Because there has been much success with these events, you may want to call the hotel early for times and dates for each event, as well as for reservations.

The Belleview Biltmore Resort & Spa is located at 25 Belleview Blvd., Clearwater. For reservations and check-in times, as well as for other special events, call 800-237-8947 or 727-373-3000 or visit their website at www.belleviewbiltmore.com.

15

Lover's Lane of Keene Road

Largo

"Still Late for the Prom"

"We stayed out most of the night that June of 1991, just sitting in the car waiting for her. We all knew the story, having heard it since middle school, so we were excited when we learned she was seen a week, or so earlier . . . Then it happened! It was around 3:15 in the morning when we saw her . . .

It was as if she was running in a fog, and she had no feet or legs!"
—Eyewitness account (e-mail)

A Little History

Alternate Keene Road, a half-mile track of thoroughfare located off McMullen Road and Fairlane Drive, and just north of Bay Road within the business district of Largo, Florida, is home to one of the more interesting types of haunting known to parapsychology; recognized as a "caveat apparent," a warning spirit that appears to those who are living foolishly.

Alternate Keene Road was once nothing more than an unfinished idea for another road that was one day to be made. This ended up serving as a second-chance road to regain one's bearings when driving in Largo's business and residential districts, where warehouses and

121

small businesses line the streets. Although the road is paved today, it was once nothing more than a simple dirt and gravel road that abruptly ended in a barren field. This road was discovered by local teenagers as a perfect site for a lovers' lane, due to its quiet surroundings and its remote location.

This story begins on one balmy May evening in 1982, when two young lovers, both students of Largo High School, were on their way to the school's annual prom. As with many other eager students waiting to model their new flowing gowns and rented tuxedos, they were ready for an evening of carefree fun before they would begin their final sprint toward graduation. Little did they know that the prom night they so desired and waited for was to end as a sad occasion.

As the prom came to an end and the echoes of laughter and merriment finally began to die down, one final hurrah of youthful glory passed through the young man's mind. He was eighteen years old and he wanted to show his girlfriend a special ending to a special night. So he and the young lady, along with two of their friends, hopped in his rust-colored 1972 Pontiac, and began their quest for a little undisturbed romance away from the prying eyes of teachers and local authorities. It would be the last thing the young couple would ever do together.

After enjoying one too many illicit libations at the prom, the young man shouldn't have been driving, but his youthful bravado told him otherwise. He and his passengers set off for the deserted Keene Road. It was while speeding down that gravel road that he decided to turn off the headlights of his car in order to get a few laughs from his passengers. And, though his girlfriend might have protested this foolish act, she was too late in her warning. Before he could turn his headlights back on, he lost control of his car and crashed head-on into an old live oak tree. Though the passengers in the back seat were injured, the young couple in the front were not so lucky, as they were killed instantly. Their lifeless bodies were slumped over the hood of the wrecked car.

Their deaths proved hard for their friends and family. At school, their classmates mourned for their friends who would never get the chance to grow up or have families of their own. It was difficult to believe that their friends were gone, but life does go on. After a time, many would forget the untimely deaths of the two teenagers almost completely. Yet, something was happening on Keene Road that would enter the realms of the paranormal.

On one summer night in 1987, a strange occurrence would befall the city of Largo that would continue to frighten and amaze people for years to come. Old Alternate Keene Road, now a darkened reminder of that tragic event, took on a sinister reputation as a visitor from beyond the grave would resurface again and again in the dead of night to warn foolish teens not to drink and drive or drive without their headlights on.

Ghostly Legends and Haunted Folklore

The haunting of Keene Road, as some have dubbed it, is actually no haunting at all. In fact, it is as one of my colleagues described it, a "caveat apparent," which is a nonsentient representation, or recording, of a once-living person playing a message over and over again. In this case it is the repetitious warnings from the young woman who was killed in the accident. I have known of this particular legend for a few years now, related to me by an old friend who lives in nearby St. Petersburg. She explained that many of the kids in the area would often go to old Keene Road late at night to see the specter of the girl, who would chase after cars who doused their headlights while driving on the road. Some of these kids would actually set up camp near the road, complete with sleeping bags and campfires, in order to spot the elusive specter. Indeed, this local legend had grown to such proportions that Largo police had to keep the road under constant surveillance just to make sure the kids weren't making the same mistakes the teens had made years earlier. To this day, when Largo's youth head off to Keene Road to catch a glimpse of this concerned spirit, many will come back having seen absolutely nothing, while others would return wide-eyed, pale, and excited, stating that they had seen something out of the ordinary. Naturally, this might be nothing more than a very creepy tale taking its toll on impressionable minds, or perhaps there is, indeed, something strange going on there.

Earlier this year, in my quest to expose this legend for what it is, I made many inquiries to several local ghost hunting organizations, most notably the S.P.I.R.I.T.S. ghost hunting group. This is a local chapter of paranormal researchers out of St. Petersburg which investigates many of the west coast's ghost stories and haunted locations. I also contacted several graduates from Largo High School to see if they knew of the legend of Keene Road. I was fortunate to receive a few intriguing stories from two graduates of Largo High, who had personal accounts to share. One story in particular, from a woman named Kathy, detailed an evening that she said she'd never forget.

It was in June of 1991, around 3:15 A.M. that Kathy had her paranormal experience. While sitting in the car with a friend waiting to see the elusive specter, she turned her headlights on and off three times to hopefully provoke it into action. Apparently this worked, for within a few seconds after the third flash of the headlights, they both saw what appeared to be a pale-white girl in a large flowing gown running up the road toward them, her arms stretched out wide and with an agonized look on her face. The apparition was fast approaching the car and it appeared as if she was running in a fog. When they looked more closely, they had noticed that this fretful spirit had no legs or feet! Wide-eyed and in shock, Kathy immediately started up her car and peeled out of there as fast as she could, trying to drive and look through the rearview mirror at the same time without crashing her car.

This is only one story, of course, but there have been many more just like it since the late 1980s. Although many similar stories have passed from one student to another over the years, we can see an eerie similarity. Even though the two teenagers were properly laid to rest, with all of the proper religious ceremonies, there still remains an essence of those last minutes before their lives were snuffed out. It's hard to say why the young woman remains earthbound; she could be trying to get the message across to other teenagers. One thing is for sure—something is startling the kids on old Keene Road.

Indeed, as this type of entity seems to be quite common in the realm of folklore and oral tradition, much like the ghostly female spirit who asks for a ride over the daunting Skyway Bridge in St. Petersburg; she too is trying to tell a story, even though she fades to a mist before she can do so. Sadly, this may be true for the girl as well. She appears to be doing the same thing—just trying to keep another from making the same mistake.

Afterthoughts

Today the once-barren gravel road and surrounding area has changed since the early 1980s. The road is completely paved now and is bordered by small houses and trailer homes. As a result, the spirit's warning is reported less and less by ghost-hunting teens. Still, on special occasions, this specter might make an appearance. If you are brave enough to sit out on the sides of this road in the wee hours of the morning, you might just have a paranormal experience for yourself. Perhaps you, too, will spot this elusive phantom racing down this dimly lit road to stop an accident from happening. One thing seems certain: if you do witness this sad vision, then you're doing something wrong, as she only appears when foolish behavior is taking place.

I had the opportunity to pay my respects to the young woman where her mortal remains rest in the Serenity Gardens Memorial Park Cemetery in Largo. She appears to be content and still in this quaint cemetery, even though her restless spirit is the subject of controversy for many teenagers, as her memory remains true to many teens preparing for adulthood. Though she has been dubbed the Queen of the Prom, this is untrue, even though many of her friends and school chums had bestowed that honor on her posthumously.

When visiting this area, remember the tragedy that took place here. Remember that someone lost their daughter and son here. Remember that although many of us may truly be invigorated by the thought of seeing a ghost or experiencing an otherworldly entity, try to show reverence. Remember also that Largo police patrol this area regularly, and they will not allow any foolish or dangerous behavior, including sleepovers and campfires. You may also need to prepare yourself for many hours of waiting, as even the most prepared paranormal researcher and ghost hunter may come up empty-handed from time to time.

When visiting the cemetery, please show respect. Offer a prayer so that her caring spirit may pass on to a better place. Lay some flowers in her memory, and while doing so, bear in mind all the dreams and goals she never lived to achieve. Know also that her endless vigil is not only to recall that fateful night, but also to offer us a lesson from beyond the grave. *Requiescat in pace, dear girl. Rest in peace.*

Serenity Gardens Memorial Park is located at 13401 Indian Rocks Road near downtown Largo. You may call the cemetery office at 727-595-2914 for more information.

16
Haslam's Book Store

St. Petersburg

"Mr. Kerouac . . . is that you?"

A Little History

Whenever I visit St. Petersburg, I make it a habit to stop by Haslam's Book Store. Though I usually end up in the metaphysical and used-book sections, hoping to find any number of rare titles, I will always explore this store's wide selection of books and magazines, which can sometimes take most of the day. Indeed, it doesn't matter if you're looking for a rare book of poetry or a recent magazine on any subject; you're bound to find it in Haslam's Book Store.

It was 1933 when John and Mary Haslam opened their little store. They sold everything from daily newspapers and flowers to candy and dolls for the kids. Although they began modestly, they slowly grew in merchandise and in reputation as a fine store, becoming a respected institution of commerce in the process. By the late 1940s, the couple added new books to their shelves, and by the 1950s they had become known as one of the better places to buy books and other reading materials in St. Petersburg. Indeed, whether technical trade manuals on cars or aircraft, books on philosophy and religion, or trade paperbacks and children's books, Haslam's always pulled through with flying colors.

To promote books and reading, the second generation of Haslams—Charles and Elizabeth, both published authors—had started a public television program on WEDU called *The Wonderful World of Books*. They would review new and old books on a variety of subjects to entice readers of all ages to get more involved with reading and writing. They got WSUN radio to spread the word; they even organized and operated book fairs at local schools to encourage young people to read. Their dedication would continue on through the years, building their reputation in the process. By 1966, Haslam's little bookstore had become so large that they had to relocate several times in order to accommodate its ever-growing stock of books and merchandise. By the late 1970s, the owners had expanded their business into the neighboring People's Gas Company complex, combining the two buildings into one store, making Haslam's one of the largest new and used bookstores in the state of Florida.

As local legend found this popular bookstore, so did famous personalities. This included authors, actors, local luminaries, and musicians, all in search of new reading material while visiting the bustling city of St. Petersburg. One such personality was the famed beatnik writer and poet, Jack Kerouac, the master of the beat generation and father of hippie philosophy. Without a doubt, this was a name proudly associated with Haslam's Book Store, and one that would go down in Florida history.

Jack Kerouac, the French-American novelist, writer, poet, and artist, was one of the most popular, writer personalities of the 1950s and 1960s. Not only was he a patriarch for the free speech movement, he was also considered one of America's most important authors. His spontaneous, confessional-style prose inspired free thinkers, musicians, and self-styled philosophers to explore beyond the limits of accepted thought. Writers and poets, including the ever-bizarre Hunter S. Thompson, and others such as Tom Robbins, Lester Bangs, Richard Brautigan, and even Bob Dylan, were inspired to create some of their best literary works, all due to Kerouac's influence. Indeed, with such works as *Big Sur, On the Road,* and *The Dharma Bums,* an understanding of post-modern thinking of otherwise taboo topics had literally changed the world, thanks to Kerouac's ideals.

Wanting to break away from the moralistic dogma of the 1950s, Kerouac traveled across the United States and Europe in order to find other like minds of the new counterculture that was finally finding a voice. He would eventually settle in St. Petersburg, where he would visit and show his books at Haslam's, as well as lecture on his personal beliefs and philosophies. Quite often the writer would visit the bookstore only to make sure his books received center attention, by rearranging the shelves the way he saw fit. In fact, he would take his books from lower shelves and place them on the top shelves to better catch a buyer's eye. He would also face his book covers outward in order to attract the customers. This, however, did not sit well with the owners, who quickly stopped the impromptu rearrangements. This infuriated the temperamental Kerouac, who would usually storm out of the bookstore in a rage, cursing and mumbling all the way up the street.

In spite of this, Kerouac would continue to write books that are today credited as the catalyst for the 1960s hippie generation, and made history in the process. Regrettably, he was also an avid drinker and experimenter of mind-altering drugs, which would eventually catch up with him. Jack Kerouac died in St. Petersburg on October 21, 1969, at the age of 47, succumbing to an internal hemorrhage caused by cirrhosis of the liver, which was in turn caused by his chronic alcoholism. Though many may have forgotten the often brilliant and insightful, as well as acidic and harsh, writings of this famed author, many feel that his unique and somewhat eccentric persona has remained in the bookstore that he both loved and hated. Some believe that his spirit continues to wreck havoc on the bookshelves of Haslam's Book Store, and that his ghost is still just as vibrant as the restless man he was in life.

Ghostly Legends and Haunted Folklore

It's hard to say just when strange things began to take place at Haslam's. Many think the first recorded incident was in the late 1970s, just after the Haslam family bought the vacant People's Gas building adjacent to their store. Others think the location of the store had always been haunted by something or someone. Still others think that the ghostly accounts are due to the many old and rare books that have passed through Haslam's shelves over the many years, where perhaps any number of these old tomes may be the reason something lurks there. Though the causes of these strange happenings remain a mystery for some, others feel it is definitely the restless spirit of Jack Kerouac, the late author of counterculture literature.

Other odd occurrences are reported to take taken place in Haslam's, ranging from cold spots in otherwise warm places to and books sent flying off the shelves by unseen hands. Low, disembodied voices are heard late at night and the unnerving feeling of being watched are the most common events reported by both staff and patrons. On occasion a customer might complain of feeling a tap on their shoulder, or a cool breeze passing by them when no one is around. Some claim to have actually seen a book or two slowly slide from its shelf and fall to the ground, as if something or someone was pushing it from the other side. This is not likely because a wall exists behind the books. It is apparent that this modest fourth-generation bookstore can boast about more than its excellent book collection—it can also brag about having a ghost or two, as well.

Having spent many an hour in this delightful bookstore, I heard about one retentive spirit that is said to dwell there. This spirit is believed to spend most of its time near the metaphysics-new age section, where the feeling and atmosphere of this area has been reported as cold and rife with other sensations. On more than a few occasions, individual paranormal research groups have taken a keen interest in Haslam's ghosts, where they make systematic surveys of the bookstore, its history and its surroundings in precise detail.

S.P.I.R.I.T.S., the ghost-hunting society based in St. Petersburg, has investigated many allegedly haunted sites across Florida's west coast. They have made an impressive database on such locations over the years, so it should be of little surprise that this organization places Haslam's Book Store on the top of their investigatory list. And, during such investigations, group members have recorded several interesting events that are directly linked to the presence of ghosts. Through digital and 35-mm photographs and video recordings, this group has captured many odd things, including the presence of popular orbs and vortex phenomena, which are those strange tornado-like anomalies believed by some to be ectoplasm in flux. Other irregularities include massive spikes and drops in temperature by as much as fifteen to twenty degrees for no logical reason. There have been high electromagnetic field readings near the do-it-yourself and home improvement section, and strange cool breezes are sometimes felt where the old People's Gas Company once had its offices. Moreover, many people, including long-time staff members, have claimed to have felt the restless but benevolent spirit of Jack Kerouac.

Since at least 1977, many strange events have taken place throughout this location. These include backroom floorboards popping and creaking when no one is present, along with temperatures falling abruptly, and staff and visitors getting goose bumps and feeling like someone was standing behind them. However, on a few occasions, there have been full-bodied apparitions experienced by those of a sensitive nature. Indeed, many psychics have entered Haslam's feeling that there was something more lingering there, and some have even claimed to have seen several spirits up close.

Sheila Cavallo, an Orlando-based psychic medium, believes one spirit which inhabits the bookstore is an older man, around seventy years of age. He has grayish hair, thinning on top, and thick whiskers around the sides of his head; he also has a bulbous nose. Ms. Cavallo said that the spirit glared at her when she was looking about the store. And though most get a feeling of malevolence when first spotting the old ghost, she felt he was simply a man who once lived in the adjacent building. When the Haslam's bought that building they cut a large hole in the wall to make an entrance to another set of rooms for their books. Some believe the Haslam's might have unknowingly "activated" otherwise dormant spirits, causing them to wander. The psychic had an impression that there is another specter in the bookstore, an entity that is just as much perturbed in death as he was in life. She believes that most spirits who cross over continue doing what they did when they were alive.

This second spirit, according to Ms. Cavallo, is possibly that of

Jack Kerouac, who makes himself more apparent in the metaphysics section of the bookstore. She feels that this entity clings to the idealistic nature of these books, where the subjects of astral projection, reincarnation, and parallel universes, along with ghosts and hauntings, are readily found. Opposite to this section are appropriately topics of religion and faith, a subject known to both entice and anger the late author. Is the spirit of Jack Kerouac haunting these bookshelves? Ms. Cavallo seems to believe so, for this is an area where many books are reputed to fall off the shelves for seemingly no reason, a behavior that seems to accompany some ghosts. Moreover, Ms. Cavallo also believes that a spirit might attach itself to a book, or series of books, which may cause this to take place.

Incidentally, Haslam's has an adopted cat named Tiptoe. This cat, like any good feline, loves to roam and explore, occasionally stopping to rub up against the legs of a patron. Though Tiptoe will go just about anywhere, he will almost never venture inside the metaphysical section of the bookstore. Tiptoe will look in that direction and survey the area, as if someone is standing there. The cat will turn his head as if looking at an unseen person walking to and fro, but then simply turn away, and prance in the other direction at a rather quick pace—coincidence?

Afterthoughts

Who walks the quaint aisles of Haslam's Book Store? Perhaps these spooky events are nothing more than an older building that is settling with age, where the floorboards are creaking and popping with time. Perhaps the cool breezes are nothing more than an overactive air conditioner as opposed to an unseen entity walking past a patron or staff member. Yet, even with such down-to-earth and reasonable answers we must, as investigators of the unknown, look just a bit further.

When we examine the background of this location, we might

begin to see a few connections. The activist-author Jack Kerouac was certainly a lively and temperamental personality in life. So much so that he might be continuing his retentive mannerisms in the afterlife, such as monitoring the bookstore where his works were once displayed, rearranging books to his liking, and popular motives. And since Haslam's was an important place for him, primarily because he could view his published works here, as well as notice the reactions of the patrons, this may very well be a catalyst for his haunting this bookstore. He was a man who wanted the best for his books, and rearranging the bookshelves was simply part of that. Though we know many things regarding the history and mannerisms of this famous writer, there may yet be a few secrets that are still unknown.

What about the other spirit that is said to lurk here? As I investigated a little more closely, going over city records and speaking to city workers and business neighbors this past year, I found that the storefronts here once allowed single families to live in the back of the stores. Though there are rules prohibiting this in many newer buildings today, this was a popular custom fifty or more years ago. When I inquired as to who might have lived in this section, I was told that there was an elderly man who once lived in Haslam's adjacent building. He was in his mid-seventies and had grayish, thining hair. He lived in a small room in what was then the People's Gas Company building long before Haslam's purchased the building. This old man was found dead in his bed from natural causes. Is this just a coincidence?

Several reputable psychics believe so. What about the strange behavior of Haslam's cat Tiptoe? This also appears to go hand-in-hand with the presence of ghosts, since animals seem to be more attuned to things people cannot see. Indeed, famed English parapsychologist Harry Price often took his dog with him on investigations, letting the animal go into a haunted location first so he could examine its reactions. He would keep the dog with him during the investigation in order to see how the dog would react. Because dogs and cats are well known by paranormal researchers to follow unseen things moving about, or will chase or bark at things humans cannot detect, many researchers and ghost hunters will often bring their dogs or cats as natural ghost detectors.

Whether or not you will have an otherworldly experience while visiting Haslam's is anyone's guess, as the spirits here tend to come and go as they please. If you're lucky, you might have a first-hand experience, where one of the two spirits will appear to you. Perhaps you will witness a book falling to the floor while perusing a book on metaphysics, or you may feel a cool breeze pass by you. Maybe you'll hear a low voice mumbling in the distance as the temperature drops, or witness Tiptoe the cat running away from that particular section of books where something or someone supernatural loiters—either way, its likely that you're not the only soul to enjoy a good book at Haslam's.

Haslam's Book Store, Inc. is located at 2025 Central Avenue, St. Petersburg. Store hours are Monday through Saturday, 10 A.M. to 6:30 P.M. To get there, take I-275 to exit 23B (old exit 11) and go straight through the traffic light at the bottom of the ramp. This is 20th Street. You'll notice the avenues count downward, 4th, 3rd, and so on—Central Avenue is the "zero" avenue. Turn right on Central Avenue and you'll see the bookstore on the right side. For more information, call 727-822-8616 or visit the Haslam's web site at www.haslams.com.

17

The Vinoy Hotel

St. Petersburg

"The Lady in White"

" . . . The Vinoy Hotel isn't just a great place to stay, and [I] have been coming here for years. . . . Over the years though, I have experienced some strange things, most notably the elevators, which sometimes seem to have a mind of their own. . . . And the fifth floor, now that's a weird place for sure. . . . You'll have to stay there to know what I'm talking about. . . . Talk about weird!"

—Hotel Guest, 2006

A Little History

The above quote came from a very pleased globe-trotting traveler who was more than happy to share his experiences as a guest of the Vinoy Hotel, though his reaction does not seem to be typical of the guests who stay here. One must actually stay a night or two to truly appreciate the gentle ambiance and vast amenities of the beautiful Vinoy Hotel. I have had the pleasure to holiday here on several occasions over the years, where every visit is always a treat. Indeed, whenever my wife and I visit St. Petersburg, we will never miss the opportunity to

stay at the Vinoy, as it is one of the friendliest and most magnificent hotels on the west coast.

The Vinoy Hotel, located in beautiful downtown St. Petersburg, was built by Aymer Vinoy Laughner, real estate magnate and noted entrepreneur of his day. Completed in 1926, and originally known as the Vinoy Park Hotel, it operated as a seasonal resort, which usually ran from December to March for northern visitors. The rates were a whopping twenty dollars a night, an exceedingly high price for those days, but because it was regarded as one of the finest hotels, and frequented by many famous people, it was considered worth the price by the "in" crowd of the roaring 1920s.

The Vinoy would entertain the rich and famous over many years, including such personalities as Presidents Calvin Coolidge and Herbert Hoover, Babe Ruth, and Jimmy Stewart. It survived the Great Depression and during World War II the hotel was temporarily utilized by the U.S. Army as a barracks and training school. After the war, the hotel was sold to Charles Alberding, who then restored the hotel to its former glory. The Vinoy would continue to prosper and service both domestic and foreign travelers happily until the early 1970s, when it finally closed its doors to financial difficulties. Most of its contents were sold off, and the once-beautiful resort hotel now stood silent and still. Sadly, the hotel became a haven for vagrants and criminals on the run; the police were there almost every day. Indeed, this once-opulent hotel was reduced to an eyesore. It wasn't until the early 1990s that this once-glorious hotel would see life again—when a celebrated rebirth took place.

The hotel, a massive and hovering building that seemed foreboding and dark, now would have some much-needed light and life restored to it. Though this would cost several million dollars in renovations, and took two years to complete, its new owners, the Renaissance Hotels and Resorts and the Vinoy Development Corporation would put the Vinoy Hotel back in service, regaining all its former magnificence in the process. The new and updated Vinoy reopened as an almost perfect replica of its former self, successfully acquiring the perfect example of Florida's golden age of resort hotels.

Today the Vinoy once again proudly boasts its Mediterranean revival–style, complete with high wall construction and imported tiles, with an eighteen-hole golf course, a twelve-court tennis complex, and a private marina equipped with personal launches. If that's not

enough, there are a multitude of first-class amenities in this meticu-
lously restored hotel that will please even the most pampered guest.
You'll find the charming Marchand's Bar & Grill, an open-air restaurant and café, along with the Terrace Room, the Promenade Lounge,
and Fred's Private Dining Room.

There is little doubt that this enchanting resort hotel will always
remain a fond memory for its guests and visitors, as this hotel's singular appeal and thoughtful staff will always make the best impressions.
Every guest is likely to leave this luxurious resort hotel with a smile on
their face, but some may leave knowing that something else is residing within the lovely corridors and stately suites here—knowing that
this exquisite hotel is thoroughly haunted.

Ghostly Legends and Haunted Folklore

The Vinoy Hotel is inclined to keep its legends of ghostly presences
and hauntings hush-hush. They are more about making sure that the
hotel remains exclusive, and remembered positively by its guests,
rather than encouraging explorations of the supernatural. In spite of
this, the Vinoy has entertained many people, both the common vacationer and the rich and famous who have walked away knowing, without a shadow of a doubt, that this beloved resort hotel has its share of
ghosts and similar shadowy entities.

There appears to be a few individual spirits here, as local legend
dictates, but only one stands out above the rest—the lady in white.
This unidentified specter, which is said to glide throughout the fifth
floor hallways in a flowing, almost transparent gown and shroud, has
made herself visible to only a few guests. Although this sad entity wan-
ders alone and in evident dismay, she apparently has a soft spot for
selected guests staying on this floor. This may include a lone male
traveler, or highly public people; but above all, she takes a shine to
baseball players.

The most popular story of the lady in white revolves around a few shaken baseball players who have had personal confrontations with this hotel's resident spirit. In each case the visiting baseball team had no idea that they were about to enter the realm of the paranormal. As the story goes, when a baseball team comes to Florida's west coast for training or for games, they often stay at the Vinoy Hotel because the players can get great massages and sit in the hot tub after a long day. On various occasions, however, when one of these athletes prepares to retire for the evening, he might just get a visit from beyond the grave.

A few years ago, Scott Williamson of the Boston Red Sox was one witness of the lady in white. He claims to have been awakened in the middle of the night by a feeling that someone was in his room. First a faint light or glow appeared, then he noticed a woman dressed in a style of clothing from the 1920s or 1930s. The spirit just stared at the shocked ballplayer until she faded away to nothingness. Mr. Williamson had to endure some razzing by his teammates later that day. Even the famous sports writer Joe Haakenson heard about the Vinoy hauntings and began a hunt for the elusive specter in hopes of proving the stories true. Unfortunately, Mr. Haakenson never received a personal greeting from the lady in white, as so many other ballplayers had, but he still keeps an ear open for more of the ghostly legends whenever staying there.

There appear to be several legends about this lady in white and who she was in life. One of the local and quite common beliefs is that she is the restless spirit of Elsie Elliott, a socialite who was purportedly pushed down a flight of stairs by her wealthy land baron husband Eugene Elliott. And, as if that's not enough like a soap opera, others believe that the apparition is actually that of Elsie's personal maid, who is said to have witnessed the murder. Not long after the event, the maid mysteriously vanished just before she was to testify to the crime. Another conjectured possibility is that the woman was a mistress of the famed baseball legend Babe Ruth. Though there is little evidence to support this theory, some feel that this lady would visit "The Babe" when he vacationed in Florida. Since he was unable to offer the love and commitment she desired, she either died regretting this or she took her life because of it. Either way, she still lingers on in the hotel she once loved.

Another spirit, said to be dressed in a tuxedo, haunts the hotel's elevators. Occasionally, this spirit makes himself known by his playful antics with the guests, and as legend tells us, when a lone gentlemen boards the elevator to go to his floor, all of the elevator number keys will light up, then go out, except for the number five; the elevator will then quickly take the confused passenger to the fifth floor. When the doors open, the passenger finds nothing but an empty hallway. Though no one is entirely sure who this playful spirit may be, some have referred to it as "the formal ghost," who is complete with top hat and tails. On another occasion, while a major league player was stay-ing in the hotel, the formal ghost made his acquaintance by standing over his bed and pressing down on his back, as if to wake him. This understandably worked, as the ballplayer turned on his side to make sure he wasn't dreaming. He let his eyes focus just enough to see a tall, thin man wearing a nineteenth-century-style top hat and frock coat, complete with tails. The mysterious visitor sported a waxed mustache and had dark eyes that just stared down at the athlete. Naturally, the poor ballplayer either thought someone was playing a trick on him or that he must have been dreaming. Thinking it was one of his baseball chums having some fun; he sat up and turned on the light next to his bed. As soon as he did, the visitor disappeared. There was no trace of an intruder and the door was locked and the deadbolt secured. Since he was on an upper floor, no one could have possibly come through a window.

Although a strange occurrence, and to date, an unsolved mystery, this was certainly not the only occasion something like this had taken place. Similar events have taken place for at least five separate baseball players over the years. Apparently, baseball is indeed the greatest American pastime—even for the dearly departed.

Afterthoughts

The stately Vinoy Hotel is certainly fit for any king and queen, a president, movie star, and even a baseball team or two. And there appear to be a few spirits residing here as well. The lady in white, who graces the hotel's hallways, seems to be more a vaporous furnishing than anything else. And though she might mysteriously impose her preternatural aspects on visitors when she appears, we ghost hunters must ask why she haunts, instead of simply banishing her presence to the nether reaches of our subconscious. Was she the ill-fated socialite who was doomed to walk these seemingly endless halls or could it be the maid who knew too much? Perhaps she is a broken-hearted mistress, a former lover of America's most adored baseball player, as some believe. And what of the strange ghostly man dressed in antiquated clothing and top hat that also appears to favor America's favorite pastime and its players? Without a doubt, these are just some of the mysteries that haunt the majestic corridors and rooms of this resort hotel.

Though these answers may never be completely revealed, we can look at a few of the obvious aspects that history has recorded for us. First, we know that many a baseball team has stayed here over the years, and unknowingly, some of these ballplayers may have brought such entities with them from their hometowns. Since there are some legends supporting the possibility that ghosts may travel along with the object of their interest, paranormal investigators must consider this possibility also. Secondly, we know that during the years when this building lay dormant, it attracted the less fortunate, along with the criminal element, as a place of refuge. Because there have been several deaths in this building, even murders as some suggest, we know that a psychic residual of such traumatic past events may have been left behind. This is known as a haunting. One thing is for sure, regardless of whether you have a ghostly encounter, you'll always have a wonderful time at the Vinoy Hotel.

If you do have a ghostly experience, you can always contact one of the many research organizations based in St. Petersburg or throughout the Gulf coast. These groups will always want to hear your story and appreciate your input. You can also pass the information along to Tampa Bay Ghost Tours, which often relates the stories of the Vinoy's ghosts on their venue. This modest organization operates out of Hubbard's Marina located on the bay waters near downtown St. Petersburg. They offer four separate guided tours throughout several Pinellas County locations, all of which are rumored to be haunted. These tours are fun for the whole family and educational too. While some of the tours tell of haunted mariner lore and lost pirate's treasure, others relate spooky tales of John's Pass and, of course, a few haunted hotels along the way. Either way, this is a great way to learn more about Florida's historically haunted side.

Tampa Bay Ghost Tours can be reached at 727-398-5200 for more information, or for an overview of their package deals, you can visit their web address at: www.allthebesthaunts.com. The Vinoy Hotel is located at 501 5th Avenue NE St. Petersburg. For reservations and information, call 727-894-1000, 888-303-4430 or visit their website at vinoyrenaissanceresort.com.

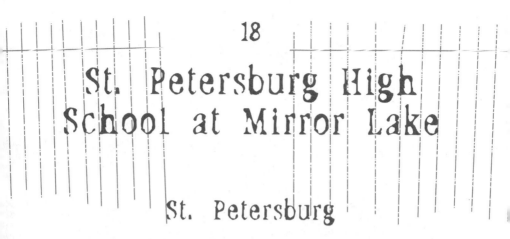

18

St. Petersburg High School at Mirror Lake

St. Petersburg

"A Little School Spirit"

"Old St. Pete High, how proudly we honor and praise you!
Time will not change you; your spirit will never die . . .
We're here to boost you in classroom and gridiron and field, too.
You are to us our own wonderful St. Pete High"

—St. Petersburg High School Alma Mater

A Little History

"Time will not change you; your spirit will never die." This simple phrase from St. Pete High's alma mater surely seems appropriate, since there seems to be more than a few spirits roaming its once-busy halls and classrooms. Of course, as this antiquated high school of yesteryear was one of the oldest and most prized schools on Florida's west coast, it would seem logical for there to be a haunted legend or two attached to it. The beautiful St. Petersburg High School, located at 701 Mirror Lake Drive in the heart of old St. Petersburg, was one of four schools originally constructed around the turn of the century, when the need for a formal school system became evident to the township's new res-

idents. Though St. Petersburg began as a small settlement of northern transplants and seafarers, the population soon grew to a city of substantial size; it wasn't long until a proper place of learning for this city's young people would be needed. During these early years Florida's west coast was just beginning to spark an interest among land and railroad barons, as well as hotel magnates from all across America. It would be such entrepreneurs and high rollers who would eventually build the grand hotel resorts like the Don CeSar, the Belleview Biltmore, Ringling Towers, and the Vinoy Hotel for the nation's elite. Indeed, the west coast would soon be on its way to becoming the much-loved metropolis it is today.

From this location's humble beginning, St. Petersburg High School at Mirror Lake would eventually serve as a public school from 1919 to 1926, as a high school from 1926 to 1931, and as the St. Petersburg Girl's Junior High School from 1931 to 1964. It also served as the Mirror Lake Adult Education Center from 1967 to 1985. In 1991, many of the building's floors were transformed into gorgeous condominiums for St. Petersburg's privileged society. Yet throughout its many incarnations and illustrious history, its primary significance in St. Petersburg will always be remembered first and foremost as an educational and cultural institution.

St. Pete High is a four-story concrete structure that faces southward toward the placid Mirror Lake. The building is designed in a square, high level-style, with the front façade set back to form an atrium, and sided with flat-roofed perpendicular sections, which are adorned with simple gable-ends shaped like parapets. The structure is designed in the Mission Revival style, exhibiting the subtle stylistic elements that dominated Florida architecture during the 1920s boom era. The building's exterior walls are clad with a stucco surface embedded with a mixture of fine, multi-colored Chattahoochee stones, giving the building a mauve hue from a distance.

This landmark's construction, with its many classrooms and massive auditorium, was certainly an impressive sight during its early years, just as it is today. But the true pride was in the school's educational reputation rather than its grand architecture. The teachers were all well trained and the students anxious to learn. As time proceeded, new sections would be added to the school; by 1926 city and county leaders raised enough money to sanction a new and improved complex for the ever-growing population of students.

The school was designed by popular architect William B. Ittner, along with County Superintendent Captain George M. Lynch. Both of these gentlemen contributed new and time-honored ideas toward the school's amenities, making history in the process. When completed, this visionary team, along with St. Pete's county commissioners and its city elders, would receive many praises from educators, parents and the media alike. In fact, the new school and its facility were written up in many trade journals, magazines, and newspapers, describing St. Pete High as:

"The finest school building in the South, with superb equipment and unique architecture, having an enormous auditorium with a stage as large as those in the greatest theaters in the world, on which basketball contests may be staged, complete with locker and shower rooms, tennis courts, baseball diamonds, a football gridiron and a cafeteria designed for 1,200 people . . . It even has its own private waterworks, electric light plant, oil-burning boilers for heat, all within a rambling Spanish architecture, which makes the three-story building look long, low, and impressive. . . . An inspiration to walk toward it to see the sun on the red-tiled roof."
—St. Pete High School Archives

Without a doubt, these aforementioned sentiments would pass down through the years from student to student and from educator to educator, inspiring pride for years to come. Having educated and inspired thousands of students and making an honorable name for itself in the process, St. Petersburg High School at Mirror Lake shall go down in Florida's history as one of the state's most historic and beloved schools. Even though this is certainly a proud dedication, this school will also be remembered as one of the state's most notable in the realms of hauntings and paranormal incidents. There have been many downright spooky events in this charming school of the past, where legends of ghostly students and ethereal shadows have been told and retold to new classmates as a rite of passage, initiating new students to the fact that St. Pete High had its fair share of the unexplained. Today the building is a luxurious condominium for the well-to-do. Some of the residents presently occupying these magnificent suites and rooms often experience the paranormal, the strange, and the bizarre—what some have referred to as the school spirit of yesterday.

Ghostly Legends and Haunted Folklore
It would be difficult to exemplify one specific cause of a haunting, or

even a hundred possible causes to such events, yet such things have been reported in the most unlikely places throughout history. Indeed, I have heard of hauntings in such strange places as old airplane hangers, bathrooms, broom closets, and even in the kitchen of a Burger King restaurant in West Palm Beach. Therefore, it should be of little surprise to find a ghost or two in a school building, whether old or new. There have been many reports of strange occurrences taking place here since at least the 1940s.

Though most of the paranormal events to take place within old St. Pete High are auditory in nature, including scratching and scurrying sounds coming from the third, fourth, and attic space floors, some have witnessed the hallway and residential lights flickering on and off as if there had been a power surge. When the maintenance crew or an outside contractor investigates, expecting to find an electrical short or similar cause, they often walk away confounded. When the St. Petersburg police arrive in response to complaints that intruders have broken in, usually late at night, they will sit outside to watch the upstairs lights flicker on and off, only to find no trace of a break-in or robbery upon investigation. What they do find are locked doors, the alarms properly set, and no sign of illicit behavior of any kind. When they walk back to their patrol cars to depart, some report seeing those same lights flickering on and off as if poking fun at the annoyed cops.

When the classrooms were in active use, however, the reports of such paranormal events and hauntings were relayed through the typical form of oral tradition, whereby the student or group of students might relate his or her ghostly experience from class to class. This being the most common manner in hearing one of St. Pete High's ghost stories, one need only ask one of these past students about the ghostly legends. Even so, you might be surprised to hear a similar tale from one of the former teachers or maintenance staff. Because these people might have worked well into the evening grading papers, preparing for an event for the following day, or cleaning, they are the ones more likely to have an otherworldly experience. Although most of the witnesses would like to remain anonymous, their stories are still fantastic and interesting.

Today, many of the paranormal reports to emerge from this massive building come from the third floor and the old gym/auditorium area. Because most of the creepy high jinks appear to be more noise-related or vocal in nature, there might be any number of logical explanations. Yet for many of the new residents who have had a personal experience with the unknown, "logical" isn't a word they would use. Indeed, more than a few residents in the past have made constant complaints about the odd occurrences and some actually moved out because of this.

While writing this story, after having interviewed several current and past residents, I found some would actually be insulted when asked if they had noticed anything strange or out of the ordinary, while others were more than happy to relate their experiences. Those more open to the unexplainable occurrences described the ghostly events more in the manner of shades and shadows rather than something definite in nature. Some said they only heard strange noises as if something was scratching at their doors like a dog, or the sound of scurrying, in an area where this sound would usually not be heard. In addition to this, some have claimed to have seen dark human-shaped images walking down a hallway or through a closed door—shapes that are almost always reported as being the size of a small person or child.

Though the third floor seems to be the primary focus of these odd occurrences and similar events, the ground-level foyer and the old auditorium area are also believed to be afflicted, as there have been several reports of a full-bodied apparition skulking through the darkness. Apparently, the ghost of a young man around the age of sixteen, sporting a short "buzz" style haircut, wearing dark pants and what appears to be a white sweatshirt with a dark stripe across the middle, is sometimes seen walking with his head bowed, on the third and fourth floors, as well as within the auditorium late at night. Such a sight might not foster much alarm if it were not for the fact that this young lad will occasionally walk through a wall or a closed door. And if that's not disturbing enough, some have witnessed this youthful specter staring down from one of the fifth floor windows, only to fade away into the darkness behind him.

According to local legend, this ethereal entity will usually be seen late at night, from around 11 P.M. until 4 or 5 A.M. He will most often be noticed looking down at the ground, as if he had lost something, or staring at his hands, as if he were holding something in them. Though this behavior is a complete mystery, many of the more open-minded residents suggest that perhaps he is looking at a photograph of his girlfriend. Some have also suggested that this spirit sulks after his lost love, and because he died too soon, missing the opportunity to confess his love, his tormented spirit continues to walk the once-bustling hallways of this city's cherished educational institution of the past. And so he continues on with his nightly walks seeking peace.

Even though finding a logical explanation for this spirit's actions is close to impossible, many researchers I have spoken to over the past years seem to believe that this is the residual spirit of a student who died tragically in the 1950s. Because there have been many tragic deaths when this location was a school, included deaths in car accidents or as casualties of foreign wars, murder, or suicide, and since majority of them were males between the ages of fourteen to eighteen, we can see a valid reason for this hypothesis. Also, because of the type of clothing this spirit is said to wear, he may have died in the 1950s. Finding a direct match is difficult in this case, especially when school records are private and difficult to secure. Regardless of this fact, most paranormal researchers and long-time local residents are certain of what they saw and heard—that of an ill-fated student who died more than fifty years ago.

Although we may never know for sure who or what is haunting this beautiful fomer school, we do know that local oral tradition and folklore are both active and long-lived. Because such legends as ghosts and spooks tend to fade away naturally over time, with new and improved thinking almost always overpowering the old, we might expect this legend to fizzle away. Yet, through time, this particular legend remains as alive today as it did many years ago, which should tell us that there is some validity to the ghostly legend of St. Pete High. Moreover, many new residents have made similar reports of the paranormal—we must take this into account.

In addition to these hauntings, there also have been stories of ghostly teachers and students walking the grounds of other local schools, including St. Pete High's sister school located at 2501 5th Avenue, another school built by the same architect during the 1920s. Here, several students have reported seeing ghostly apparitions in the second-floor classrooms, as well as within the cafeteria and main auditorium. There have also been reports of toilets flushing by themselves in the boys' restroom, and female students have reported seeing faces in the bathroom mirrors. There have been reports of cold spots being felt in the classrooms, and even disembodied voices being heard from the heating vents throughout the school. Because similar reports have been made by teachers and staff alike, it's safe to say that something very much out of the ordinary is going on here. Apparently, St. Petersburg has its share of ghostly incidents—not to mention a restless student body.

Afterthoughts

St. Petersburg High School can boast many positive aspects to its contribution to education and society. Among its more famous alumni are

Florida's Governor Charlie Crist; Ashlee Kidd, track and field athlete at the Georgia Institute of Technology; and Antonio Quarterman, a football player at Thiel College in Greenville, Pennsylvania. Though a humble school by most respects, where a genuine passion for learning was offered at a time when the now bustling city of St. Pete was a mere township, we can surely see a proud dedication to its placement and significance.

Though most of the former students went on to create their fortunes, have families of their own and generally lived out their lives, some were not so fortunate. Many died before they had the chance to live, leaving emptiness where fulfillment should have been. When we look at the history and methodology of what we think of as a ghost or what causes a haunting, we know by now that tragic events and strong emotional feelings can oftentimes leave an indelible mark in the place where such events have taken place. Such appears to be so with the ghostly legend of St. Petersburg High.

What many psychical researchers believe is that a place, whether a grand castle or a humble home, or an office building, a hospital, or even a school building, and the materials used to make these places, somehow hold or encode past events in a form of cyclic fashion, playing, and replaying over and over again. This idea seems to be true with this school's haunting, as the ghostly image of a young man is seen pacing to and fro. Perhaps in life this young student suffered somehow before he died. Perhaps he pined over a girl that did not return his favors, or perhaps he was the casualty of a broken romance? In either case, this somewhat gloomy specter continues his nocturnal lamentation from time to time in the school that was probably very much a part of his daily life.

Residual hauntings have been evident for ages and do not limit themselves to stately manor houses or foreboding castle keeps in Europe. We can find such hauntings in everyday places just like St.

Petersburg High School. Since this building, much like the aforementioned places, is also constructed of stone, glass, and wood beams, we might see the connection, as some minerals and building materials are said to act as recording devices for strong psychic responses. Perhaps those long-dead students of yesteryear are still concentrating on one particular subject with such potency and tenacity that this may have engrained emotional and spiritual vibrations within the very foundation of this location.

Today, though the old St. Pete High School sits overlooking the beautiful Mirror Lake surrounded by quaint homes and newly constructed apartment complexes and condos, some of this area's original buildings are still there. If you walk around this area you may get a feeling for the past, as some of the early architecture remains intact. The sturdy Carnegie Library, for instance, as well as the old Lyceum Church and the steadfast Coliseum Theatre Forum, where you can still see classic shows, echo an illustrious past.

While investigating the old St. Petersburg High School, remember that it is now a private location and trespassing is still trespassing. Therefore, before you begin your investigation, be sure to get the proper permission first, as the residents here will probably not tolerate an intrusion. Although this location is off-limits to the public, an interview about the old school's past, and perhaps permission to tour the grounds may be possible. So, be sure to acquire the proper authorization before entering. This is doubly true if visiting the St. Pete High School campus on 5th Avenue, as you must get permission first from the front office before any investigation takes place. Once done, you may be surprised at the history that envelops both of these locations and, perhaps, you will catch a glimpse of an elusive specter or two.

St. Petersburg High School is located at 701 Mirror Lake Drive in the heart of old St. Petersburg, near the Coliseum and the Carnegie Library.

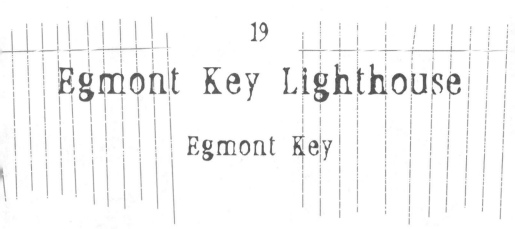

19

Egmont Key Lighthouse

Egmont Key

"When I heard doors slamming shut, I knew I had to check the area out. . . .
This is my job, and even though I was along here, I had to check it
out. When I got to where the noise was coming from, the doors were all
shut and locked, but when I saw a man dressed as a Civil War soldier, that
was it for me . . . I got the heck out of there fast!"
—Anonymous Park Ranger, 2006

"Beacon for the Dead!"

A Little History

It was during the late 1700s, when Florida was under British rule, that land surveyor George Gauld named Egmont Key after Lord John Perceval, the Second Earl of Egmont, honorable member of the Irish House of Commons. Egmont Key, though well worth a visit by naturalists, historians, and ghost hunters alike, is a somewhat barren location and remains a haven of obscurity to most Floridians.

This tiny island silently rests at the mouth of Tampa Bay, just southwest of Fort DeSoto beach. It is a lush paradise that has survived through history, having served as a valuable resource since the first settlers arrived more than two hundred years ago. Having functioned as

Egmont Lighthouse, Egmont Key,
near St. Petersburg, Fla.

Florida State Archives

a lighthouse, refuge, prisoner camp, military base, and finally becoming an almost-forgotten natural preserve, home only to birds and indigenous turtles, this unique island has much to offer. Although access is only possible by charter or private boat, Egmont Key will always prove a restful and educational outing each and every time.

During the late 1830s, when the shipping lanes were increasing, many ships were grounded and destroyed on the abundant sandbars that surround Egmont Key. Having lost far too many ships, which in turn resulted in losing commerce, Congress authorized enough money to build a lighthouse on the tiny key. The original lighthouse, a forty-foot brick tower, topped with an octagonal thirteen lamp lantern with twenty-one-inch reflectors, was finally completed in 1848, and was first activated and operated by Sherrod Edwards, the first lightkeeper. The Egmont light served as the only beacon between St. Marks and Key West. Just a few months after its grand opening, the entire west coast of Florida was hit by what is now known as the Great Hurricane of 1848, believed to have had winds equal to those of Hurricane

Katrina in 2005. With over eighteen-foot storm surges ravishing the tiny island, the lighthouse received a great deal of damage, which left it in poor repair.

When another hurricane hit in 1852, the damage was far too severe, prompting Congress to rebuild the lighthouse, as well as construct a new permanent residence for the lightkeeper and his family. All went as expected, and life proved relatively simple until the end of the Third Seminole War in 1858, when Egmont Key was commandeered as a detainee camp for the U.S. Army. Here, Seminole prisoners were held until they could be shipped off to reservations in Arkansas. The island became a place of dread.

The lighthouse was reconstructed once more, this time to withstand any storm. The new tower stood eighty-seven feet high, complete with an Argard-class kerosene lamp with a new Fresnel lens. It was the pride of seafarers everywhere, maintaining safe navigation for countless vessels. During the Civil War, Confederate troops temporarily commandeered the island, but when they could not hold off Union ships, they quickly evacuated Egmont Key, including the Confederate spy and current lighthouse keeper, George V. Rickard, taking the expensive Fresnel lens with them when they left. Soon thereafter, the Union Navy took command, utilizing the island as an outpost for their Gulf coast blockade against the Confederacy. After the war ended, the lighthouse and the tiny island would return to a more subtle existence, being occupied by a new lightkeeper, his assistant, and their families from 1866 to 1898.

By the dawning of the new century, the Spanish-American War had started, shifting the quiet and reserved nature of the island to that of a military outpost once more. The impressive Fort Dade was soon established, and by 1906 a modest yet efficient community was built around it. A city of more than three hundred people lived here, complete with simple homes that lined red brick roads. There was even electricity and telephone service in every home. The city also had a hospital, a diner, a bowling alley, tennis courts, and even a town jailhouse and small cemetery. Indeed, this quaint community served its purpose nicely until the war ended, at which time servicemen and their families returned back to the mainland, leaving only a handful of people on the island. Later, as the need for such a township dwindled, the fort and its tiny community were disbanded in 1923; the island would soon become a desolate and forgotten jungle once again.

In 1974, Egmont Key became a national wildlife refuge, and has been managed by the U.S. Fish and Wildlife Service ever since. The island was added to the National Register of Historic Places soon thereafter, and the lighthouse became fully automated in 1989, taking away the need for a lightkeeper. Today, the majority of the modest homes are gone, their places occupied only by empty foundations that line deserted red brick streets, which are shadowed by huge palms and heavy vines. The ruins of the old fort, as well as the old gun batteries, sit in silent decay, reminders of a bygone era. The empty and somewhat foreboding dark windows and doorways leer at visitors, as if something unseen waits within, just waiting to pounce. When walking down the streets here, such as Palmetto Road, which is today nothing more than a manmade tunnel cut through vines and thickets, one can't help imagining that something wholly unnatural watches with curious eyes. Without a doubt, this place fits the definition of the word "creepy."

The rest of the island, 328 acres in all, is open year-round from sunrise to sunset for any seafaring visitor. The steadfast lighthouse continues to lead ships to safety, as well as pin-point coastal airports to pilots as they approach the west coast, where all are brought to safety by the new high-intensity aero-beacon light installed in 1985. The original lightkeeper's home was torn down for surplus many years ago. Its skeletal frame believed by some to have burned to the ground by a lightning strike during a late night thunderstorm. In its day, the home was a large two-story colonial-type home with a wrap-around balcony. It had many rooms fit for a large family, complete with several fireplaces and a large front porch, all painted bone white and topped with a dark green shingle roof. It was a graceful and beautiful home reminiscent of Florida's past. Indeed, this is a beautiful location perfect for a day trip and suitable for the whole family. But, as the sun goes down on this tiny island, it is said that the island takes on a life of its own, as if the ghosts of Florida's rich and illustrious past are reclaiming the island for spectral parties and spirited mischief—it's as if the entire island is alive with the strange and unnatural.

Ghostly Legends and Haunted Folklore

Egmont Key, though a fun getaway for the day and a wonderful spot to snorkel or collect a wide variety of shells, is nonetheless considered by many paranormal researchers to be one of the more haunted places on the west coast of Florida. And, as strange as that may seem, far too many people have reported paranormal events here over the years. Indeed, these were frightening things that have had many leaving this tiny island in a hurry. One such person, a park ranger, related one such event that had me and my companions looking at this quaint island paradise a little differently. This park ranger, who I will call "John," described his experience as follows:

> "It was when I was inspecting the southern section of the island, where the fort and gun batteries are located, that I started hearing things. I stood there a few moments just to see if anyone would walk out, but no one did. It was pitch-black outside, and no one else should have been there, outside of another park ranger. As I walked toward that area, I began hearing doors slamming shut, over and over, and, even though I was a little nervous, I knew I had to check the area out. This

is my job after all, and even though I was alone here, I had to check it out. When I got to where the noise was coming from, the doors were all shut and locked, which was very strange. I began to think someone was playing around, and when I saw a man dressed as a Civil War soldier, complete with all the regalia, I began to think 'okay, what is this—this has to be someone's idea of a joke.' But, when this character started walking toward me, stopping about four feet from me and just staring intensely at me, then turning around and walking away, only to finally vanish altogether, that was it for me. I got the heck out of there, and fast!"

The park ranger's testimony seems genuine enough, and the possibility of there being a spirit or two from the Civil War era is plausible in theory, for such a conflict that ended up as the worst this country had ever experienced a ghost or two would seem to make sense. Indeed, perhaps this entity was the spirit of a Confederate soldier that did not leave the island in time to make it to safety, or perhaps he was one of the several soldiers who died from one of the many diseases or other ailments that were so prevalent at the time. Any guess might suffice. But what of the other creepy events said to take place here, since not all the spirits on Egmont Key are necessarily from the same era.

Undeniably, it would be difficult, if not impossible to identify a specific ghost or spiritual personality here, as properly identifying a particular personality in Egmont Key's history is simply not possible due to poor record-keeping. One suggestion of a possible identity might be that of George V. Rickard, the lightkeeper in 1861. Rickard was known to be in a struggle with military factions and others to control the lighthouse as the war began, and because there was a conflict in loyalties from people throughout Florida, such a thing might constitute bad blood between one's friends and family. As the war escalated, and rumors of a takeover surfaced, Rickard soon fled the island with the lighthouse's expensive Fresnel lens. This might also suggest a strong emotional tie that somehow binds Rickard to this island. Other Civil War–era specters have been seen walking within the deep thickets there, as well as platoons of gray-clad soldiers standing guard as if ready to engage in combat. If that's not enough, several people over the years have reported hearing someone whistling *Dixie* long after the island is empty of visitors late at night. Indeed, park rangers and park volunteers alike have been hearing the ghostly whistling since at least the 1970s. To date, no one has been brave enough to chase down this phantom whistler. Most simply credit this musical ghost to a proud Confederate of more than 135 years ago.

Other ghostly possibilities include Indian prisoners who were held here during the Seminole Wars—some died from disease and violence, and perhaps their spirits linger there. Though there are no marked graves to support this, nor are there any surviving records to indicate the locations of any graves, this may point to the ghostly goings on here, nonetheless. Since this island would have been of interest to sailors and pirates long before the Spanish and English arrived, it stands to reason that many spirits of bygone eras might remain as eternal memories that linger on this tiny island, repeating past actions over and over again.

Because several lightkeepers, their assistants, and their families had lived on the island for many years, it is safe to assume that each of these individual souls may have left something behind long after death. Some of these families were simple in life, while others were eccentric. Some may have been loners, while others were strong-willed zealots on one side or the other of the Civil War conflict. Regardless of personalities, however, some may have left their personal imprint on the very grounds they once called home. Some believe that Sherrod Edwards, the first lightkeeper on Egmont Key, continues to activate the light as he did years ago, climbing stairs that no longer exist or pacing the shores making sure there are no derelict ships approaching the dangerous shoals and sandbars. Others believe that a few spirits from the Spanish-American War have made their homes here as well, having returned to occupy the places where they once lived. Indeed, many a visitor has claimed to see strange movements and dark figures walking around on vacant foundations where those modest homes once stood. Yet the most widely believed theory is that the lighthouse is, in fact, a beacon for the dead, calling in all those who died at sea. This legend, as intriguing as it sounds, is actually quite ancient in origin. Early seafarers believed that if one died at sea, one must find the caring glow of the lightkeeper's flame, since doing so was the only way home. Once the soul finds the pulsating beacon of a lighthouse, the spirit will go towards it to find safety. If this is true, then the tiny island known as Egmont Key must assuredly be a haunted place—a place that is acting as a beacon for the dead.

The most active times to witness these paranormal events are said to be during the twilight hours and in the early dawn just before light. Of the activities reported, including out-of-place voices and similar sounds, running noises that come from nowhere, strange dim lights emitting from where the lightkeeper's house once stood, and unseen things flying past late-night workers and visitors are the most common reports. Though there may be logical explanations attached to these strange events, to the witnesses they are most certainly spirits and uncanny things. When visiting the lovely, if a little spooky, island of Egmont Key, be sure to embrace the gorgeous nature that surrounds you. Be sure to visit the abandoned fort and the many gun batteries, the rustic remains of military quarters, and, of course, the lighthouse—the lonely beacon that constantly stands guard over the Gulf coast. Explore this unique Floridian jungle with its forgotten red brick roadways and its white sand beaches. As you explore all the wonders this island has to offer, try to recall the active past this tiny island can boast. Remember the many people who lived and died here. Recall the stories of the lost souls who made their way to this tiny island from their watery graves; souls that may be walking behind you as you investigate this seemingly forsaken island of Florida's rich and diverse past. Know that when the sun goes down on Egmont Key, hosts of spirits and ghosts here are just waking up.

Afterthoughts

What haunts this tiny islet off Florida's bustling Gulf coast? Do the spirits of the dead return here from watery graves? And do the restless spirits of Florida's warring past still walk this barren island in the wee hours of the night? We may never know for sure. What we do know is that this island has seen far more history than most people realize. Though it would be difficult to know for sure what haunts Egmont Key, the simple fact that so much unrest and intrigue had occurred here may be the reason behind such paranormal experiences; that is to say, history might be repeating itself, as seen in the Civil War spirit observed by the frightened park ranger. For some, such an experience might suggest an intelligent entity that is aware of its surroundings, rather than a simple instant replay. Indeed, the fact that this specter had confronted the park ranger with a questioning look, and then walked away in disgust over of the changes in the fort he and the other soldiers had once manned, might seem to prove the existence of some kind of intellect. Yet such an event might well have been something more along the lines of a recording playing over and over again in a loop.

Several of my colleagues seem to believe that the island itself is acting as a kind of resonator, which holds various forms of information stored in the stone and masonry ruins of the old fort. If this is indeed possible, then perhaps the whole island is acting as a massive recording device, whereby past events such as physical, psychological, and intense emotional vibrations have left their scars here—etched in the ruins themselves.

As the remains of Fort Dade and the old foundations forever rest upon the deserted brick streets of this long-dead community, they are, in some way, saving these memories to play and replay in cyclical fashion. Perhaps when the living make their presence known here, they are in some way activating the strange activity reported over the years, where the spirits are actually interacting with the living visitors to this island. In either case, visitors may very well find more than they bargained for—they may come face-to-face with the ghosts of Egmont Key.

When visiting Egmont Key, you can spend the day basking on the beach, swimming in the warm bay waters, or just walking through the historic ruins of Fort Dade and the old gun batteries. Or you can walk the brick paths that remain from when an active community once thrived, where a wide variety of tortoises and seabirds now call home. Egmont Key State Park is managed by the Florida Department of Environmental Protection, the U.S. Fish and Wildlife Service and the U.S. Coast Guard, so it's safe and fun for the whole family, Remember that the island is accessible only by boat; if you don't have one of your own, you can charter one from one of the many Tampa Bay area charter boat companies.

During the summer months, you should bring sunblock, as well as insect repellent, because this is Florida, after all, and biting insects just love it here. You may also wish to bring a packed lunch and drinks with you and, of course, a camera. Who knows? You may just catch a ghost or two when the sun begins to go down. When you visit, be sure to have fun, but also remember that this is one of Florida's best-kept natural secrets, so always be sure to keep Egmont clean for everyone by throwing away trash in the proper place, so we can keep this spooky little paradise safe and enjoyable for everyone's family to enjoy for years to come.

To visit Egmont Key State Park, you may contact one of the following charter services for launch schedules and prices: Cortez Lady 941-761-9777, Capt. Bill 727-867-8168, Capt. Dave's 727-367-4336, Capt. Frank's 727-345-4500, Capt. Kidd 727-360-2263, Dolphin Landing 727-360-7411, and the Hubbard's Sea Adventures at 727-398-6577. Most of the day cruise lines depart from St. Petersburg area and the beaches, so getting to the island is relatively simple. For more information on the park, write to Egmont Key State Park 4905 34th Street South #5000 St. Petersburg, FL 33711 or call 727-893-2627. For a look at Egmont Key, visit the website at www.floridastateparks.org/egmontkey.

20

The Ritz-Carlton Hotel

Sarasota

"Loitering Phantoms of Ringling Towers"

A Little History

The magnificent Ritz-Carlton Grand Hotel, located at 1111 Ritz-Carlton Drive in Sarasota, is without a doubt one of the prize resort hotels in Florida. Indeed, the very name of Ritz conjures up the romantic era of world-class hotels that once dominated the land. From Hollywood, Florida, to Palm Beach, this much-loved resort chain has inspired and dazzled people for over a hundred years. The stunning Ritz-Carlton Sarasota boasts a AAA five-diamond rating and has catered to the rich and famous—starlets of film and stage as well as countless presidents and dignitaries—for generations.

Billed as a stylish and sophisticated blend of cosmopolitan hotel and beach resort, the Sarasota Ritz-Carlton is truly a luxury landmark of Florida's west coast, which is conveniently located near the center of Sarasota as well as some of the beautiful beaches that line the coast. There are 266 suites, each with a private balcony and view of Sarasota Bay, a private marina, and the beautiful city skyline. Though this is certainly worth the stay in itself, the Ritz-Carlton is famous for its per-

The John Ringling Towers in the 1920s.

sonalized service to the point of pampering, as well as for its award-winning dining.

The Ritz-Carlton can claim its contribution to fine cooking by way of the elegant El Vernona Restaurant, a huge golden-yellow and white dining room that echoes the grand dining ballrooms of the 1920s. There is the Beach Club Grill, the Boutique Chocolat, and the beautiful Ca d'Zan Bar. As soon as the guests walk across the lobby breezeway, atop hand-carved imported marble, their experience with the hotel's excellence begins. Although guests of the Ritz-Carlton may be amazed by its exceptional class and hospitality offered here, they may be completely unaware of this location's deep history, or of its many incarnations as a hotel and apartment building. Likewise, guests may also be unaware of the close ties this hotel's existence has to the Ringling Bros. & Barnum and Bailey Circus, the world's foremost circus entertainers. Undeniably, the efforts of master entertainer, builder, and entrepreneur John Ringling are quite extensive in Sarasota. Here he and his wife, Mable, designed and oversaw the construction of some of the west coast's most elaborate and gorgeous architectural masterpieces ever to exist.

During the 1920s, at the height of his renaissance, John Ringling began work on several projects, including Bay Haven Elementary School, Sarasota High School near the newly constructed Tamiami Trail, Southside Elementary School, and the El Vernona Hotel, later to be known as the John Ringling Towers. John Ringling's prime masterpieces-to-be were the El Vernona Hotel, and the fantastic Ca d'Zan, his personal retreat, which was co-designed by architects Dwight James Baum and Owen Burns. The architectural style for both structures is based on the late nineteenth century Venetian and Turkish revival. The Ca d'Zan, which cost more than $1.5 million at the time, was to be the Ringlings' home for retreats and winter holidays. John Ringling would later relocate the Ringling Bros. & Barnum and Bailey Circus to Sarasota for its winter quarters, after which he would begin new architectural projects such as the Ritz-Carlton Hotel, which was to be located on the southern end of Longboat Key. Sadly, his final architectural vision was never completed, nor would he ever open a Ritz-Carlton in his lifetime, as his dreams and aspirations slowly came to a halt.

By the time the Great Depression began, John Ringling's health began to fail, and having felt a severe financial blow to his empire, he lost virtually everything. He was, however, able to keep his beautiful home and the museum, which contain his extensive art collections. To make matters worse, his beloved wife, Mable, died soon thereafter. By 1932 he was voted out of control of his once-flourishing business, leaving him a distraught and broken man. John Ringling died on December 2, 1936, leaving the Ca d'Zan and the museum, as well as his entire art collection, to the state of Florida. Although John

Ringling's magnificent home and museum remain a highlight in Sarasota and throughout the Gulf coast, his once beloved El Vernona Hotel would experience many changes. It sat unused for a good portion of the Depression era. Once the nation regained its strength, the old hotel would undergo extensive renovations and reopen as The Ringling Towers Hotel. This would last throughout the 1950s, when it began taking on a feeling of despair, as newer and more elaborate hotels were being designed. It then closed for a few years, only to re-emerge as the Ringling Apartments in 1964. Although this proved positive for several years afterward, the building itself became run-down and faulty, claiming more problems than services, not to mention attracting a less than wholesome clientele. Indeed, the once state-ly hotel had fallen in such despair it finally closed its doors for public use in 1991. There it would sit, apparently dead to the world.

As this former beacon to society and culture sat in a cloud of mystery and dust, many vagrants and down-on-their-luck souls would find shelter within its now-empty hallways and darkened suites. It also attracted the worst kind of criminals, ranging from drug dealers and rapists to killers on the run and even devil worshipers. Thus, the old El Vernona fell even further in despair. In fact, the Sarasota Police Department spent many an hour surveying the hotel's old remains in order to capture these scoundrels. It should be of little surprise to learn that more than a few murders had taken place there, as well. Yet, regardless of these events, it was during this time that John Ringling's dream would finally come true, in a matter of speaking.

As the popular and successful Ritz-Carlton Hotel Corporation had seen the old El Vernona Hotel's property to be exquisite in area and location, plans were soon made to build the resort hotel we see today. So, the old hotel that had once been a city eyesore and haven for illicit behavior was finally leveled to the ground. Although this monument to the Ringling empire was gone, a newer and better-designed hotel would soon rest very close to the old El Vernona's original foundation. In 2001, the doors to the elegant Ritz-Carlton Hotel Sarasota were opened, ushering in a new generation of the rich and powerful, the jet-setters and the world travelers to its time-honored amenities, where a stay is never second-best nor ordinary. And, even though the guests here will no doubt have an enjoyable stay, they may also have an experience or two from the realms of the past, as many have reported—for indeed, it seems that the restless spirits of the old El Vernona and Ringling Towers have refused to check out.

Ghostly Legends and Haunted Folklore

The belief that spirits remain in a location where once a different building or home had existed is very common. In fact, one could attribute this form of haunting to at least four out of ten hauntings, because so many locations are augmented, refitted, or completely changed over the course of the years. This is certainly the case for the Ritz-Carlton, as the original structure of the old El Vernona had been totally destroyed. Still, there seems to remain an essence of past events lingering in this now entirely modern structure. Perhaps there are, indeed, spirits coexisting in this newer structure. It seems more likely, however, that the paranormal events experienced here are more replay and spectral vibration than actual intelligent entities.

There have been many reports of illicit behavior taking place where the old hotel once stood; this suggests that such past negativities have left a psychic residue here that replays itself from time to time, perhaps igniting other spectral activity in the process. Though this hypothesis is speculation, other investigators, as well as myself, know from past surveys that several paranormal encounters have taken place here since at least the mid-1990s. Reports of a construction foreman and workers hearing voices saying "Don't do this. Please, don't do this" when surveying the old hotel's interior, are well documented, as are reports of tiny sparks being seen from the dark regions of the hotel at night, as if someone were trying to ignite a lighter. When investigated, no one is ever found. In addition to this, various pieces of equipment would be found in strange places, such as under debris or teetering from a window ledge—in one instance, when workers arrived in the morning, an expensive drill and diamond-head bit, which had been locked in a large metal toolbox, were found in the middle of the floor, with the drill itself lying upright on top of the toolbox. Because this drill was locked in a box and only the foreman had a key, this caused a lot of talk among workers. The fact that this drill, which cost more than $1000, was not stolen, makes this even more peculiar. If that wasn't enough, construction workers found evidence of a more sinister activity—Satan worship!

As soon as the construction company and crew entered the old hotel, walking through all the rooms to make sure no one was hiding out or living there, they found that the downstairs rooms and the lobby had a lot of graffiti spray-painted on the walls. They also found a makeshift altar, complete with glasses and various herbs and plants strewn all around it, as if a ceremony had taken place. But this wasn't all. As the workers continued to search, they found the remains of several dead animals scattered around that looked as if they had been placed there on purpose. Once law enforcement came in to inspect the area, they concluded that kids must have broken in and used the hotel as a hang-out, sometimes using the lobby as a place for satanic black masses. Although it was strange and disturbing, nothing more came of the dark discovery. The strange paraphernalia was removed and progress continued.

All during the demolition process, which took a little over a week, both day and evening crews reported odd things occurring. After the area was cleared of the rubble and dust, new foundations were laid to add to the original location, and new construction began. A private security firm was hired at night to watch over equipment and tools to make sure nothing was stolen, and to keep vagrants out. At this time a lot of strange activity took place. When the security guard walked around, or when an officer sat at a desk that served as his outpost, he would hear knocking sounds and glass breaking, as well as footsteps and breathing coming from different areas. And, if that's not unnerving enough, running and tapping sounds were heard coming from the floor overhead. This was too much for the poor security guard. In the end, a total of eight separate security guards came and went in a three-week span of time—all because they were too frightened to work there.

Shortly after the doors opened at the Ritz-Carlton in 2001, other paranormal events were reported by guests and staff members alike. From cold spots being felt in otherwise warm places to footsteps being heard in the corridors, many left the Ritz feeling a little different about the unknown. When guests stayed in the luxurious penthouse suites, they sometimes woke up at night freezing cold, as if the windows were open in the middle of winter. Even when the air conditioner was turned off, guests complained about cold winds being felt in the rooms.

Many also complained about being watched by someone lurking behind a corridor or in the stairwell. In fact, several guests over the past few years have called down to the front desk to report that a strange, poorly dressed man was observed walking around the hallways. When hotel security sent one officer up in an elevator and another one up the stairwell to make sure the possible intruder didn't get away, they found no one. When guests reported a man described in the same manner skulking around the pool area late at night, security was once again dispatched to investigate, and, once again, they found nothing.

During the off-season, with only a few guests staying there, some of the guests would get a chance to have a little quiet time with their family and friends before they would have to head back to their businesses and busy lifestyles. Some, however, did not get this chance, as they would hear odd mumblings and indistinct questions from unseen people. A few slightly bewildered guests reported hearing odd voices and what seemed to be questions coming from the walls, as if someone were standing behind them. One past guest, a personal friend of mine, told me of her experience.

It was while she was staying at the Ritz that she had an odd, but not uncommon, experience. She was walking from the main lobby area to one of the corridor elevators and she was asked a question. She did not hear the entire question, so she turned around to say "excuse me;" when she did, she found no one there—just an empty corridor. This was weird enough, but when she got off on her floor, as she was nearing her room, she once again heard what sounded like a question being asked. This time, when she heard the voice, she turned around as quickly as she could to see this elusive person, and once again, no one was there—just empty hallway.

My friend continued to tell me that though such things would not deter her from staying at one of America's finest hotels, there was another feeling that might have others wanting to check out early. She went on to tell me that though everything else at the Ritz-Carlton was exceptional in every respect, she always felt uneasy in the lobby area. She said that she just could not shake the spooky feeling she got whenever she went through the lobby. She would always get bad feelings, as if she were being watched by someone or something.

To this day, there will be those who experience the strange and bizarre, as if something or someone else resides within these beautiful hallways and exquisite suites. Even though the building itself is relatively new, there does indeed seem to be something there, as if those long-dead continue to loiter in the place they once called home.

Afterthoughts

The Ritz-Carlton Hotel in Sarasota certainly offers the best of both worlds—a cosmopolitan hotel set within a lush, tropical resort destination on Florida's Gulf coast. Indeed, this gorgeous resort that elegantly rests on the crystal waters of Sarasota Bay, makes any vacationer long to stay just one more day. Yet, with all of this, the guest might just get a little extra something in their vacation package—ghosts.

What lurks within this beautiful resort has not been determined or authenticated. Whether actual, semi-intelligent spirits are intermingling and co-existing with the living is indeed a mystery. Perhaps an unfortunate soul or two who may have died here continues to exist on the premises. Perhaps, these strange emanations are nothing more than the engrained vibrations, ethereally etched in timeless groves. Or maybe the nearby body of water somehow activates and propels spirit emanations, as many psychical researchers suggest. Regardless of such hypotheses, many a traveler has had personal experiences which point toward the strange events that simply cannot be explained.

When visiting the Ritz-Carlton in Sarasota, be sure to acquire the proper permissions before beginning your investigation, as this may prompt a negative response from the proprietors. Once permission is secured, you might want to walk the halls, and especially the lobby area, as these are allegedly the best locations to experience the paranormal. Moreover, you may wish to bring your audio equipment, as many have reported hearing strange voices recorded on new audio tape after their investigations. Similarly, photographs that have been taken during the evening and early morning hours, both inside and outside, have shown many examples of orb activity, vortex phenomena, and unexplainable dark shadings near and in the elevators.

If staying at the Ritz-Carlton, be sure to visit the elegant cocktail lounge and bar on the main floor, as many of the guests will gather here; some may even relate personal experiences with the paranormal.

Either way, be sure to respect the guests staying here, as they may not share your enthusiasm for the supernatural. In fact, it's likely that they may not want to know they have an unseen guest from the past residing in the room next to theirs.

The Ritz-Carlton, Sarasota is located at 1111 Ritz-Carlton Drive. For information call 941-309-2000; fax 941-309-2100. Or, visit their website at www.ritzcarlton.com/resorts/sarasota. For an interesting photo of the old Ringling Towers just before in demolition, visit the following private web site http://www.fenichel.com/Ringling.shtml.

21

Ringling School of Art and Design

Sarasota

"Mary"

"Mary is a typical haunt . . . Most often, the supposed ghosts you encounter simply seem to be playing out the activities they did thousands and thousands of times when they were alive . . . not aware that some things have changed around them . . . They are a residue or imprint, without any real awareness or consciousness that is still there."

—Dr. William Heim, associate professor
of literature, University of South Florida, Tampa

A Little History

The Ringling School of Art and Design, located at 2700 North Tamiami Trail, near downtown Sarasota, is a private, four-year college in the areas of art and communications. This not-for-profit college, fully accredited by the National Association of Schools of Art and Design, and the Southern Association of Colleges and Schools, offers various degrees in computer animation, graphic and interactive communication, fine art, illustration, interior design, and the photographic sciences. There are minors and concentrations in the fine arts, digital imaging, and game design, as well as in the business of art and design. Undoubtedly, the Ringling School of Art and Design ranks

176

Sarasota County History Center

The original Bay Haven Hotel circa 1928. This is now Keating Hall . . . it has changed somewhat.

very high among the schools and colleges that offer art education nationwide.

The picturesque thirty-five-acre campus includes seventy-eight buildings and enrolls more than a thousand students from forty-three states and twenty-eight countries, and more than half of them live on the residential campus. Additionally, the college's 130 faculty members are professional artists and scholars who actively engage in art production outside of the classroom, offering the chance to not only lend valuable insight to their students, but also set many worthy examples for Florida's future artists. Today many modern amenities are available for the students, as well as various resources and organizations that will not only ensure a proper education to advance in our fast-paced society, but also the chance for the student to make a name for himself or herself in the process. And, though this is a thoroughly modern and aesthetically pleasing institution by all accounts today, housing and amenities in the early years were far less remarkable.

The original school was founded in 1931 by master entertainer, builder, and entrepreneur John Ringling of the famous Ringling Bros. & Barnum and Bailey Circus. Along with Dr. Budd Spivey, President of Florida Southern College in Lakeland, Florida, this joint venture produced the School of Fine and Applied Art of the John and Mable

Ringling Art Museum, an institution based on the preservation and advancement of the arts. It became a beacon for artists and connoisseurs of the arts in Florida's ever-growing Gulf coast area. During the early years following its grand opening, many of the school's first buildings and dormitories were older structures, either already in use or vacant and ready to sell. As this was the best and most logical way to begin financially, one of the first buildings utilized to serve as the new school was the vacant Bay Haven Hotel.

Built in 1925 by the Echols Construction Company, this hotel boasted an architectural style reminiscent of the Spanish Mission Revival, which was popular during the early part of the twentieth century. This hotel remained in use for several years, catering to travelers coming to Florida for leisure or business, maintaining usefulness until the nation's economy began to falter. As times got hard, the hotel suffered, and when its high-class clientele departed, a lower-class and far more dangerous clientele took over. Gambling and prostitution became dominant where a gentle population once stayed, reducing Bay Haven's character to one of regret. But there was hope.

Because the Bay Haven Hotel offered enough room to accomplish the college's intended goals, John Ringling quickly bought it and the surrounding property and renovated it for use as classrooms and student housing. Today, the former Bay Haven Hotel, now known as Keating Hall, is used primarily to house administrative services and classrooms, as well as being used as a dormitory. The single and double rooms here are nicely maintained, with refinished hardwood floors and many built-in amenities. Each room has telephone and internet access, cable TV, and furniture. The rooms are air-conditioned and have laundry facilities to serve the student in every need. Other classrooms and buildings, as well as four separate art galleries, are all within college grounds for the use of the students.

For nearly seventy-five years, the Ringling School of Art and

Design has encouraged the creative spirit in the arts, where students from around the world are transforming the visual arts. Yet, even with all their advances and technology, there is an essence lingering in the architecture here, where past impressions and lost memories are somehow transfixed to these buildings. This is especially noted in Keating Hall, where the memory of a long-dead lady of the night is said to wander and pout. Though her exact place in history, her life, and her death shall remain an everlasting mystery to the students and faculty, the faint shadow of a woman named Mary has been noticed here for decades.

Ghostly Legends and Haunted Folklore

As with many schools and campuses across America, the Ringling School of Art and Design has developed a well-rounded ghostly legend that has attracted attention from many seasoned psychical researchers and amateur ghost hunters over the years, not to mention major television producers looking for a fine ghostly tale. In fact, the legend of Mary, the specter of an ill-fated prostitute from the 1920s, was nicely portrayed by the Travel Channel in 2004. The program is usually shown around Halloween.

The legend of Mary, though somewhat vague in most documented accounts, can be traced back to when Keating Hall, the college's first classroom building and dormitory, was operating as the Bay Haven Hotel. It is believed that she was a live-in prostitute who occupied a second-floor room, along with other ladies of the night. Because rent was low, and travelers staying at the hotel made work easy, Mary evidently had a good thing going. But, as time went on and her life became more and more discouraging, Mary slipped into a deep depression. To make matters worse, Mary allegedly fell in love with one of her customers who could not return her affections because of his marriage. This, along with her depression, made life too difficult for Mary to bear, so she decided to end it all. And, as local legend tells it, Mary took a cloth cord from the draperies which hung in her room, tied one end to the railing of the third floor stairwell, and the other end around her neck, and flung herself between the two floors. She died instantly, swinging between the third and second floors. Though this is only one of several stories of Mary's decision after an accumulation of pain, regret, and depression, there are other beliefs as to how and why she took her life that late afternoon. Regardless of the details, however, one thing is for certain—Mary's spirit still remains.

Ringling's Keating Hall is considered by many paranormal researchers to be one of the most haunted buildings on any campus in the United States. Even though some believe she was successfully exorcised by a local priest a few years ago, many of the students living in Keating Hall know better. In fact, many students over the years have witnessed a woman in her late teens or early twenties gazing out one of the second-floor windows. She has been reported as just staring down on the students walking back from late classes, sometimes smiling, sometimes grimacing. She is seen wearing a cream-colored dress with ruffles on the sleeves, sporting a short, dark "pixie" haircut. Others have reported this apparition as wearing a lavender "flapper-style" dress, wearing one small blue shoe and a tight-fitting skull cap-hat common in the 1920s. Some have even claimed they saw this apparition as a skeletal figure wearing tattered clothing and having long rotting hair, with two dark eyes peering out. This is certainly a frightening image, yet the most horrific visual image of this sad spirit is noticed as a pair of feet dangling down the stairwell. This section is now completely sealed off to public use and can only to be used as a fire escape.

Over the years, Mary's presence has both inspired and frightened students, and her presence has become a staple of this institution's unique folklore. According to one graduate, Mary became attracted to a male student who constantly complained of smelling perfume and hearing giggles and soft laughter echoing from the hallway late at night. When this student returned to his dorm after class, he would sometimes find a slight impression on his bed, which he neatly made each morning before he left for class. The impression, he said, was very much like that of his girlfriend, who swore she never went into his room when he wasn't there. The dorms have locks and this student's girlfriend did not have a key to his room, so it would seem that Mary did visit while he was out—it certainly makes for an interesting addition to Mary's legend.

In addition to this, students living in what was once room 12 of the old Bay Haven Hotel and throughout the old women's dormitory, have reported room and hallway lights flickering on and off by themselves, cold spots in strange places, televisions turning on and off in the middle of the night, and door knobs rattling. Also, personal objects have been moved or have disappeared altogether. If that's not strange enough, some students would enter their rooms to find paper and other supplies falling off their drafting tables and paint brushes swirling by themselves in mugs of water. Spooky for sure, but also consider some hapless student lying in bed attempting to get some sleep, who is awakened by passing footfalls outside the door in a seemingly endless pattern. The student gets out of bed to see who was making all of the commotion, and when the student opens the door and finds absolutely no one there and no logical reason for the noise, the student in question may become understandably unsettled.

Since at least the early 1990s, Mary has been seen less and less as a full-bodied apparition, and more as a shady, shadowlike presence. Those who witness her say she is seen through the corners of their eyes, like a foggy outline that moves along with the witness, as if following them. When that person turns to look, the image will fade away altogether. On other occasions, the hallway in Keating Hall may prove a little foreboding, especially when the lights flicker and the area becomes strangely dark. When this happens, toward the end of the hallway, a student might witness a thin, shadowlike frame standing there, only to dart away to the closed-off stairwell. When someone follows in order to see who's lurking in the dark, they find nothing except the light scent of a lady's sweet perfume. Indeed, during the 1990s a priest was said to have exorcized Keating Hall by sprinkling holy water and reading from the Roman Rites and Rituals, which is designed specifically to clear a location or object of a demon or earth-bound spirit. In addition to this, several of the female students living in the dorms took it upon themselves to burn white sage throughout the hallways and rooms. Because such an action is a common ritual to release negativity among many Native Americans, the students felt this might release Mary from her earthly bonds and help her to find peace. And though this seemed to work for a while, the gentle spirit of Mary continues to walk the corridors of Keating Hall.

Although some of the odd occurrences experienced in this dormitory and across the campus have certainly spooked a good number of students over the years, most of the student body, as well as the faculty, have accepted Mary as part of their family, regardless of her haunting ways. Even though the spirit of this hapless girl lingers on in a harmless, almost playful manner, she has become a silent example of a timeless legend, which shall no doubt continue through history, along with the Ringling School of Art and Design.

Afterthoughts

Legends like that of Mary are reminiscent of classic folktales, where the spirit of a tormented soul lingers on long after the corporeal body has turned to dust. This type of legend, which may in fact be based on a true experience, is prone to grow over the years, finally settling in our subconscious minds long after we had heard the legend. Perhaps this tale was initially told to new students preparing to lodge in a strange room for the first time. Because that student will be sleeping in such a room all alone, the primary reason for telling such a tale is to simply frighten the new student into hearing and seeing things that may not actually exist. Such a thing, however illogical, does indeed take place. This is known as "sympathetic magic," and can make even the most down-to-earth person see a ghost where no ghost exists. That's not to say that Mary does not exist. Quite the contrary, as there have been many witnesses of the haunting who were completely unaware of any such entity haunting this dormitory, and not aware of a suicide which took place there more than eighty years ago.

Is Mary a sentient spirit, able to co-exist with the living, watching the students day in and day out? Most professional psychical researchers will say no, believing instead that Mary is simply a vibration of past events, which were most likely potent and powerful while she was alive. This seems to be a more logical theory. The images of a sad girl looking out a window, and the hanging apparition, complete with dangling feet, are good examples of powerful past events personally important to the spirit in question. Imagine, if you will, that when a person is hanged, he or she will have active electrical responses and thinking capacity for an estimated thirteen seconds after the body dies. Now imagine what is going through that tormented mind in those final thirteen seconds. As Mary was obviously suffering both mentally and emotionally, her final thoughts were probably not happy, and in this case remained long after her body was removed from the stairwell. What is more, as these emotions and feelings are believed to be permanently etched in the fabric of our reality, we can see the reasoning for Mary's spectral return.

When visiting the Ringling School of Art and Design, be sure to get the proper permission to walk the campus. Although the dormitories are off-limits to the public, you can always talk with the students, as they are usually happy to relate a story or two.

The Ringling School of Art and Design is located at 2700 North Tamiami Trail, Sarasota. For information call 800-255-7695 or 941-351-5100; fax 941-359-7517. You may also visit the school's web site at www.ringling.edu.

22
Cracker Barrel Restaurant

Naples

"Nothing but Bad Memories"

A Little History

The Cracker Barrel Restaurant—store #117, located at 3845 Tollgate Boulevard, just off I-75 in beautiful Naples, Florida—is just another fine example of family-style restaurants. Indeed, Cracker Barrel Restaurants have been cooking fine meals for hungry Americans across the land for decades, offering every kind of down-home meal imaginable.

Though this restaurant chain had been doing great business for years, and most of the workers were basically happy, some were decidedly not. Perhaps it was just a matter of time until something truly horrible would take place here.

It was during the early morning of November 15, 1995, when the appalling incident took place—an incident that would rock the Naples community and devastate the staff of this humble restaurant. When two assailants broke into the kitchen in the early part of that morning, they had not expected to find a trio of employees already hard at work in there. These hapless employees, Vicki, Jason, and Dorothy, were preparing for another busy day at the Cracker Barrel

when the robbery began. And it didn't take long for these malevolent thieves to realize that they had a problem on their hands—witnesses.

A mere robbery paled in comparison to the viciousness of the crime that followed. Indeed, taking a monetary loss would have been one thing—desirable, in fact, compared to what the other employees found as they came in to work an hour later. Sadly, the bloodied and lifeless bodies of the three employees were found on the floor of the kitchen freezer, their hands tied with electrical tape and their throats cut. Vicki, Jason, and Dorothy were murdered in cold blood. When police arrived soon thereafter, they found bloody shoe prints leading from the freezer, and throughout the kitchen area, as well as within the manager's office. There the office safe was found open, surrounded by scattered money and plastic money wrappers. At the rear of the restaurant, where the assailants had broken in, they found more scattered money, a large Buck knife, an air pistol, and a pair of blood-stained gloves. Thankfully, the local police and their C.S.I. forensic unit were on the ball, and within three weeks they had apprehended the two murderers in Las Vegas, Nevada. A justice of sorts had been accomplished.

The assailants, two men named Brandy Jennings and Charles "Jason" Graves—both ex-employees of the restaurant they robbed, later directed the police to a nearby canal where they disposed of other pieces of evidence. There the police found gloves, bloodied clothes, shoes, socks, packaging from a pellet air gun, and a money bag marked "Cracker Barrel." And, though the two assailants now remain in a Tallahassee prison serving three life sentences for the convictions of first-degree murder, and fifteen years for the conviction of robbery, nothing will ever make up for their unspeakable crimes. Even though justice has successfully removed these two killers from the streets, this does little to comfort the families of the three employees who lost their lives for a few hundred dollars. Nothing will ever remove that horrible incident from the minds and hearts of the local residents of Naples, nor the employees of the Cracker Barrel Restaurant.

As time went on, however, and business got back on track after a brief hiatus of healing, the restaurant reopened. Things would slowly return to some manner of normality. Yet even with the allotted time for employees to heal, there are some things that just cannot fix themselves. Indeed, some memories, like good times and close companionships that can never be renewed, must be the biggest issues here. But other memories, no matter how ugly and despairing as they may be, sometimes reappear in the most frightening of ways, as a few sensitive people had noticed. When such bad memories resurface to remind us of a horrible event in history, they seem to come alive. Even the most stout-of-heart will be spooked. Although the horrible events of this restaurant's past are certainly horrific in every sense, there have been more than a few strange things to have taken place here over the years since those murders—events that make some of the employees here take note.

Today, many employees will look over their shoulders when closing the restaurant, when the last light is being turned off. Others have claimed to see strange things out of the corner of their eyes as they get something from the freezer, or hear strange, out-of-place noises after the last customer has left. Without a doubt, something out of the ordinary seems to be lurking around every corner here—something downright unnatural.

Ghostly Legends and Haunted Folklore

Though it's been more than a decade since the Cracker Barrel murders, the bad memories of that day have seemed to survive in the form of an ongoing oral tradition. When new employees begin their training here, they will undoubtedly learn of that tragic morning in exhausting detail. They will also learn of the alleged hauntings that occur as a postscript to that horrible event. These new recruits will no doubt be treated to a practical joke or two regarding the spirits that appear to be attached to this location. And though this behavior serves as a method to ease the trauma of that horrible event, as well as pay homage to the victims and create an better atmosphere in the process, it is, nonetheless, quite normal in all respects. Therefore, the reasoning for a "haunting" at such a location is not only logical; it's plausible in almost every regard.

Strange occurrences were first reported just after the employees returned from the restaurant's hiatus, occurrences that took place immediately after the murders. Though these events—which included lights flickering on and off and the freezer door being found open from time to time—are frightening and seem to be paranormal, they could be from natural causes. In addition to these events, a general feeling of uneasiness and dread has been felt by almost every employee and manager since the murders, though such feelings should be considered normal and quite understandable, bearing in mind the circumstances. Yet, even with such an understanding, strange and preternatural events have been reported ever since that terrible day. Events like objects moving by themselves and feelings of being watched appear to be the most common experienced, as well as an overall uneasiness when entering or departing the freezer rooms—events that have seemingly been increasing in strength and frequency.

Having interviewed several employees claiming to have observed many extraordinary events over the years, and a few being more than happy to relate them to me, I am able to see how such legends begin and maintain themselves throughout the years, acquiring minor deviations in the process. Though the following examples will serve as the primary paranormal activities said to occur here, other aspects and behaviors have also been noticed by both employees and customers alike. While these employees were for the most part pleased to share their personal accounts, I have chosen to keep their identities private for the sake of business relations and professional respect.

Throughout this restaurant, which is almost identical to any other Cracker Barrel Restaurant in the United States, there is a large dining area, divided into sections by walls adorned with farm tools, road signs, and decals popular in the days of general stores and small American towns. There is usually a large fireplace to give the place a homey atmosphere, and the entrance to the large kitchen is in plain sight so the patron can see the cooks and waitstaff working away. And of course, there is the large lobby area, which contains a gift shop filled with knick-knacks. Though each of these areas is said to contain some form of paranormal activity, the kitchen area and the women's restroom appear to be the most active—especially the large walk-in freezer and cooler units. It was here that the cold and lifeless bodies of the three employees were found that early morning in 1995, and it is here that several employees have had more than a few fearsome experiences.

Since that fateful day, a few employees have gone into that freezer unit to get food and condiments, only to race out of there because of something they had seen or felt. Apparently, as these hapless employees were busy working, the freezer lights would go dim, flicker a few times, and go out altogether. If that's not creepy enough, when the employees would push the release knob on the door in order to get out, the door would not budge. As this employee might at first suspect a practical joke taking place, he or she would soon find out that no earthly person was responsible for holding the door shut from the outside. Moreover, while that employee is standing there, he or she might hear a soft, nearly inaudible voice coming from a corner of the freezer room or perhaps feel a light touch on the face or arm—alarming for some.

The ladies' restroom has also been reported as being unnaturally rife with odd occurrences. Once, after the restaurant had closed for the evening, as an employee was cleaning the restroom for the following day, the toilets began flushing by themselves over and over again, as if someone were repeatedly activating the eye of the automatic-flush sensors. When the employee went in the stall to investigate, the flushing would stop altogether. Then the lights would flicker on and off occasionally, followed by cool blasts of air rushing through the stalls as if someone or something were running past them. Others reported hearing a woman having a conversation within one of the restroom stalls, only to have the stall found unlocked and empty when inspected. In addition to this, a general feeling of uneasiness is felt here, as if someone is constantly watching from some unseen place.

The dining room, too, has been reported as being a creepy place long after the patrons have gone home, and when it's dark outside. Here the employees will set out supplies such as sugar, sweeteners, salt, pepper, etc. for the following day. They will fill each container and then move on the next table, going as fast as they can in order to get home at a reasonable hour. The night crew will sit at one of the tables and fold forks, spoons, and knives into napkins, then walk around to make sure that each table is wiped down and ready for the next busy work day. On occasion, after the containers and napkin dispensers have been filled, the tables cleaned and all the chairs placed in their proper positions, and the floors mopped, the night crew would leave for home knowing that the store would be ready for the morning shift the following day. When the morning waitstaff arrived, however, they might find sugar and sweetener packets tossed about and the chairs moved out of their spots, as if someone had taken a seat in them during the night. Sometimes, miscellaneous newspapers and other papers will be found flung about the floor, and on occasion, music boxes and other electrical lights and toys will light up or turn on by themselves. Though understandably strange and a little unnerving, no living person has taken credit for such disturbances.

Despite the fact that the kitchen and freezer area of this restaurant, as well as the ladies' restroom, have certainly been the focus of many strange occurrences over the years, the front lobby and display area have apparently undergone a few psychic changes as well—adjustments made by unseen hands. As local legend has it, many of the front façade pieces, which are set up according to corporate guidelines, will often be found in different locations from where they were originally placed. When the morning shift arrives, they might find the displays altered or missing all together. Whether it is a display of cookbooks, checker boards and novelty toys, or a collection of Halloween or Christmas housewares, many have been found in entirely different locations. Some of the smaller items, like votive candles and similar assorted knick-knacks, might disappear altogether and were thought to be stolen. That is, however, until the items were found a few days later under a display case, behind a shelf of jellies and condiments, or in other unexplained locations. Though understandably annoying for the management, such a paranormal event, known as an "apport" (in which inanimate objects vanish and then reappear in a completely different location), has been observed over the centuries around the globe.

During the past few years, the Naples Cracker Barrel restaurant has been attracting quite a bit of attention. Whether from newspaper reporters or television crews, the many eerie occurrences that have been observed here over the years have made many paranormal investigators, as well as the general public, take notice. As to the identity of the spirit, or spirits, haunting this location, only they will know for sure. Indeed, though many self-styled ghost hunters and psychics have come here in search of spirits, most have returned empty-handed and unaffected. A select few, however, have walked away knowing that there is indeed something unearthly taking place here.

Afterthoughts

Because of the strange and spooky events that have been reported within this restaurant since at least the late 1990s, from moving objects to disembodied voices echoing from the freezer, it seems safe to assume that this location is indeed haunted. Nevertheless, as proposed earlier, such incidents may instead be the strong and active memories etched upon an unseen surface that continuously echo past events over and over again. As this location has a violent past, such an assumption does appear logical. Though such a hypothesis may seem likely, especially to a seasoned psychical researcher, we must at least bear in mind the almost human qualities of these aforementioned manifestations. The movement of objects from one location to another, and the eerie, disembodied voices heard in unlikely places do indeed seem to point to an intelligent source. Regardless of most accepted viewpoints of such events being psychic recordings and nothing more—this is truly the mystery of paranormal research and ghost hunting, and the provides spice for my folkloric research.

The unfortunate loss of life should, above all, be the primary focus within every researcher's inquiry. Whether the researcher is investigating from a psychical or paranormal viewpoint or a folkloric point of view, the lives lost on that sad morning in 1995 should be remembered first and foremost. From a psychical and paranormal point of view, we may surmise that such odd, preternatural occurrences must emanate from the murdered victims. From a folkloric point of view however, such odd events might be nothing more than the aftermath of the crime itself, where that tragic event may be enticing more imaginations than that of ghosts or paranormal activity. In the end, without positive proof of there being intelligent entities at this location, or any scientific evidence supporting a psychical reality, for that matter, such reports of spirits and hauntings will always be considered subjective—always to remain in the realm of the supernatural.

When visiting Naples, Florida, be sure to enjoy what this beautiful community has to offer. Whether enjoying the gorgeous white sand beaches, visiting friends and family, or just passing through, make a date to eat at this restaurant. If you're especially lucky, you might actually sense something of the unearthly here, as many people have over the years. Perhaps you will detect a faint voice echoing from the corner of a vacant room, or perhaps you'll observe your cup of coffee move by itself across the table. Just remember the lives lost here that bleak day in this restaurant's history, and the irreparable damage it has left on the minds and hearts of the survivors. For indeed, as legend tells us today, the spirits of these victims most assuredly remember.

If you are planning a ghost hunt here, keep in mind the issues are still a matter of controversy and sadness for many of the workers there, so be sure to show the proper respect. Because the areas where most of the hauntings take place are for employees only, you will probably not be able to access them. However, you may be able to get information about the paranormal incidents to have occurred there by speaking with your waiter directly.

The Cracker Barrel Restaurant is located at 3845 Tollgate Boulevard, just off I-75 in Naples. The restaurant's hours of operation are Sunday through Thursday 6:00 A.M. to 10:00 P.M., and Friday and Saturday 6:00 A.M. to 11:00 P.M. For more information you may call 239-455-6588.

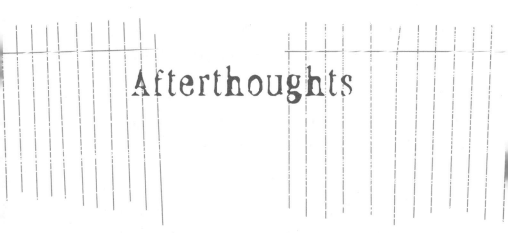

Afterthoughts

As we complete our ghostly journey along Florida's amazing Panhandle and beautiful Gulf coast, we should be able to appreciate all the wonders our great state has to offer. From the cascading waves of the Gulf of Mexico to the white sand beaches of St. Petersburg and Sarasota, we have investigated some of the most potent and chilling stories of the cities and townships that rest on these shores. Now that we have taken a closer look at the preternatural side of the Sunshine State, hopefully becoming more aware of the fantastic legends and folklore that exist here, perhaps we will view this state in a different light, knowing that something ethereal lives here too. Though the word Florida will conjure visions of a tropical paradise, where Americans vacation each year to enjoy the climate, the nightlife, and the unique nature we Floridians often take for granted, there is indeed something out of the ordinary going on here.

Florida has a direct attachment to the supernatural. Indeed, while many of us might be familiar with ghost stories from older civilizations such as the United Kingdom and much of Europe, *Florida's Ghostly Legends and Haunted Folklore* hopefully lends a little more credence to our state's ghostly significance. Knowing that these stories only represent a fraction of the many legends and historical accounts of such supernatural events to take place here, let this collection of time-honored folklore and somewhat peculiar oral traditions be your invitation into the little known, and seldom seen, haunted side of this great state.

Having lived in Florida since childhood, I have been fortunate to have heard some of the best, and certainly the most captivating, stories of ghosts and hauntings in the state. As I journeyed throughout the state, from Pensacola's active naval bases to Largo's gentle neighborhoods, I have seen the truly amazing. From small graveyards in Cocoa Beach to the bustling cities of Tampa and St. Petersburg, I had experienced the unbelievable. Yet, throughout it all, I was afforded the chance to visit some of the most frightening locations, as well as the most beautiful places imaginable. Places like the Pensacola Village and Seville Quarter, which has a ghostly bartender who haunts the festive Rose O'Grady's Bar & Grill after the sun goes down. This story has echoed throughout Florida's northwest corridor since the unfortunate barkeep was found dead in one of the restaurant's huge freezers, a spirit that continues to spook and inspire ghost hunters everywhere. Other, more notable locations, such as the many magnificent examples of colonial and Civil War–era homes in Pensacola's older community, where many a spirit is said to walk the antiquated hallways and well-manicured gardens, are just a sampling of the ghostly lore that has been told for over a century. Indeed, who can forget the legend of the long-dead church rectors of the Old Christ Church and their dancing bones that are said to have jumped around in the nearby Lear-Rocheblave Home? How about the translucent spirit of Clara Barkley Dorr, who continues to walk the staircase and veranda of the house she will always call home. These are just a few illustrations of Florida's haunted history that will forever live in both legend and infamy.

As I traveled southward from the Panhandle down the Gulf coast, I discovered quaint rural communities such as Cedar Key and Egmont Key, as well as cities such as St. Petersburg and Sarasota. Though both offer a wide selection of haunted folklore that has been told and retold for close to two centuries, I knew there was so much more than meets the eye. When I visited the beautiful Island Hotel and Restaurant in Cedar Key, I found a genuine threshold to Florida's rich and interesting past. Here, legends of the ghostly manager who walks the corridors to see that his guests are comfortable, or the spirit of a long-dead lady of the night who drops by to kiss single male guests goodnight in the wee hours of the morning, are legends that are almost as old as the hotel itself. When I explored the tiny island of Egmont Key; an island with abundant history, albeit shrouded in historical mystery, I learned of the active spirits that walk the ruins of its long-abandoned city, and the frightening specters that have terrified more than one lone park ranger over the years.

Later, as I traveled throughout the Gulf coast, I discovered the incredibly delightful Biltmore Belleview Hotel near Clearwater, a hotel equal in beauty to any in the world. Here casts of time-honored spirits grace the hallways and suites in order to keep this hotel's vast history alive and well for countless generations to come, all eager to tell their own story. The Vinoy Hotel in St. Petersburg and the Ritz-Carlton in Sarasota, both brimming with ghostly tales and otherwise unheard histories, denote a particular and unique essence that shall always belong to Florida, and Florida alone. As I explored the beautiful pieces of Florida's past, such as the opulent Royalty Theatre in Clearwater, and the Ringling School of Art and Design in Sarasota, I found myself actually experiencing Florida through the caring restoration and devoted maintenance of these places, as well as through the time-honored folklore being told by those I met there. When I walked the beautiful terraces and mezzanines of this grand theater, or the grounds of this notable college campus, I knew that there was more truth to the ghostly anecdotes than many would like to believe. I can honestly say that I believe in ghosts.

Because the concept of folklore and the urban legend is based on a factual event in one manner or another, it would be foolish to assume a folktale or urban legend to be mere folly. For even if the facts have changed a little over the span of time, taking on new aspects in order to enhance that folktale or legend, it is still based on an actual event regardless of such additions. Indeed, if we were to exclude the entire legend of our nation's first president and his encounter with chopping down a cherry tree, then we must exclude the very existence of this legend's protagonist too—that being George Washington, of course. Because we all know that George Washington did indeed exist, and that some kind of encounter with the cherry tree had taken place, then we must at least acknowledge that some part of that legend must be true, regardless of the historically harmless fabrications added to redirect the story. In short, though many of the ghost stories you have read in this book may have been a fanciful illustration added to an original account of an actual event in history, and then retold as factual, it should not disqualify the story. Instead, we should take these stories for what they are—legends that have been relayed over a period of time in order to instruct, enlighten, enthrall, and even frighten a little.

Although there may be a thousand or more ghostly stories still remaining in Florida alone, many that will lapse in history, and many that are never to be heard, I feel I have offered at least a goodly portion of such stories for your enjoyment. And though many of these ghostly legends and haunted folktales shall remain nothing more than a spooky story to be told on stormy nights when the lights go out, try to remember the truly horrific aspects to these stories, beyond the creaking floorboards and squeaking doors, or the alleged specters lurking behind them—remember that there may indeed be more truth to that spooky yarn than mere legend.

When visiting Florida, be sure to enjoy the many amenities the Sunshine State has to offer. Enjoy the many amusement parks, the fine restaurants, and the fast-paced nightspots our beautiful cities have to offer. And don't forget to bring your suntan oil when relishing our magnificent beaches. Although you will enjoy what Florida has to offer, just keep in mind that there is so much more here. As you explore Florida's haunted wonders, don't be surprised if you experience the uncanny, the strange, or the supernatural, for there is no doubt that Florida truly is a haunted place!

If you're still interested in Florida's ghosts and haunted locations and want more, be sure to read my first two books: *Florida's Ghostly Legends and Haunted Folklore, Volume One: South and Central Florida* and *Volume Two: North Florida and St. Augustine* for even more true-to-life tales of the supernatural, tales that will keep you awake at night, when the lights go out, and the mood is just right for a ghost story.

Happy Ghost Hunting!

Appendix A
Tools of the Modern Ghost Hunter

For the ghost hunter today, whether a highly-educated scholar with a university grant to fund his or her research or a stout-of-heart amateur hoping to find evidence of life after death, the need for scientific equipment is necessary. Indeed, such equipment is as important as the bravery these people need in order to walk through the deserted cemeteries in the dead of night or explore the abandoned, reputedly haunted houses or buildings during a stormy night. Having the proper equipment can make the difference between that of a successful ghost hunt or just another walk in the night.

There are only a few organizations and businesses that sell these rather fascinating items. From flashlights, electromagnetic reading devices, and remote motion sensors to smudge sticks for cleaning a haunted area and dowsing rods for finding a ghost, these department stores of the paranormal will outfit you and your team. Here are a few of the best places to find these high-tech toys: the Ghost Store (www.ghosthunterstore.com); the Parascience Shop (www.parascienceshop.com) and Ghost Hunter Store (www.ghosthunter.com).

The following examples are tools used by many paranormal investigators in their research, and although many are expensive, most of these tools are quite common and available at many department stores today:

Air-Ion Counter: This is an expensive piece of equipment used to measure the amount of positive and negative ions in the area. Ghosts can cause a lot of positive ions because they give off high amounts of electromagnetic discharges.

Baby/Talcum Powder: Used in order to find evidence of ghostly footsteps or hand prints.

Barometer: Ghost hunters have used barometers to look for paranormal activity. Some believe that some paranormal events can affect barometric pressure.

Cameras/Video Recorders: A Polaroid 600, Polaroid 2400FF 35 mm, Pentax Auto-Focus 1QZoom 80-E, 400 speed (black and white film), and an Olympus digital video recorder are all suitable items for the modern ghost hunter today. A 35mm camera is an excellent camera to use because it can eliminate the chances of odd things showing up on the photo, which may happen due to camera anomalies found on many digital cameras. Color film is the easiest to buy in stores, as well as black and white and there are many one-use cameras as well. Film speeds of 400, 800 and 1000 are the best choices. Black and white film and infrared film have been used for interesting results. Remember to bring extra rolls of film and batteries for the camera. Often, when you are on a ghost hunt, camera film and batteries sometimes malfunction, so be sure to have a good stock of batteries before all investigations.

You can use a camera tripod to help you eliminate moving the camera so that you can get a better picture. Make sure to advise your film developing company to develop your film as is, as developers often think the pictures of ghosts are camera mistakes. When you are taking photographs ALWAYS take off the camera strap so there no chance it will get into the photo. Be sure to secure long hair too as this can get in the way.

Candles: If your flashlight and equipment stop working you may need to resort to candles and matches/lighters.

Cell Phone: Cell phones can be useful if you have an emergency and need to call for help. Cell phones can also be affected by electromagnetism, such as the presence of a ghost, so be prepared.

Compass: Some people may use a compass, as they may show a change in point in the presence of a spirit or ghost and it, too, can be affected by an electromagnetic disturbance.

EMF (Electromagnetic Field) Detector: Likely the most important piece of equipment, EMF detectors are excellent tools. EMF detectors will pick up electronic fields over various frequencies. A digital readout is preferred on an EMF detector, and some detectors have an alarm that will sound to alert you. The cost for this piece of equipment is usually inexpensive, ranging from $40 to $150.

Tri-Field Natural EM Meter: Designed expressly for use in paranormal investigation, this amazingly sensitive device is one of the favorite portable instruments of researchers around the world. In the magnetic setting, the unit has a sensitivity of 2.5 milligauss, which is less than 0.5% of the earth's field. In the electric setting, it has a sensitivity of 3 volts per meter, which is well below the level at which static electricity (10,000 volts per meter) forms. This instrument has a setting that will alert the investigator to the earliest stages of paranormal manifestation.

This meter can detect changes in electrical magnetic currents long before they become obvious to people. It will detect approaching thunderstorms and even the presence of a person behind a wall. The alarm tone is proportional to the amount of change in the field and can be set for any desired threshold; it also measures radio and microwave waves from 100 kHz to 3 GHz in milliwatts of energy.

Extra Batteries: You should always bring many extra batteries. Ghosts are believed to be electromagnetic in nature and can cause your batteries to run down rather quickly. Remember to bring batteries for both your flashlight and camera.

Flashlights: Since a lot of ghost hunting is done at night in places like cemeteries and battlefields, it's imperative that you have a flashlight in order to find your way around and to avoid falling.

First-aid Kit: Take along a first-aid kit just as a precaution in case someone is injured on the ghost hunt. Old buildings, graveyards, and battlefields can be hazardous in the dark.

Film: Take lots of extra film with you on the ghost hunt. The electromagnetic discharges can affect your film and you may have to replace it. Use 400, 800, or 1000 speed film, as this will provide the best photographs.

Gaussmeter or Cell-sensor and the Multidetector II: An excellent tool for the modern ghost hunter, the cell-sensor, or gaussmeter, is a highly sensitive meter, which features both a cell phone frequency RF measurement, as well as a single axis ELF Gaussmeter. The Gaussmeter is calibrated around 50/60 Hz and also offers two scales: 0–5 and 0–50 (mG). Remote probe with two-foot extension cord allows the user great flexibility and reach. Both RF and gaussmeter provide audio sound and a large flashing light, which corresponds to field strength so you can hear and see in the dark when you are getting a positive reading. It includes complete documentation on how to conduct proper measurements.

The Multidetector II measures electric and magnetic fields and is highly sensitive. It has extending power cables that can be extended more than one-meter distance, able to detect the presence of TVs, computers, and other electronic devices from a distance of more than three to four meters, and high voltage cables at more than 350 meters. It features an 11 LED display, which provides a high luminosity to enable measurements even in dark areas like cellars, attics, and, of course, graveyards.

Headset Communicators: Headset communicators can provide you with a method to communicate with the rest of the ghost hunting party. This equipment is good for distant communication on a site and provides you with the benefit of leaving your hands free to use your other equipment and to take notes.

Infrared Thermometer: This is a noncontact infrared thermometer that emits an invisible infrared beam, which reads the temperature of anything the beam comes in contact with. Researchers have found that this type of thermometer can detect cold spots, both moving and stationary, in under a second.

Motion Detectors: A useful tool for ghost hunters. They work great when left in a room during the time when no investigator is present. Many motion detectors that are used by paranormal investigators project an infrared beam. When the beam is disrupted by spirits, an alarm will sound giving the investigator a clue that spirits may be present. When switched to alarm mode, it will sound a siren when it detects motion up to thirty feet away, and may include optional wall mount brackets.

Night Vision Scopes: Some people like to use night vision equipment on their ghost hunting expeditions. There are monocular and binocular types to choose from; both are useful, especially in areas where there is absolutely no artificial light. Binocular types are a better choice because they add the benefit of depth perception. Night-vision adapters are available to put on your cameras and camcorders, ranging from $200 to $1,000.

Notebook and Pen: You need a notebook and pen to record your investigation, as it is vital to describe weather conditions, the temperature, and what happened on your ghost hunt. The ghost hunter will need to document EMF and thermal scanner readings. The date, time, and who was present on the ghost hunt, as well as what was seen, heard, or felt, are all important things to note for future investigations.

Omni-directional Microphones: An excellent tool when investigating for electronic voice phenomena. Paranormal investigators recommend external microphones. The use of these microphones will make it possible to avoid tainting the recording with noises from the internal parts of the tape recorder. Omni-directional microphones are ideal because they pick up sounds from every direction equally and can be used with standard, micro-cassette, and digital recorders.

Spotlights: Spotlights are always good because they can help you set up your equipment to get ready to do your ghost hunt when it's dark, as well as to give you an added level of security.

Tape or Digital Recorder: Take along a tape recorder to pick up electronic voice phenomena (EVP). When you turn on the tape recorder and let it run for the entire hunt or investigation, occasionally strange, ghostly voices may be captured. Be sure to speak in a normal voice, as this will prevent confusion about whether your whisper was really a ghost. You may not always hear the voices during your investigation but if you review your tape afterward, you may hear voices or other almost-human sounds on the tape. Take an eternal sensitive microphone to allow you to pick up sounds.

Thermometer-hygrometer: This indoor thermometer/hygrometer allows one temperature reading and checks the humidity. Complete with a digital humidity/temperature gauge, and able to read a humidity range of 20 percent to 90 percent, this device is an excellent addition. As high humidity can also have an effect on your camera and cause your photos to appear to have orbs or mist on them, this device will help in the investigation.

Thermal Imaging Scopes: This device provides you with an actual image of what your thermal scanner sees. It provides the exact shape of a particular temperature anomaly. If for example, someone or something is walking behind a wall, you will see that person's shape and size.

Thermal Scanner: This device measures temperature changes instantly for a specific area. As temperature changes are common in haunted locations, the importance of this tool is clear. Infrared thermal scanners are equally beneficial. Because ghosts are believed to be electromagnetic in nature, and in order for them to materialize they need energy, there will be a noticeable change in temperature and atmosphere. There may be a severe drop in temperature that could range from twenty degrees or more. "Cold spots" are good indications of what many believe to be a "portal" haunting, which can appear and disappear quickly, so this tool would also be a good choice.

Walkie-talkies: The new and improved walkie-talkie will provide the ghost hunter with a better method of communication during the ghost hunt. It also adds a sense of security.

Watch: You need to take a watch with you on a ghost hunt to record the time that events take place.

Web Sites: One of the best and most effective of all the tools listed is the internet. As important as the telephone today, the internet and the massive database of ghost research and related web sites, both professional and amateur, are all excellent resources of information, regional legends, and folklore, as well as an outstanding source of photographs of alleged ghosts and spirits.

Appendix B
Glossary

The following list presents some of the many terms used by ghost hunters, paranormal investigators, and parapsychologists today. Although these examples represent only a sampling, these examples are the most commonly used terms today.

Agent: A human being who is unaware that she or he is directing poltergeist activity. The agent is often a prepubescent teenager, usually a female; it is believed that a poltergeist or similar entity will attach itself to a child, the agent.

Altered States of Consciousness: Any state of consciousness that is different, either altered or reduced, from a typical state of normal consciousness.

Amulet: An object believed to have the power to ward off evil spirits or other malevolent demons; usually in the shape of a charm or talisman worn around the neck.

Apparition: A disembodied soul or spirit from the deceased, which may be seen or heard as a supernatural appearance. Apparitions may appear and disappear very suddenly, seemingly at will. They may pass through walls, cast shadows, and produce reflections in mirrors. They may appear real or sometimes appear foggy or completely transparent. Sometimes they are accompanied by smells or produce cold spots or drafts. Most apparitions seem to have some sort of purpose, such as communicating a message, known as crisis apparitions. These entities usually appear during a severe family crisis such as when someone has died. The term collective apparitions refers to apparitions seen by more than one person.

Apport: When a solid object manifests in different locations, without physical assistance; supposedly done by a spirit or other paranormal force.

Astral Body: The soul of a person that is projected outside of their body, but remains attached as if by an invisible umbilical cord.

Astral Plane: The level of existence through which spirits of the dead pass or a level of existence in which an astrally projected spirit travels naturally.

Astral Projection: The separation of the astral body, or spirit body, from that of the physical body. This astral body may travel in the astral plane and possibly beyond.

Aura: An energy field that surrounds all living creatures, similar to that of Kirlian photography.

Automatic Writing: This is the communication with a spirit in which the spirit controls the hand of a writer, usually a medium or psychic, and writes out messages. This medium may produce written material while controlled by this spirit and may not be conscious of what she or he is writing. Most often, this person may write a page or pages of words that they do not remember writing when they are back to their conscious state.

Automatism: Spontaneous muscular movement believed to be caused by a ghost. Automatic writing is one example of this, as well as involuntary movements or spasms during sleep.

Banshee: A spirit or omen of death, usually indigenous to Scotland and Ireland. The banshee is more often heard than seen, and is almost always synonymous with a death in a family.

Black Magic/Black Mass: The practice of conjuring preternatural forces for a specific evil purpose. The mass is held in honor of Satan, the Prince of Darkness, at the witches' Sabbath, primarily by Satanists.

Caveat Apparent: A type of warning spirit that appears to be concerned for the welfare of the living. *See Crisis Apparition.*

Channeling: A form of communication in which a spirit communicates through and sometimes possesses a psychic medium. The entity being channeled is believed to be that of a deceased human being, angel, or demon.

Clairaudience: The psychic ability to hear sounds and voices normally not heard by most people.

Clairvoyance: The psychic ability to see objects, persons, places, or events regardless of time or distance.

Conjuring: The process of calling preternatural forces into aid or action through the use of necromancy or black magic.

Crisis Apparition: A spirit that shows itself to a living family member or friend just after that spirit's corporeal death. Thought to be a sentient form of spirit that engages with the living in order to ensure peace of mind for the living or to relay a message.

Demon: A lower-level evil spirit, or drone, working for Satan or an evil entity hostile to humans, through trickery or attack.

Demonologist: Involved in the study of demonology.

Demonology: The study of demons, including their characteristics, classification, and effect on mankind.

Discarnate: Existing outside a physical body, in spirit form, possibly in a form of astral projection.

Disembodied Spirit: A spirit functioning without the use of the physical body.

Doppelganger: Doppelgangers appear to be the ghostly duplicates of a living person. The doppelganger will often be invisible to that person, and in some cases that person will come upon his own doppelganger engaged in some future activity. Doppelgangers are traditionally believed to be omens of bad luck or death of the living counterpart.

Earthbound: A spirit being trapped to remain on the earthly plain against its will or desire.

Ectoplasm: An unknown substance that emanates from the bodies of mediums, correlating to supernatural phenomena. It is also believed by many parapsychologists to be ethereal in nature.

Elemental: A lesser spirit bound to the fundamentals of nature, such as earth, wind, water, and fire, or perhaps even seen as the remains of the dead.

Entity: A term used to describe a disembodied spirit or ghost.

Exorcism: The process of expelling or removing an evil spirit by a religious ceremony. Exorcisms may be performed by a priest, minister, rabbi or shaman, each using similar ceremonies to disrupt or banish an evil spirit or entity.

Exorcist: One who conducts the rights of exorcism, such as a priest, rabbi, wiccan, or shaman.

Ghost: A ghost can best be described as a form of spiritual recording, similar to an audio or videotape. Although there is no life force left; a ghost may replay the same scene or action over and over. A ghost may be the residual energy of a person, animal, or even an inanimate object, repeating itself for eternity. It is widely believed that if a person has performed a repetitious act for a long period of time in life, he or she may leave a psychic impression or "psychic scent" in that area. This psychic scent may stay in the area long after the person who created it has moved on or died. This paranormal event is very vivid when first encountered and appears to be sentient. Over time, this psychic scent, or spirit, will get weaker over time, but is believed it can recharge itself under the right circumstances.

Ghosts/Spirits: There are many theories that try to explain what ghosts are. Many believe that there is a residual energy left behind by a person of emotional strength, a person who wanted more life, or a spirit that revolves around a specific traumatic life event. Many believe that there are various specific electromagnetic impulses that pulse and are expended during periods of high excitement or stress and that this energy may last long periods of time, or even feed on similar forms of electromagnetic energy, such as a power plant or where high levels of electricity pass. Some believe that ghosts are telepathic images that may be picked up by a particularly sensitive person, such as a psychic; the person may also pick up or receive vibrations, most likely from strong past events or from the area where it appeared many years ago. Such an event may also explain instances whereby a person sees a loved one at the moment or near the moment of that loved one's death, where the dying one might be unconsciously projecting their thoughts to a receptive person, such as a family member. It is also believed that ghosts might also be the result of time slippage, where an event that happened in the past might be seen briefly in our present time because of a fluctuation in our space-time continuum.

Ghost hunting: Where a person or group of people investigates a location where there have been alleged sightings of ghosts and attempts to find evidence of said ghosts. These people often use a wide variety of equipment, such as video recorders, cameras, and audio recorders, to capture visual evidence and sounds. Graveyards are the number one place to begin, followed by churches, schools, or any structure reputed to have ghostly activity.

Ghost lights: These anomalous balls of iridescent or glowing lights have also been called will o' the wisps, earthlights, and spook lights. They appear largely in the southern and western United States, and are specific to one area or common location. Although thought of as nothing more than swamp gas, or the decaying of plant and animal remains during the summer months, ghost lights are reliable throughout the year and in some places these lights have been the subject of scientific study, such as the Greenbrier lights in Jacksonville, Florida, and the Snow Hill Road lights in Oviedo, Florida. Of the many theories and legends revolving around these mysterious lights, the typical folk tale involves ghostly, disgruntled Indian braves, phantom trains, and UFOs.

Ghost Ships: Although rare, these ghostly sea vessels have been seen throughout the ages, most notably the *Flying Dutchman,* or the ghostly burning ship of Block Island, Rhode Island, and the ghostly fishing ship of Mayport Village, Florida.

Ghostly Sounds and Lights: Sometimes a haunting will consist entirely of the sound of footsteps or ghostly music. There are also many legends of ghost lights, often said to be caused by a ghostly lantern, a spectral motorcycle, or a phantom train. The music heard at the Myrtle Hill Mausoleum in Ybor City, Florida, constitutes a phantom sound in the form of a hazy yet audible music box.

Haunted: In the context of parapsychology, a building, house, or area is considered haunted when paranormal activity can be documented repeatedly over a period of time. Paranormal activity, however, can vary dramatically from case to case and some paranormal activity is not associated with the presence of an entity or ghost.

Incubus: A demon that, according to ancient lore, assumes the form of a man and lies on women, possibly engaging in sexual intercourse with the woman while she is asleep. The female version of this demonic entity is known as a succubus.

Inhuman Spirit: An entity or spirit of a being that has never lived in the earthly realm, such as a demon.

Levitation: The raising of a body or object without any physical or visible means, found in some poltergeist cases and hauntings.

Magic/Magick: Not to be confused with stage magic, this is the art, science, and practice of producing supernatural effects, in hopes of causing change to occur. The controlling of events in nature with one's own will.

Medium/Channeling Agent: A person who can make contact with discarnate or inhuman spirits on the astral plane.

Occult: Pertaining to the supernatural, that which is beyond the range of natural knowledge.

Orbs: Although highly controversial amongst serious psychical researchers and parapsychologists, the concept of orbs is fast becoming the most common aspect of paranormal and ghost research, these faint balls of transparent light resembling magnified dust spores or droplets of water are known exclusively among psychical researchers as ghost orbs, spirit globules, and spirits in transit. Orbs are believed to be the main transportation mode for spirits because they require little energy in this state. One of the primary distinctions between ghosts and globules is that ghosts are imprints of the dead bound in an endless loop of repetition. Globules, in comparison, are mobile and very much sentient entities that can change their frequencies and locations at will.

Ouija Board: Oui means yes in French and *ja* means yes in German. The Ouija Board consists of letters of the alphabet, numbers one through ten and the words "yes," "no," and "goodbye." It is used as a tool for communicating with spirits. Although used by many as a game or form of entertainment, many feel that the Ouija board is an unwise form of communication to take part in, as it may open up corridors or portals to unfriendly spirits or even misleading demons.

Out of Body Experience: Also known as astral projection, a person can purposefully or unconsciously leave his or her body in spirit form.

Parapsychology: "Para" means above or beyond and psychology is the study of man, his psyche and the human condition. Parapsychology is the scientific study of phenomena that natural laws cannot explain.

Pentagram: The magical diagram, such as the seal of Solomon, consists of a five-pointed star, which is the representation of man, as well as the five elements. Considered by occultists to be the most potent means of conjuring spirits, the pentagram is said to protect against evil spirits.

Phantomania: An occurrence in which the victim is held paralyzed while being subjected to preternatural attack, such as an attack from an incubus or succubus.

Planchette: The indicator, pointere, or empty reversed glass used in association with the Ouija board.

Poltergeist: From the German word for "noisy ghost." It is a spirit associated with the movement of objects and general mischievous activity. Poltergeists are the only spirits who may leave immediate physical traces. Poltergeists are best known for throwing things about and producing rapping sounds and other noises. Poltergeists often occur where there are children on the brink of puberty and may often interact with people.

Possessed Objects: Sometimes inanimate objects are said to be cursed, or possessed. An example of a supposed cursed object is the Hope Diamond, which is most likely a form of sympathetic magic or an urban legend designed to frighten potential thieves.

Possession: The state in which a living person is controlled by a foreign, malignant energy such as a demon.

Preternatural: Considered associated with inhuman, demonic, or diabolical spirits or forces.

Psychic: Having the ability to see, hear, feel, and sense beyond the average human ability.

Psychic Cold Spot: The cold sensation received when a spirit is present, usually having defined boundaries.

Psychic Photograph: Supernatural or preternatural images, from ghostly images to orbs, appearing on a photograph.

Psychical Research: The study of psychic phenomena, including Earth mysteries, ESP, and ghosts and hauntings.

Psychokinesis (PK): The movement of objects without the use of physical means.

Repetitious spirits: Some apparitions are believed to repeat the same motions or scenes over and over with no apparent intelligence. Many classic hauntings fall into this category. The Lady in White seen walking the bafflements of Derbyshire, England; the Brown Lady of Raynham Hall, who is seen walking down a hallway with a swaying lantern; the ghostly seventeenth-century soldiers continuously fighting on the Marsden Moors in England; and the ghostly sentry who walks guard on the Turnbull fort in New Smyrna Beach, Florida, are excellent examples of repetitious spirits.

Shadow People: A relatively new form of entity, said to be a nocturnal spirit, having human form, and prone to filtering on the walls and ceiling of a house. Time-honored subject of the *Art Bell Show,* the famous AM radio nightly talk show, shadow people, whatever they are, are believed evil, possibly demonic in nature.

Specter (Spectre): A ghost, or supernatural entity (*see Spirit*).

Spirit: A spirit is the actual essence, or soul, of a person that has remained after their physical body has died. Spirits usually appear for one of three reasons. First, if a person died suddenly or with little warning, as in the case of a car accident, he or she may not actually realize that they are dead. Second, a person could be confined to this world by an unkept promise made to a loved one. Third, he or she may have some unfinished business, usually pertaining to a loved one. A variation of this reason would be if the person were murdered at an untimely point in their lives. Spirits, unlike ghosts, can communicate with the living. Usually, if a person frequents a place where the deceased spent much of his or her time, a form of psychic communication can occur. Sudden and unexplained feelings of sadness or melancholy are common indications, especially if encountered only in one particular room or area. Another way that a spirit can communicate with the living is through dreams. Although much more rare, a spirit can make itself appear as an apparition or make small items physically move.

Succubus: A female form of the incubus. This spirit, most likely demonic, will attempt to engage in sexual intercourse with a sleeping male. It is also said to drain the sleeping male of his vital energy and stamina.

Talisman/Charm: Also known as a fetch, these may be drawings of various shapes and sizes, which have specified purposes of good luck, protection, health, etc., and can be worn as a necklace or key chain.

Telekinesis: The movement of objects by psychical means.

Telepathy: Psychic communications between individuals.

Teleportation/Apport: Objects moved or materialized by supernatural forces.

Will o' the Wisps: Also known as ghost lights, will o' the wisps are believed to be a natural phenomenon, such as pockets of swamp gas that hover and rise over swamps, ignite by natural causes, and glow blue or green. Also known as corpse candles, fox fire, elves' light, and *ignis fatuus,* which is Latin for "foolish fire." Some believe these lights to be omens of bad luck or death.

Appendix C
Ghost Research Organizations

The following is a listing of the most prominent psychical research organizations devoted to scientific inquiries, parapsychology, and related paranormal research today. Several of these organizations, such as the American Society of Psychical Research, are membership-based societies, but may share resources with nonmembers. Several of these societies also publish online journals and printed periodicals in the field of parapsychology and paranormal research, which may be of interest to Florida ghost hunters. The Florida-based web sites herein are an excellent resource for organized ghost hunts, investigation studies, and ghost hunting tours throughout the state of Florida.

American Society for Psychical Research (ASPR)
  5 West 73rd Street, New York, NY 10023
  212-799-5050

The American Institute of Parapsychology
  www.parapsychologylab.com
  Dr. Andrew Nichols, PhD, Director

Society for Psychical Research (SPR)
  49 Marloes Road, Kensington, London W86LA,
  United Kingdom

Florida Psychical Research Group (FPRG)
  Folklore and Urban Legend Collection
  Dr. G. Jenkins and Lynda Knight-Jenkins, R.N.
  arkham1964@yahoo.com

Psychical Research Foundation
c/o William G. Roll, Psychology Department
West Georgia College, Carrollton, GA 30118

Parapsychological Association, Inc.
P.O. Box 12236, Research Triangle Park, NC 27709

Parapsychology Foundation
228 E. 71st Street, New York, NY 10021 212-628-1550

Parapsychology Research Group
3101 Washington St., San Francisco, CA 94511

Foundation for Research on the Nature of Man
Institute for Parapsychology
P.O. Box 6847 College Station, Durham, NC 27708

Graduate Parapsychology Program: Department of Holistic Studies
John F. Kennedy University, Orinda, Ca. 94563
510-254-0200

Division of Parapsychology
Department of Behavioral Medicine and Psychiatry Box
152 Medical Center, University of Virginia
Charlottesville, VA 22908

Center for Scientific Anomalies Research (CSAR)
P.O. Box 1052, Ann Arbor, MI 48103

Society for Scientific Exploration
c/o Dr. Henry Bauer
College of Arts & Sciences, Virginia Polytechnic Institute
Blacksburg, VA 24061

Committee for the Scientific Investigation of Claims of the Paranormal
(CSICOP, Skeptical Society)
1203 Kesington Avenue, Buffalo, NY 14215

Association for the Scientific Study of Anomalous Phenomenal
www.assap.org

Coast-to-Coast Radio with George Noory
www.coasttocoastAM.com
A great late night A.M. radio show and an excellent resource for ghost stories and related paranormal information.

Big Bend Ghost Trackers
http://www.bigbendghosttrackers.homestead.com
An excellent group in the Tallahassee area that conducts research in the Big Bend/Panhandle area of Florida.

Center for Paranormal Research and Investigation
http://virginiaghosts.com

Daytona Beach Paranormal Research Group
www.dbprginc.org

Florida Ghost Chapter
www.floridaghostchapter.com
Great site, which also offers various "ghost walk" information.

Florida Paranormal Research Foundation
www.floridaparanormal.com

Florida Paranormal Research Hotline
www.FloridaParanormalResearch.com
LeadInvestigator@FloridaParanormalResearch.com
Covers Lee and Collier counties and the Florida Everglades. This group is based in southwestern Florida.

Haunts of the World's Most Famous Beach (Daytona, FL)
www.hauntsofdaytona.com
Another great organization that features a ghost walk in the Daytona Beach area. Look for the Daytona Ghost Walk information.

International Ghost Hunters Society
www.ghostweb.com

Obiwan's UFO-Free Paranormal Page
found at *www.ghosts.org*
An excellent site with hundreds of resources for ghost hunters everywhere.

The Shadowlands
www.shadowlands.net/ghost/
A well-done page on many aspects of the paranormal, including an extensive section on ghosts and hauntings.

Southern Ghosts and Southern Ghosts Radio AM 540
www.SouthernGhosts.com

The Ghost Investigators Society
http://www.ghostpix.com
An excellent source for information on Electronic Voice Phenomena (EVP). Proprietors will correspond with those truly interested and may conduct investigations.

S.P.I.R.I.T.S. (Servicing Paranormal Investigators Reporting Information Through Study)
http://centralflghosts.homestead.com/home.html
An excellent group in St. Petersburg, Florida. They are a voluntary organization that investigates local paranormal activity within west central Florida. This group conducts public presentations covering many aspects and terms of ghosts and ghost hunting.

Miami Ghost Chronicles
http://www.miamighostchronicles.com
Available to assist any group that needs help in south and central Florida. They have stories and links on their website.

South Florida Ghost Team

http://floridaghostteam.com/

A paranormal team located in southern Florida. They investigate hauntings, gather evidence of paranormal events and conduct research. Their website contains photos, ghost tour information, investigation results, and information on the paranormal subjects.

The Florida Paranormal Group

www.floridaparanormal.com

Florida Ghost Hunters

http://www.floridaghosthunters.com

The International Ghost Hunters Society

http://www.ghostweb.com/links.html

GHG Ghost Hunters

http://www.ghgghosthunters.com

Appendix D
Ghost Tours

Ghost tours and ghost walks have become all but customary in almost every great city in the United States today. Most of these tours are filled with the haunted or ghostly history of a particular location, usually a location of some historical significance. Sometimes, these walking tours are specifically designed to be entertaining accounts of speculative incidents that may revolve around a particular ghost or haunting. On occasion, these tours will cover actual documented histories that report paranormal activity, but sometimes these groups will embellish an actual story or legend, creating an urban legend within an urban legend.

This process of telling a good story and making a little money as a result may prove to be the hobgoblin to serious paranormal researchers as well as scholarly folklorists. So, with this said, I would like to kindly recommend that you be cautious when braving the busy streets and downtowns in search of ghosts. Although your guide might be wearing a top hat and a flowing black cape, and his or her story may sound wonderfully exciting, please keep in mind that there may be many falsehoods in the anecdotes. Although entertaining, there is always the possibility that the story is incorrect, or simply designed to capture your attention and your money. Therefore, respectfully, take the story with a grain of salt and do the research for yourself—you might be surprised what you'll find.

The following listing of Pensacola and west Florida's ghost walks and haunted tours is current and up-to-date as of this writing. Over time some businesses may close and new ones may appear. Always check before you go on a tour. The best way to learn of new ghost tours in your area is on the internet or by calling that city's chamber of commerce.

Pensacola

"The Haunted Ghost Tour"

The Pensacola Historical Society operates this ghost tour, which normally operates two weekends in late October, usually starting around 6:30 P.M. on a Friday and lasting until about midnight. The Historical Society has been collecting local Pensacola ghost stories and folktales for many years, and presents many of them during the annual Haunted House Walking and Trolley Tours. Visitors can walk or ride to the various places that have a supernatural history while costumed guides share tales of Pensacola's historical and haunted past.

To find about dates, times, and locations of tours and story times, call or visit The Historical Museum of Pensacola, 115 E. Zaragoza St. Pensacola. 850-433-1559 or call The Historical Resource Center at 850-434-5455.

"Big Lagoon State Park Haunted House & Trolley Ride"

Located in Big Lagoon State Park in Pensacola, near Perdido Key on Gulf Beach Highway, the park operates a yearly haunted house with twenty rooms of spooky things for young and old alike. They also operate a haunted trolley ride that travels through the swamp with a tour guide telling both historical tales and tales of paranormal interest. In the past, this function served as a fund-raiser to build a Marine Environmental Center in the park, so it has a good cause.

The Haunted House, which has more than twenty scary rooms, offers a lighter side of the Halloween season for the whole family. The guides will also relate some interesting folklore of strange swampland creatures and even the tale of a ghost of a missing park ranger of long ago. Big Lagoon State Park is located in Pensacola off Gulf Beach Highway on the intersection of Bauer Road. For more information, call 850-492-2785. Fax: 850–492–2785

Monticello

"Historic Monticello and Cemetery Ghost Tours"

"Monticello, Florida, is well known for its historic values, but what many people don't know is that with all the history, there are ghosts hiding in every history page. The "Old Hanging Tree," the "Opera House," and even private homes have been haunted by ghosts for centuries.

This is a wonderful and educational ghost walk in charming Monticello, Florida, operated and overseen by Big Bend Ghost Trackers out of Tallahassee, and the Jefferson County Chamber of Commerce. There are two separate tours offered, starting at 7:30 P.M. and 9:00 P.M. from the Monticello/Jefferson County Chamber of Commerce. Tickets are $10 for adults and $5 for children. Price of a ticket includes refreshments at the Chamber of Commerce. For more information on the Monticello tours, contact the Jefferson County Chamber of Commerce at 850-997-5552 or visit them at 420 W. Washington Street, Monticello, Florida.

Big Bend Ghost Trackers also offers other events throughout the northern section of Florida, including ghost tours and investigations in Pensacola, St Augustine, San Marcos de Apalache in St. Marks, and the Natural Bridge Battle Site in Woodville. Each ghost tour offered by this organization donates its proceeds to various good causes throughout the state, so enjoying one of their events will do more good than simply getting a great lesson of our state's heritage and ghosts. For more information on investigation, dates, and times, call 850-562-2516 or visit www.bigbendghosttrackers.homestead.com.

St. Petersburg

"The Original Ghost Tour of St. Petersburg"

Billed as the original ghost tour of St. Petersburg, and one which is based on the book *Ghost Stories of St. Petersburg,* offers a professionally guided, narrated walking tour through historical St. Pete. With tales of Spanish conquistadors and buried bodies, legends of the phantom hitchhiker on the Sunshine Skyway Bridge, and the "Lady in White" who lurks at the Vinoy hotel, of lost cemeteries and hidden treasure, this tour will offer visitors a chance to hear some of the less common stories of the west coast. The tour begins every Tuesday at 8 P.M. Tickets are $18 per person and include refreshments. Reservations are required and you may purchase tickets in advance. Visa, Mastercard, and American Express are accepted. For more information, call 727-894-4678

"The Ghost Tour of Jungle Prada"

The Jungle Prada Ghost Tour claims to offer one of Florida's most mysterious and mystical locations on the "haunted side" of St. Petersburg, with legends of lost burial grounds, hidden treasure, bootleggers, murder, mayhem, and ghostly sightings on the shores of Boca Ciega Bay. This two-hour tour includes a stroll through The Jungle followed by a storytelling gathering inside the haunted Al Capone Room inside Saffron's Caribbean Restaurant. Refreshments are served.

Tickets are $15 per adult, $8 for kids ages four to twelve. Visa, Mastercard, American Express, and Discover are accepted. Reservations required and you may purchase tickets Tuesday nights at 7:30 P.M. The Jungle Prada Ghost Tour is located at 1st Street, NE & 2nd Ave. St. Petersburg, across from Baywalk, outside the chamber of commerce building. For reservations or further information, call 727-894-4678.

"The Downtown St. Petersburg Ghost Tour"
This ninety-minute tour of the city's most haunted locations covers many west coast locations, from the historic 1880s hotel where a debonair sea captain is said to lurk to the gorgeous Vinoy where the Lady in White haunts the lofty hallways. This tour is entertaining and offers a good history lesson along the way. The tour guides tell fun and fascinating tales of specters and haunted places throughout St. Petersburg. Tours begin each evening at 8:00 P.M. across from Baywalk, at the Chamber of Commerce building: 1st St. NE & 2nd Ave. N, St. Tickets are $15 per adult, $8 for kids ages four to twelve. Tickets are by reservation only. Call 727-894-4678 or visit www.ghosttour.net.

"John's Pass Tour"
Here's an interesting ghost tour that covers the folklore of a more sea-worthy nature, with legends of oceanfaring specters and tales of pirates, this tour is fun for people of all ages. One can buy tickets directly at Hubbard's Marina and then meet in front of the information booth on the boardwalk, next to the Friendly Fisherman Restaurant. A costumed tour guide will meet you by the red and white lighthouse on the board-walk. Dates and times change, so call for more information 727-398-5200 or visit http://www.hubbardsmarina.com/ghost.html.

"Tampa Bay Ghost Tours"
These fun and educational ghost tours offer a somewhat serious, and somewhat spooky, look into the darker side of downtown St. Petersburg, which highlights the Vinoy Hotel and other local haunts. They also offer the Maritime Mysteries & Pirates of the Pass; Haunted Halls and Horrifying Hermits (St. Pete Beach and Pass-a-Grille); and the Gulfport Guys and Ghouls—all fun and full of creepy information on the haunted west coast. Tickets are $14 for adults, $10 for children.

For information on all events, times, and group packages, and for reservations, call 727-398-5200 or visit www.allthebesthaunts.com.

Fort Myers

"Ghost Tours of Fort Myers"

This lantern guided tour takes you on a ninety-minute stroll through the city. This tour offers a well-researched tour that both entertains and educates, and is great for the whole family. You will hear stories of the man who was buried in a bathtub, the spooky history of Fort Myers beach, and the creepy secret behind the Mermaid Club. All in all, a fun and entertaining ghost tour. For information, call 239-949-3644. Web site: www.hauntedfortmyers.com.

Bibliography

Clearfield, Dylan. *Floridaland Ghosts.* Michigan: Prism Stempien Thomas, 2000.

Cool, Kim. *Ghost Stories of Sarasota: The Heart of the Cultural Coast.* Venice: Historic Venice Press, 2003.

Cool, Kim. *Ghost Stories of Venice.* Venice: Historic Venice Press, 2003.

Guiley, Rosemary Ellen. *The Encyclopedia of Ghosts and Spirits.* New York: Facts on File, 1992.

Hiller, Herbert L. *Guide to the Small and Historic Lodgings of Florida.* Sarasota: Pineapple Press, 1986.

Moore, Joyce Elson. *Haunt Hunter's Guide to Florida.* Sarasota: Pineapple Press, 1998.

Research Sources

The Pensacola Lighthouse, Pensacola

Steitz, George C. *Haunted Lighthouses and How to Find Them.* Sarasota: Pineapple Press, 2002.

Powell, Jack. *Haunting Sunshine.* Sarasota: Pineapple Press, 2001.

Interviews by author, 2005–06 (anonymous sources)

Interviews with Betty Davis, Big Bend Ghost Trackers, 2006

The Naval Air Station and Naval Hospital, Pensacola

Interviews by author, 2004–05 (naval liaisons and anonymous sources)

Interviews with Betty Davis, Big Bend Ghost Trackers, 2006

Fort Pickens, Pensacola

Interviews by author, 2007 (United States National Parks Service)

Interviews with Betty Davis, Big Bend Ghost Trackers, 2006

The Seville Quarter & Rosie O'Grady's, Pensacola
Interviews by author, 2005–06 (anonymous sources)
Interviews with Betty Davis, Big Bend Ghost Trackers, 2006

T. T. Wentworth Jr. Florida State Museum, Pensacola
Interviews by author, 2005 (anonymous sources)
Interviews with Betty Davis, Big Bend Ghost Trackers, 2006

Dorr House, Pensacola
Moore, Joyce Elson. *Haunt Hunter's Guide to Florida*. Sarasota:
    Pineapple Press, 1998,
Interviews by author, 2006 (anonymous sources)
Interviews with Betty Davis, Big Bend Ghost Trackers, 2006

Pensacola Little Theatre, Pensacola
Interviews by author, 2005–06 (anonymous sources)
Interviews with Betty Davis, Big Bend Ghost Trackers, 2006

The Lear-Rocheblave House, Pensacola
Moore, Joyce Elson. *Haunt Hunter's Guide to Florida*. Sarasota:
    Pineapple Press, 1998,
Interviews by author, 2005–06 (anonymous sources)
Interviews with Betty Davis, Big Bend Ghost Trackers, 2006

Museums of Industry and Commerce, Pensacola
Interviews by author, 2005–06 (anonymous sources)
Interviews with Betty Davis, Big Bend Ghost Trackers, 2006

Old Christ Church, Pensacola
Moore, Joyce Elson. *Haunt Hunter's Guide to Florida*. Sarasota:
    Pineapple Press, 1998.

Interviews by author, 2005–06 (anonymous sources)
Interviews with Betty Davis, Big Bend Ghost Trackers, 2006

Island Hotel and Restaurant, Cedar Key
Interviews by author, 2005–06 (anonymous sources)

The Royalty Theatre, Clearwater
Interviews by author, 2005 (anonymous sources)
Interview with Brandy Stark, S.P.I.R.I.T.S., St. Petersburg, 2006

Belleview Biltmore Resort, Clearwater
Powell, Jack. *Haunting Sunshine,* Sarasota: Pineapple Press, 2001.
Interviews by author, 2006 (anonymous sources)
Interview with Brandy Stark, S.P.I.R.I.T.S., St. Pete., 2006

Lover's Lane of Keene Road, Largo
Clearfeild, Dylan. *Floridaland Ghosts.* Michigan: Prism Thomas, 2000.
Interviews by author, 2001–02 (Kimberly Penkava)

Haslam's Book Store, St. Petersburg
Powell, Jack. *Haunting Sunshine.* Sarasota: Pineapple Press, 2001.
Interviews by author, 2006 (anonymous sources)
Interview with Brandy Stark, S.P.I.R.I.T.S., St. Pete., 2006

The Vinoy Hotel, St. Petersburg
Interviews by author, 2004–05 (anonymous sources)

St. Petersburg High School at Mirror Lake, St. Petersburg
Interviews by author, 2001–02 (Kimberly Penkava)

Egmont Lighthouse, Egmont Key
Interviews by author, 2002 (Kimberly Penkava)
Interviews by author, 2005–06 (anonymous sources)

The Ritz-Carlton Hotel, Sarasota
Interviews by author, 2006 (anonymous sources)
Interview with Brandy Stark, S.P.I.R.I.T.S., St. Petersburg, 2006

Ringling School of Art and Design, Sarasota
Interviews by author, 2005–06 (anonymous sources)
Interview with Brandy Stark, S.P.I.R.I.T.S., St. Petersburg, 2006

Cracker Barrel Restaurant, Naples
Information via Tallahassee Courthouse Liaison
Interviews by author, 2006 (anonymous sources)

Index

(Boldface numbers refer to photographs)

Adams, President John Quincy, 14
African American Heritage Society, 58
Alberding, Charles, 139
Apple Annie's, 35
Astaire, Fred, 104

Barin Field, 14
Barrancas National Cemetery, 25
Baum, Dwight James, 168
Bay Haven Elementary School, 168
Bay Haven Hotel, **177**, 178
Belleview Biltmore, 88, 111–20, **112**, 146
Bense, Dr. Judith, 82
Bernard, Simon, 22
Blue Angels, 1
Branded Hand, The, 50
Bronson Field, 14
Burns, Owen, 168
Bush Sr., President George, 113

Ca d'Zan,168
Cadwell Manwaring, Mae "Maisie", 117
Carter, President Jimmy, 113
Cedar Key, 87, 91–102
Charos, Socrates, 105, 107, 108
Civil War, 5, 7, 22–24, 51, 79, 92–93, 96, 157
Clearwater, 87, 88, 103–20
Coolidge, President Calvin, 139
Corry Air Field, 13, 16
Cracker Barrel Restaurant, 185–94, **186**
Crist, Governor Charlie, 153

Davis Jr., Sammy, 104
de Luna, Don Tristan, 12
DiMaggio, Joe, 113
Don CeSar, 146
Dorr, Clara Barkley, 49, 51

Dorr, Ebenezer, 49–50
Dorr, Ebenezer Walker, 49
Dorr House, 34, 49–55, **50**
Duke of Windsor, 113

Edison, Thomas, 113
Edwards, Sherrod, 156
Egmont Key, 88, 155–65
Egmont Key Lighthouse, 155–65, **156**
El Vernona Hotel, 168, 169 (*see also* Ritz-Carlton Hotel)
Elliott, Elsie, 141
Elliott, Eugene, 141
English, Charles, 94
English, Shirley, 94
Ellyson Airfield, 13
Escambia County, 49–50

Feinberg, Simon, 93, 97–98
Flower, Rev. David D., 82
Ford, Henry, 113
Ford, President Gerald, 113
Fort Barrancas, 1, 12, 22, 28
Fort Dade, 157
Fort DeSoto beach, 155
Fort McRee, 22
Fort Pickens, 1, 22–32, **23**
Fort Sill, 25

Gauld, George, 155
Geronimo, 24–25, 26, 27–28, 29, 30, 31
Gibbs, Bessie, 94–95, 99–100
Gibbs, Loyal "Gibby", 94–95
Great Depression, 93–94, 96, 139, 168
Great Hurricane of 1848, 156–57
Greenleaf, John, 50
Gulf Islands National Seashore, 30

Haakenson, Joe, 141
Hale, Francis E., 91–92

Hall, Captain Guy, 16
Haslam, John and Mary, 128
Haslam's Book Store, 128–36, **129**
Historic Pensacola Village, 1
Hoover, President Herbert, 139
Hope, Bob, 104
Hope Diamond, 45
Hulse, Dr. Isaac, 14
Hurricane Ivan, 30
Hurricane Katrina, 157

Ingraham, Jeremiah, 5, 7–8
Ingraham, Michaela, 5, 7–8
Island Hotel and Restaurant, 91–102, **92**
Ittner, William B., 147

Julee Cottage, **34**

Kaleidoscope Ballet Company, 58
Keating Hall, 178, 179, 180, 181–82
Kerouac, Jack, 130–31
Kidd, Ashlee, 153
King Tut, tomb of, 45
Korean conflict, 14

Largo, 88, 121–27
Lavalle Home, 34
Lear, John and Kate, 64
Lear-Rocheblave House, 64–70, **65**
LePaite, Henri, 5
Lili Marlene's World War I Aviators Pub, 35
Lynch, Captain George M., 147

Markham, Marcus, 93
Menéndez de Avilés, Pedro, 33
Minnelli, Liza, 104
Montgomery, Alabama, 5
Museums of Industry and Commerce, 34, 71–78, **73**

Naples, 88, 185–94
National Museum of Naval Aviation, 1

National Register of Historic Places, 95, 158
Naval Air Station, Pensacola, 12–21, **13**, 25
Naval Hospital, 12–21

Oklahoma, 25
Old Christ Church, 65, 66, 79–85, **80**

Palace Oyster Bar, 35
Parsons and Hale General Store, 93, 96–97
Parsons, Langdon, 93
Parsons, Major John, 91–92
Peake, Rev. Frederick F., 82
Pensacola, 1–85
Pensacola Children's Chorus, 58
Pensacola Cultural Center, 35, 56, 61
Pensacola Historical Museum, 1, 41
Pensacola Historical Society, 41
Pensacola Lighthouse, 3–11, **4**
Pensacola Little Theatre, 35, 56–63, **57**
Pensacola Museum of Art, 35
Pensacola Opera House, 58
Pensacola Village, 33–36
Perceval, Lord John (Earl of Egmont), 155
Pickens, Andrew, 22
Plant, Henry B., 111, 117
Plant, Morton, 117
Ponce de León, Juan, 33
Poole, Hosea, 59, 62–63
Powell, Gary, 82–84
Presley, Elvis, 104

Quarterman, Antonio, 153
Quayside Gallery, 35

Revere, Paul, 50
Rickard, George V., 157, 160–61
Ringling Bros. & Barnum and Bailey Circus, 167, 168
Ringling, John, 167–68, 177
Ringling, Mable, 168

Ringling School of Art and Design, 176–84
Ringling Towers, 146, **167** (*see also* Ritz Carlton Hotel)
Ritz-Carlton Hotel, 88, 166–75
Rocheblave, Benito, 64, 68–69
Rogers, Ginger, 104
Rosie O' Grady's, 35, 37–42, **38**
Royalty Theatre, 103–110, **104**
Ruth, Babe, 113, 139, 142
Ruth Eckerd Hall Opera House and Theatre, 105

Santa Rosa Island, 22, 30
Sarasota, 87, 88, 166–84
Sarasota High School, 168
Saufley Airfield, 13
Seville Historic District, 1
Seville Quarter, 37–42
Shanahan's, 35
Sherman Airfield, 28
Sinatra, Frank, 104
Spanish-American War, 65, 157
St. Petersburg, 88, 128–54

St. Petersburg High School at Mirror Lake, 145–54, **146**
Stewart, Jimmy, 139

T. T. Wentworth Jr. Florida State Museum, 34, 43–48, **44**, 77
Tampa Bay, 155
Thatcher, Margaret, 113
Third Seminole War, 157

U.S. National Park Service, 25

Vinoy Hotel, 137–44, **138**, 146

West Florida Literary Federation, 58
Wharton, Sarah, 39–40, 41
Whiting Air Field, 12, 14
Williamson, Scott, 141
Woman of Lemb statue, 45
Woolsey, Commodore Melanchton B., 16–17
World War I, 13, 16, 104
World War II, 13, 104, 139